UNEARTHED

A NOVEL BY MICHAEL COLE

SEVEREDPRESS

UNEARTHED

CHAPTER 1

Boom!

"There they go blasting again. Maybe they'll get through that layer of granite by the time we retire."

Corporal Lon Bergis looked up from the leg of the M3 Scorpion. His sergeant, a grizzled guy named Galloway, was looking to the northwest. Somewhere beyond that patch of island jungle, Unit Three was detonating another twenty pounds of T-6 explosives at the mine.

"You heard what the geologist said. The meteor is comprised of the most dense rock known to man. Basically, the universe's idea of an anvil. Anything within a thousand miles of this bad boy when it hit the Earth eighty million years ago had a real bad day."

"I guess. Then again, they probably didn't even know what hit them," Sergeant Galloway said.

Bergis shook his head. "The ones within a mile or two of the point of impact certainly didn't. But everything all around that area? The air pretty much ignited, cooking them alive. Then there was the shockwave, wind gusts, and ejecta matter."

The Sarge turned to face Bergis, his face conveying a sense of bemusement.

"You sure *you're* not the geologist?"

Bergis twirled his wrench. It was a little out of the norm for a simple gun-for-hire to be into geology and meteorology. Aside from the explosions, it was a fairly quiet job. One of the few avenues of acceptable entertainment when on the clock was reading. And most of the material had to do with science relevant to the dig.

"I guess we should count ourselves lucky the meteor wasn't any bigger," he said. "If it were, it probably would have done more damage than the big one that wiped out the dinosaurs."

1

"Wouldn't have made a difference to us, considering we weren't here back then," Dennis Lergee said.

Corporal Bergis snorted. The twenty-something year-old security operative was always a know-it-all. Judging by his remarks during their assignment on Delta-5 Caprona, Lergee knew everything there was to know about geology, astrophysics, demolition, politics, billion-dollar corporations, and a dozen other things. His source of information: his own opinion.

"If it was a true global killer, yeah it would affect us," Bergis said. "Evolution can't really continue if the planet is sterilized. Had the Chicxulub asteroid been made of the same kind of rock as the meteorite we're digging up, you and I would not be having this conversation."

He took notice of the half-smirk on Sergeant Galloway's face and the way he was scratching his head. It was the look of a man whose mind was cycling through a thousand different thoughts.

"I'm starting to question whether that'd be a bad thing," he said. "How 'bout you finish up there. At this rate, by the time you get the repairs done, Earth will be hit by another meteor."

Bergis took a moment to self-reflect. Here he was thinking Lergee to be acting like some know-it-all, yet for the last couple of minutes, he went on a long-winded lecture about meteorite mass. He was considered an odd duck by his fellow company men, and a wannabe scientist by the actual PhDs and lab nerds on the island— the few who even knew his name, that is.

With that in mind, he got back to work. Their dig was already delayed as it was. If he took too long getting the machine back up and running, the engineering foreman and the supervising geologist would be up everyone's ass.

The hierarchy within the Globus Enterprise tended to be brutal to its lower ranks. It was the epitome of corporate culture. Everyone seemed to carry some sort of superiority complex. Funnily enough, Bergis had overheard political discussions in which the administrative staff verbally patted themselves on the back because they 'supported the little guy'. Yet, when push came to shove and the mess hit the fan, they were more than eager to throw the 'little guys' to the wolves. Additionally, they rarely socialized with anyone outside of their air-conditioned cubicles and personal quarters. Of course, they all got private quarters, while the majority of the regular staff had two or three people in a room.

Another thing Bergis found amusing in the company culture was the attitude toward the security staff. They were treated as incompetent mall guards who had no real skill sets or authority. In reality, the security on this island had a very thorough vetting process. Veterans and police-trained personnel were preferred. A four-week training program had to be completed before new hires could work assignments. It was basically a mini police academy, with its share of firearms training, some close quarters drills, and classroom sessions.

It was not as though the guards stood around doing nothing but idle patrols either. They assisted with the digging, maintenance, and other roles. Like the regular military, Globus wanted to utilize their lower staff in as many ways as possible. As a result, they carried a lot of responsibility on their shoulders. Still, the suits and blouses on the third floor of Operations looked at guys like Bergis as little more than disposable 'uneducated' chess pieces.

Right now, this chess piece needed to get the damn M3 Scorpion *Old Buster* running again.

The great machine, used by the company for both tunneling and extracting minerals, was originally a weapon for field combat. It had seen a great deal of action in its time. Its green chrome had lost its shine, especially around its eight legs, multi-purpose arms, and underside. As its name suggested, its design was based on the actual arachnid, right to the flexible tail. Instead of a stinger, the tip was armed with an L16 laser. A weapon designed for cutting through enemy troops and armor, it proved useful in tunneling through tough granite.

Bergis knew the machine like the back of his hand. During his service in the West Atlantic Army, he piloted it during the Campaign of North Africa. The conflict itself was something he didn't care to dwell on. A year of his life had been spent firing cruel weapons at strangers who wore a different flag and spoke another language, in a country where neither he nor they belonged in. Like most wars in human history, it was just another instance of nations not getting along—or rather, their *leaders* not getting along—and alliances forcing other countries to join the fray.

Despite his attempts to distance himself from the horrid memories, one thing Bergis did cling to was *Old Buster.* Having been assigned to the vehicle in his service, it was essential to his survival in North Africa. Its hull protected him from a storm of shrapnel that cut down infantrymen around him. More importantly, it allowed him to save the lives of many of his brothers.

After the war, *Old Buster* was decommissioned, due to be dismantled and sold as scrap. It lived to fight another day after Globus, the company who made and sold the machine to the military to begin with, bought it back at a sixth of the price.

It was the newly hired Lon Bergis who informed them of the Scorpion's status, thus saving his mechanical friend.

"Piece of junk," Private Lergee said. "Damn thing's broken down on us three times this month."

"It does most of the hard work," Bergis said. "We can't begrudge it for having a little wear and tear. Especially after all it's been through."

"Who am I to judge?" Sergeant Galloway said. He moved his right leg to the side and leaned forward to stretch his hip. "Won't be too long before I'm gonna need some maintenance."

Bergis looked over at him. He was aware of the arthritis building in the sergeant's lower back and joints. Years of competitive athleticism followed by his draft into the Army took a toll.

"How much longer until you rotate out?"

Galloway finished his stretch, his face tensing from the gravelly sensation in his hip.

"Two months." He pulled a cigarette out of his shirt pocket. He knew his good friend Bergis already knew the answer, and knew the true purpose of his asking. "You're still flirting with the idea of staying on longer. Just cut the cord and go back to the mainland."

Bergis shook his head. "There's nothing for me there."

Galloway took a draw of his smoke. "Nothing for you here, either."

"There's work."

"Work." Galloway scoffed at the word. It was the very thing that drew him to this place. Enough time in the heat and humidity had a way of lessening the majesty of the island paradise. "Two months to go on this damn island. If the pay wasn't so good, I'd be staring at the mirror, asking God why some geologists had to discover portions of some ancient meteorite under the surface. And why I was dumb enough to sign on."

"You'd be part of making history, of course!" Lergee said. "That's what they told me!"

Bergis chuckled. It was what everyone was told. It wasn't just an asteroid they were uncovering. It was the answer to a brand-new power source. Supposedly, a kilo of rock from the inner layer of the asteroid could power a city block. The outer layer was thick, as was the sediment that formed over it over the many millions of years since the impact. Hence the need for explosives and laser weapons.

Boom!

An echo from the northwest broke his train of thought.

"Whoa!" Galloway exclaimed.

Lergee turned towards the sound. "Okay, so it wasn't just me who noticed that."

"Yeah, that blast was way too shallow," Galloway said. "It should've been at least thirty feet deep. That explosion almost sounded like it was on the surface." He grabbed his radio off the hood of the V12 Force Application Light Reconnaissance Vehicle, nicknamed the Boar. "Site Three to Site Four; you forget how to set the charges over there?" He smiled and awaited a sarcastic response from the supervising officer over there. Except, nothing came.

Boom!

All four men of Site Three shuddered. That blast, too, was surface level.

The fourth team member, a quiet demolitions specialist named Walton, broke his silence.

He pointed thirty degrees skyward. "I see smoke."

Bergis could see it too. A little bit of smoke and dust was nothing too unusual after a demolition charge had been set off. But this was not some mild plume of brown dust and grey smoke. This was asphalt black and thick, not originating from a deep pit, but the surface ground around it.

Galloway made another attempt. "Site Four? The hell's going on over there?"

No response came.

"Central Command to Site Three? What's happening?"

It was only a matter of time before the voice of Colonel Tarsus came through the receiver.

"We're seeing smoke from Site Four's location, sir. They're not responding to our transmissions. We registered a couple of blasts from their site, and unless I'm mistaken, they sounded as if they detonated on the surface, not in the pit."

"Copy that. We've got a bird heading that way right now. Stand by for a moment, Sergeant..."

They could hear the twin rotors of the Dragonfly gunship whirring in the northwest. It moved about for a couple of minutes before moving off.

"Site Three, our bird has sighted the smoke. The canopy is too thick, they can't set down and check it out. I need your team to get your gear together and take a look, ASAP. You're the closest unit that can respond."

Galloway snapped his fingers at his men. "On it, sir."

Bergis placed his tools down and went for the Boar. Walton pulled their T-4 Python rifles from the back compartment and handed them out.

"You don't think it's more bats, do you?" Lergee asked.

Bergis bit his lip. The thought of those creatures and their six-foot wingspans was an unpleasant one. It was not solely because of their size and ravenous fangs, but the reminder of why Globus wanted their own private military to handle this dig. It was not just meteor fragments the dig had unearthed, but a dormant clan of winged creatures. And they did not take kindly to being woken up from their slumber.

Once upon a time, such a discovery would have been cherished. For Globus? They were a hindrance that needed to be eradicated.

"I doubt they would know how to set off the charges," he said.

"Not unless they learned to spit fire," Galloway said. He slipped into the driver's seat. "Sooner we get there, the sooner we figure out what's going on."

With that said, the rest of the team boarded the vehicle. Galloway stomped on the accelerator and took them northwest.

Straight toward that plume of smoke.

CHAPTER 2

Normally, driving through the jungles of Delta 5 Caprona was the favored part of the assignment. Riding on the Boar meant the unit could socialize, smoke, and rest unhindered by work. Plus, there was little risk of getting blown up. It was considered the downtime of everyone's workload, so much so that some units took their sweet time moving from site to site.

Today, Bergis and his fellow teammates had no desire to drag out this drive. With Site Four still not responding, Galloway floored the accelerator.

Walton was on the mounted M41 Piranha Chain-gun. A weapon designed for eliminating threats in the air and on the ground, it provided the team with a fair sense of security as they approached that ugly tower of smoke.

It grew increasingly larger, both in perspective and literal size. A smell of burnt metal, oil, and gunpowder permeated the jungle surrounding Site Four, furthering Team Three's dread of discovering what had occurred.

Galloway steered the vehicle through a bend in the trail, bringing them on site. All four men stared in dumbfounded silence, gradually taking in the details of a horrific aftermath.

The excavators, machines that stood forty feet high and weighed ten tons, were spread across the site. Smoke billowed from the can and treads of one of them, the yellow paint blackened by the heat of the thermal detonators. And there was no doubt the source of the smoke was caused by the thermal detonators. Two craters indented the ground at the center of the small space. The larger of the two was the mine from which Team Four extracted minerals from the buried *Fukuda* meteorite fragment.

The smaller one was new. Less than ten minutes old, in fact. Surrounded by charred debris from Team Four's Boar, excavators, and mineral carrier, it was undoubtedly the result of the case of thermal detonators having gone off accidentally.

"Oh, God," Lergee muttered.

"Fan out," Galloway said. "Look for survivors."

Lergee snorted. "You not seeing the same thing I see, Sergeant? I can't see how anyone could have survived—"

"Lergee, I didn't ask for commentary," Galloway said in a grisly voice.

Bergis stepped off the vehicle. "Come on, Private."

The soldier blew raspberries, then stepped off the Boar. He slowly approached the wreckage, rifle pointed downward, ready to be raised at any moment.

"Walton, stay on the gun. Provide cover," Galloway ordered. "The rest of you, on me."

The sergeant shouldered his weapon and approached the dig site. Bergis took the right, making sure to keep his eyes on the canopy in case any of those bat things were around. He hated the idea of gunning down the poor creatures, but his compassion did not override his sense of self-preservation.

While it did not add up, an attack by those creatures was the best explanation they had for the explosion. The second greatest possibility was human error, but given the safety measures installed in the explosives, it was difficult to imagine Team Four being so incompetent that they would blow themselves up.

An accidental discharge of a pulse rifle into one of the thermal detonators in the heat of combat, while unlikely, made the most sense. Maybe one of the guys was trying to shoot when he got swarmed by a couple of flyers, resulting in him losing balance and discharging his firearm in the wrong direction.

Then again, I don't recall hearing any gunfire.

Sure, it would have been faint, but unmistakable all the same. And an attack of any kind would have resulted in at least a few shots popped off. One shot possibly could have been undetected by Bergis' ears. Multiple ones would have been impossible.

In that case, Bergis' assumption was wrong. An accidental gunshot to the detonators was not plausible if no shots were actually fired.

It only proved to be one of many questions rising from this horrible aftermath.

Galloway raised his fist, signaling to the fireteam to stop. After a few moments of observation, he moved toward the wrecked excavators.

Between the nearest one and the charred crater was a skeletal corpse, blackened by plasma flames. A pulse rifle remained clenched in the dead soldier's grasp, its grey metal barrel and frame now jet black.

Bergis, needing to put to rest his theory of the gunshots, knelt by the dead man and checked the weapon's magazine. Though damaged beyond use, the payload was still intact.

"He didn't fire a single shot."

"Nor this guy."

Bergis looked at Lergee, who stood over the remains of another corpse. Corpse proved too generous a word, for the poor guy was nothing but a collection of parts scattered southeast of the dig site. His weapon was in the middle of the carnage, its magazine full.

Galloway was visibly uncomfortable as he tilted his mic to his mouth. "Team Three to Central Command?"

"Colonel Tarsus here. What'd you find, Sergeant?"

"Colonel, Team Four is dead. Their entire explosive supply appears to have detonated. All their equipment is destroyed. Furthermore, we've got fires spreading on the northern side. Given the fact the island hasn't gotten rain in the past three days, there's a significant possibility our operation will be in a state of emergency unless we get it under control."

"Copy that, Sergeant. I've already got an EMS team en route. I'll instruct them to stop by Pump Seven and get water flowing to that area. A flight response team is prepping for liftoff as we speak."

"Understood, sir." Galloway took another look at the flames, only to realize his corporal had moved closer to them. "Bergis?! What the hell's the matter with you? Unless you plan on joining these fellas for barbecue, I suggest you get back here!"

Bergis knew he would garner such a response from the sergeant when he first noticed the oddity in the ground. While Galloway spoke with Tarsus, Bergis could not help himself. The curiosity proved too great, plus, given the situation, he didn't want to leave any stones unturned.

Except, in a twist of irony, his inspection did not provide any answers. Just more questions.

A series of small craters dotted the earth, coming from the northeast, stopping a few yards from the second excavator. Each one went a couple of inches deep, were roughly two meters in width, and had jagged formations on one side.

"Sergeant, you might want to look at this."

Galloway had a moment in which he considered dismissing the corporal's concerns, but reconsidered. The Scorpion operator was not one to point out insignificant details and waste time.

He moved closer and laid eyes on the markings in the ground. His eyes moved from the nearest one to the next, following the series of craters far into the jungle.

"Those weren't there before, were they?" he said.

Bergis shook his head. He pointed the muzzle of his rifle at the blackened ground between the nearest crater and the excavator. It almost resembled a 2D illustration of a tornado, with the far end being narrow like the tip of a cone, gradually widening as it stretched farther.

Bergis followed the charred funnel to the excavators and the skeletal body. From there, the trail bent to the left, concluding in the large indentation where the thermal detonators had been.

He took a knee and touched his fingers to the earth, confirming the obvious. A river of fire had cut across the area, resulting in the detonation of the explosives.

What wasn't obvious was the cause of the fire. In his time in the military, Bergis had seen more than his fair share of literal scorched earth. As advanced as the species had grown in technology, its ancient brutality never evolved with it. On the contrary, it devolved, reinventing brutal weapons that were once done away with due to being considered inhumane.

One of those weapons were flamethrowers. Streams of burning fuel fired from handheld nozzles, they were the very essence of cruelty, igniting everything they touched. That included the ground itself, whether it be a grassy plain or a sandy desert. In inspecting the haunting aftermath of battles, Bergis always noted the zigzagging markings on the ground where a flamethrower had swept back and forth.

He forced aside the memories, returning his mind to the equally disturbing evidence in front of his face.

"We need to alert the colonel."

"He's already been briefed," Galloway said. "He's got EMS and Fire Response en route."

"No," Bergis said. "He needs to sound a red alert. This wasn't an accident. Not all the fire we're seeing was caused by the blast. These marks here are the results of an extremely concentrated flame."

"Flame?" Lergee said. "You suggesting something unloaded a flamethrower on the guys here?"

"Not suggesting. I'm stating it," Bergis stated bluntly.

"Let's not get ahead of ourselves," Galloway said. "We don't have flamethrowers on the island, so we know it's not some crazed staff member. And there's no way anyone is gonna sneak onto the island with this kind of equipment. Not without getting detected."

"You have a better explanation?" Bergis asked.

Galloway glimpsed at the destruction, then shook his head. "Maybe not. But it doesn't make your theory suddenly make sense. And if there was a hostile force on the island, why would they start their attack here? A dig site with only a handful of security personnel. It doesn't make sense, especially if they have the element of surprise."

Bergis could not answer that. There was no denying that logical fallacy. At the same time, he knew the results of a flame blast when he saw it.

Boom!

The fireteam turned to the west, each of them experiencing an increased heart rate.

"There's no digs over that way," Lergee pointed out.

"No, there's not," Galloway said.

"Central Command to Team Three. Do you have eyes on Dragonfly-Three? We've received a partial distress signal, but the transmission died, and we can't reach them."

Bergis and Galloway looked at each other.

"Sir, did they happen to be west of our location?" the sergeant asked.

"Affirmative."

Galloway pursed his lips. Bergis' hypothesis suddenly became much more credible.

"Colonel, we just heard an explosion from that location."

There was a moment of dead air, during which they envisioned the colonel barking orders throughout the station. When he returned to the radio, his voice was almost mechanical. He was mentally prepped for combat, the change in demeanor indicative of a man who knew he had to possibly send people to their deaths.

"Get over there now," he said. "I'll send Team Two as backup."

"Copy that." Galloway turned and hurried to the Boar. "This just keeps getting better and better, doesn't it?"

Bergis hopped in the passenger seat. "Not sure if 'better' is the word I'd use."

CHAPTER 3

"There it is!" Bergis pointed a finger to his one o'clock.

"I see it," Galloway said.

The presence of flames surrounding the large grey fuselage in the distance confirmed the worst. Just as Bergis had feared, the situation was not getting better in the slightest. Whatever was going on, it was escalating quickly, with no explanation in sight.

Galloway took the Boar through a thick patch of jungle, carefully weaving through the many obstacles between them and the downed Dragonfly aircraft.

"What the hell happened?" Lergee shouted over the rumbling of the engine and crunching of undergrowth. "You think it's the Russo Chinese?"

Galloway shook his head. "Not likely."

"Not likely my ass," Lergee said. "We've got a whole private military on this island for a reason, and it isn't just to repel bats. The guy in charge is a decorated colonel who led an armored division through Botswana. He was obviously hired for a reason. Hell, we've got an entire mech unit in addition to our Scorpions. They're not here for show."

Galloway and Bergis shared a glance, their impatience mirrored in each other's eyes. Lergee was a decent soldier—security operative being the technical term in this case—but he was very green. He was one of the hires who came without a military or police background. Not that it was an issue in itself. He did his job without a fuss and received no negative judgement from his teammates. But his lack of pre-Globus experience showed in his occasional naivety.

"Makes no sense for the Russo-Chinese to risk diplomatic relations for a meaningless attack on us," Galloway said.

"To my knowledge, Globus has contracts with them," Bergis added. "There're other threats out there, and some of them do not carry flags. For example, there's the Saradia Corporation, which supplies fuel to much of Eastern Europe. If they figured out what we're digging for out here, they wouldn't be too pleased."

The radio crackled.

"Team Five to Team Three, we're en route to Dragonfly-Three's last known location. Is that smoke I see over there?"

"Are you referring to the one west of Site Three?" Bergis replied.

"Affirmative."

It was as good of an opportunity as any to update the island colony.

"Team Three to all units. Dragonfly-Three is down. I repeat: Dragonfly-Three is down."

The Boar punched through a wall of fern and veered to the left to avoid the flames. They had arrived.

The entire port side of the Dragonfly gunship's grey hull was jet black. The rocket pod on that side had exploded, leaving the interior wide open.

Bergis watched the ground-level flames. They were surprisingly few in comparison to the raging fire on the treetops directly above. He went to the back of the Boar and pulled an extinguisher out.

A white fog jetted from its nozzle, gradually eradicating the fire around the wreckage.

"Team Three, what's your status?" Colonel Tarsus asked.

"Sir, we've arrived at the crash," Galloway answered. "We were able to get control of the ground-level flames, but sir, the treetops are ablaze. We're gonna need aircraft to dump water from above to put them out."

"Copy that. Any survivors?"

Bergis took a peek through the cockpit's shattered windscreen. It was empty, save for a ripped-up pilot's seat and some blood.

He looked at Galloway and shook his head.

"Negative, sir," the sergeant said. "So far, no sign of the cause of the crash either. But I think it is safe to say it was not an accident."

"Took the words right out of my mouth. All units are on Red Alert. I want mech units mobilized right now. All off duty personnel are on duty. All personnel without security certifications are confined to the main compound."

An engine rumbled from the north. Team Three, being on edge, pointed their weapons in that direction. To their relief, the approaching vehicle was the Boar carrying Team Five.

The vehicle came to a stop by the Dragonfly's tail rotor. The four men stepped off.

Bergis struggled to recall the names of the three security operatives. Only their sergeant, a guy named Dore, was familiar.

"Mother of God," the sergeant muttered. He gazed in awe of the fallen aircraft. He had never seen a Dragonfly in ruins before. Only in dogfights over the Mediterranean had he even heard of the awesome vehicles being shot down.

"Okay, can someone explain this to me?" Team Five's gunner said. He was looking straight up at the burning canopy. Like everyone else, he had taken notice of how only the tops of the trees were on fire. The rest of them were relatively untouched, save for the bases and small vegetation between them. And all of that was easily explained by the crash landing. "How exactly does this happen?"

"Rocket, maybe," Lergee said. "Or a laser. Dragonfly exploded, resulting in the fire."

"If that was the case, there'd be debris from the trees everywhere," Bergis said. "Aside from the fact they're burning away, the treetops look relatively intact. Meaning the Dragonfly exploded *above* the canopy."

"I agree," Sergeant Dore said.

"Doubt it was a laser," Galloway said. "Only large vehicles like the Scorpions possess the capability of energy weapons. Plus, the concentration in energy would have cut through many of the branches. No, this looks more like someone flat out torched the place."

"With what, a flamethrower?" Lergee said.

Bergis checked the burnt side of the Dragonfly's hull. "Starting to look like it. This wasn't just caused by the explosion. Only a concentrated flame could char the metal like this."

"It'd have to be molten lava," Walton called out from the Boar's machine gun.

"Chimera-S4 flamethrowers practically are," Bergis said.

"Geez o Petes," Galloway muttered. "Bergis, you and these flamethrowers! Get a room already."

"You have a better explanation?" Bergis shot back. "Incendiary rounds fired up from ground level would have resulted in more widespread flame, given most of them would have missed."

"Last I checked, flamethrowers aren't necessarily anti aircraft weapons," Galloway said. "More to the point, if the Dragonfly was as high as you suggest, it would've been well beyond the range of most flamethrowers. Only the ones on a Goliath V2 battle tank would have a chance at hitting it, and guess what? Those things would not be able to move through this jungle without leaving an obvious trace."

That word 'trace' jumped out at Bergis. Galloway, seeing the way his corporal perked up, had the exact same thought. All of them had been so fixated on the fallen Dragonfly that they did not think to look for any other clues elsewhere.

They combed the perimeter with their eyes, settling on a grove of trees on the northeast. One of them was split in two, its top half leaning heavily to the right. The others nearby were covered in heavy abrasions from the base of the trunk to the sixty-foot mark. Branches littered the ground, nearly obscuring the series of strange craters.

Bergis and Galloway stared at the bizarre markings.

"Look familiar?" Bergis said.

Galloway nodded. "Same markings we saw at Site Four."

"Markings is one word," Bergis said. "I dare say we're looking at footprints."

Galloway's brow wrinkled. While he could not deny the shallow craters resembled such things, he had a difficult time acknowledging it. It seemed too implausible, even as he laid eyes on them in real time.

Lergee, standing a few feet behind them, started sniggering.

"Footprints. Ha! That's a good one, Bergis. As much as I'm fascinated by the possibility of Sasquatch being real, I think we need to not let our imaginations run rampant."

"Whatever moved through here was much larger than Sasquatch," Bergis said.

"Whatever it was, it can't be too far from here," Galloway added. "We've got a golden opportunity. We can track it down and put an end to it."

Lergee's grin vanished. "Wait, you believe something stomped its way through here?"

"Could be a mech unit," Galloway said. "Maybe a new model nobody knows about. One that has a flamethrower in its armament."

Sergeant Dore signaled for his men to regroup at their vehicle. "We can track it down and put an end to it. What do you think, Galloway?"

Galloway looked at his weapon, then at the .50 cal on his team's Boar. Team Five's Boar had a similar setup, except they had an even cooler toy mounted up there. Instead of a machine gun, they were equipped with a Striker-12 grenade launcher. Most people considered it to be overkill for this island assignment. Today, Galloway and Bergis were both thinking differently.

Bergis saw his sergeant's eyes move in his direction. It was Galloway's way of asking 'what do you think?'

Normally, Bergis would give either a nod or a head shake to convey yay or nay. This time, he simply shrugged. On the one hand, they had a lead on the perpetrator and had an opportunity to take it down. On the other hand, they were not sure what it was they were hunting. Whatever it was, it wiped out a four-man unit and took down a Dragonfly gunship.

On the other hand, there only appeared to be one bogey. The element of surprise was diminished. At the very least, it stood to reason they would be able to inflict some kind of damage to the thing.

After giving one more look to the wreckage, he made a choice.

"I think we're capable of putting some hurt to the thing."

That was good enough for Galloway, who turned to face the others.

"Mount up. We're going after it."

CHAPTER 4

For a quarter mile, the two teams followed a trail of crushed vegetation. Tree limbs as high as forty feet above the ground had been snapped off like toothpicks. Underneath all of the ruins were those strange tracks.

Whatever made them was both large and fast, the latter casting further doubt on the theory it was some sort of battle mech. They were agile enough, but were not known for plowing through thick groves of trees. Only a certain few stood at a forty-foot height—two of which were stationed here on the island. The standard height was twenty-five feet and an armament of eight rockets, twin machine guns, and a Bushmaster cannon.

After another hundred yards, the trail was reduced to mostly tracks, with the occasional flattened bush or abrasion on a tree.

"We're getting closer," Galloway said. Hearing his own words, he slowed the vehicle and grabbed the mic. "Team Five, reduce speed. Keep your eyes peeled. Whatever's out there is probably aware of our presence."

The man in the passenger seat of Team Five's vehicle gave a thumbs up. Sergeant Dore eased off the accelerator and trailed a few meters behind Three. The gunners on both vehicles swept the surrounding jungle with their weapons, ready to unload on anything that might dare emerge.

After another couple hundred feet, there was barely a trail to follow.

A droning sound drew all eyes to the sky. Three dragonflies passed overhead, en route to the crash site with intent to put out the flames.

Another two Dragonflies could be heard southeast of the group's present location, unloading water and fire-retardant aerosols on the flames around Site Four.

"This is Colonel Tarsus. I want all excavation units to report to Command Central for briefing and reassignment. As stated before,

all non-combat personnel are restricted to the compound until further notice."

Bergis leaned forward to watch the ground as best he could. There did not appear to be any more tracks in this direction.

"Stop the vehicle."

Galloway made a face as though about to say 'Oh, you're giving the orders now?'

Except, he agreed with the corporal. He eased on the brakes and veered slightly to the right to allow Sergeant Dore to pull up alongside them.

In the moments following their departure from the wreckage, Lergee pointed out the names of Dore's squad. A social butterfly, he tended to chat with anyone in his proximity, especially when bored.

The gunner was Honda. He was a former security specialist for the Air Force before hiring into Globus. Like Walton, he was the no-nonsense type. Evidently, those kind of guys were drawn to gun-duty while on mobile patrols.

The guy in the back passenger seat was Corporal Kanner. There wasn't much said about him that wasn't known just from looking at the guy. His addiction to tattoos was evident just from looking at his face—literally. The guy was a true walking piece of art. Not that Bergis considered Kanner's designs artistic, per say.

Lastly, there was the man in the passenger seat who Lergee identified as Dyson. Lergee, being the type to give a little too much detail, admitted to owing the guy two hundred credits.

Bergis wanted to smack the private upside the head. Of course he would be dumb enough to waste his wages on pointless gambling, especially against a pro like Dyson. Though this was the first time Bergis saw the guy, he had heard of his reputation in the mess hall.

"What now?" Sergeant Dore asked. "Should we rendezvous at Command Central with everyone else?"

"We may have lost the trail, but we're likely still pretty damn close to the target," Dyson said. "I'd say we still have a shot at finding it… then, whatever we're looking for."

Spoken like a true gambler, Bergis thought.

"Let me guess, you bet someone we'd locate the threat?" Lergee asked. Dyson shrugged, pretty much confirming everyone's suspicion.

"Who'd you bet? And how much?" Kanner asked.

Dyson shrugged again. "Ishiro from the galley. Hundred credits that we inflict the first casualties on the threat."

Bergis clenched a fist. People had died in the last several minutes and for all they knew, the entire colony was under attack. Yet, this jackass was placing bets and playing games. The urge to subtract a tooth from his skull was a mighty tempting one.

A sharp whistle from far off in the distance cut his internal debate short. The others heard it too and perked up all at once.

The sound devolved into a strange mixture of gravelly and dull droning noises.

Galloway was the first to look east in the direction it was coming from. "Sounds like a falling projectile… or an…"

BOOM!

A shockwave rippled underneath the vehicles.

Galloway cut the wheel to the right.

"…aircraft going down."

Bergis switched frequencies to those of the air patrol units. A frenzied barrage of transmissions spat from the receiver by a group of equally confused pilots and dispatchers.

"…from the trees. I repeat: Dragonfly-Six is down. I lost the target."

"Copy that, Seven. Can you confirm identity of threat?"

"I… Stand by, Central. I want to get another look at the thing first. I need to make sure my eyes aren't playing tricks on me."

Bergis could hear the rotors of Dragonfly-Seven as it moved northwards. Neither he nor his teammates could see it, but judging from the vibrations, it was roughly seven hundred meters away.

"Let's assist," Galloway said. He stomped on the accelerator and took them east. Team Five followed suit, its gunner Honda equaling Walton in his determination to blast something.

"Central! I've got a visual. Rockets armed and ready to go. Jesus! Central, the target… I can't believe I'm saying this. The target is a—AGHHH!!!"

BOOM!!!

The sound of eight rockets simultaneously going off in their pods was unmistakable, as was the whirring of ravaged engines and the crashing of treetops, getting closer and closer to the two Boars.

Bergis looked up, his heart practically jumping into his throat when he saw the trees shuddering, and a huge burning projectile coming straight at them like a meteorite.

"Good God!" Galloway swerved to the left, sideswiping the trunk of a tree in his effort to evade the falling Dragonfly.

Sergeant Dore veered in the opposite direction, only to regret it one moment later when a huge broken branch smashed down in his path. The front of the vehicle lurched over the wooden limb, flattening the two front tires. With the vehicle lodged halfway over the trap, the men could do nothing but hope for Lady Luck to be on their side.

The blazing Dragonfly punched through the trees and smashed down thirty feet behind the group. Its tail rotors broke into razor sharp fragments that shot from the stern of the aircraft like buckshot. Metal projectiles punched through the jungle, shredding vegetation and embedding themselves in tree trunks.

Bergis was the first to pop his head up. The shockwave from the impact could still be heard rolling farther inland, spooking local animals from their habitats.

To his relief, the four men on the other vehicle were all in one piece. A piece of rotor impaled the tailgate just inches below the rim. Honda, still mounted on the grenade launcher, was staring at the shard, which was perfectly lined up with his ass.

"That probably would have hurt," the gunner said.

Galloway swung back and drove over to Team Five. "You guys alright?"

"Yeah." Dore stepped out of the damaged vehicle and ran to the downed Dragonfly. The others quickly followed, the gunners remaining behind to keep a lookout for the threat.

Dore looked through the smoldering cockpit, catching a glimpse of the pilot inside. He quickly turned away.

"Oh, Jesus!"

Bergis didn't bother looking for himself. Just the sight of the torched aircraft, which barely resembled its original shape at this point, was enough for him to know the pilot and crewmen were goners.

"This is insane!" Lergee said. "That's *three* Dragonflies down now! What's going on; who's doing this?!"

Thump!

Thump!

Thump!

All eyes turned to the east. Walton and Honda swiveled their weapons in the direction of the thunderous sounds. They came two to three seconds apart, all originating from the ground, and each one closer than the last. Cracking tree limbs and undergrowth accompanied the rumbles.

"Footsteps," Dore said. "Gotta be a mech!"

"Coming this way," Galloway added.

Bergis shouldered his weapon and pointed his muzzle upward. "Looks like you're about to win your bet, Dyson."

The soldier no longer appeared gleeful about that fact. If the look on his face conveyed anything, it was a rare regret for winning.

The noises drew closer.

"Bergis, get in the driver's seat of the Boar," Galloway said.

"We won't all fit," a nervous Dyson muttered.

"Shh!" Galloway hissed. "We've got one working vehicle, and it's a sitting duck. Bergis, move!"

The corporal was not going to say no. He sprinted to the Boar and climbed into the driver's seat.

Thump!

SNAP!

A tree, already damaged by burning debris from the Dragonfly crash, leaned westward. Bergis looked up at the towering plant, its trunk splitting twenty feet above the ground. Everything above that point was coming down, right in the path of his Boar. Worse than that, some of its branches were on track for smacking down across the vehicle.

The quiet Walton let loose a frantic "WOAH!"

Bergis, with only a split-second to respond, put the Boar in reverse and floored the accelerator. The vehicle shot backwards, narrowly evading the falling tree, only to smash against the trunk of another.

Walton sounded off again, this time with a "Shit!"

Bergis rocked in his seat, momentarily jarred by the impact. Another *thump* and *crash* drew his eyes to the coming monstrosity.

Walton readjusted his aim. For the third time in a row, he broke his silence.

"God Almighty!"

It was a phrase shared by many of his fellow security operatives.

From the jungle emerged the threat. What they saw was not a machine, but a gargantuan living organism staring back at them.

It walked on two hind legs, its body parallel to the ground. In this posture, it was a little over thirty feet in height, with an overall length that easily exceeded a hundred feet. Three toes, tipped with long black talons, extended from each foot.

It took another step, leaving behind a small crater with a jagged side.

Two long forearms with three clawed digits, were half-coiled under its chest. Two black eyes nearly blended in flawlessly with the dark grey skin. Extending from that skull where those eyes were located was a set of crocodilian jaws. Lining those jaws were intertwined eight-inch conical teeth. A long, nimble tail swayed back and forth behind its massive bulk.

From the center of its back was a bony sail-shaped structure. Formed by extensions of its vertebrae, it ran from the base of its neck to the start of its tail.

Bergis froze in his seat.

Am I seeing what I think I'm seeing?

Walton exclaimed a fourth time. "A freaking dinosaur!"

The beast parted its jaws and voiced its response with an earth-shattering roar.

Fear took hold of the gunner. Even now, fleeing was not in his nature. When it came to fight or flight, Walton chose the former.

A stream of bullets flew from the barrel of the .50 cal onto its flesh. The reptilian beast lurched in pain and anger, the booming sound waves under its footsteps doubling in intensity.

Bergis shrieked. The same unspoken question went through his head a second time.

Am I seeing what I think I'm seeing?

The creature roared in anger and stepped towards him. Its flesh, aside from some scrapes from the bullets, was unaffected by the turret.

Walton kept up the bombardment. Personal stubbornness and disbelief in the ineffectiveness of his weapon against the beast.

It made another step, then accelerated into a full sprint, arms uncoiled.

Bergis put the gear in forward drive, cut the wheel to the left, and hit the accelerator. Bark and sawdust flew as the rear tire spun between two roots.

The Boar was going nowhere.

"Bail!" Bergis was halfway out of the vehicle as he shouted. Walton failed to hear him over the sound of gunfire and his own screaming. His hands remained closed over the butterfly grip, either from steadfast determination or crippling tension.

The creature lowered its head and snapped its jaws over the gunner. After it yanked up, Walton's hands still remained on the grip. The rest of him proceeded to be munched into pulp between those jaws.

"Light it up!" Galloway shouted.

Rifle shots pelted the creature's flesh. Like the .50, they failed to do anything except agitate it.

It pivoted sharply in the team's direction, whacking the Boar with its tail.

Bergis had just started to sprint when he heard the sound of metal tapping the ground like a giant softball. He looked over his shoulder just in time to see the vehicle barreling toward him.

He went to the left to get out of the way. It was a maneuver which was so close to being successful. A split-second would have made all the difference.

As it turned out, the corner of the engine smacked his right shoulder. Bergis went into a tailspin and fell flat on his face. His head bounced hard against the rough soil, ringing his ears worse than the recent Dragonfly crash.

Shockwaves from heavy footsteps swept underneath the corporal, sparking just enough willpower to fight through the pain and brain fog.

Hazy senses detected the warped sound of screams accompanying the rifle fire. He lifted his head and saw fuzzy images of men running in different directions.

The creature turned to its right to pursue Dore and Lergee. Its tail swung with the motion, its low arch deliberately aimed at Kanner. The corporal was launched like a softball off a bat and sent straight into the burning cockpit. Gargled yells from a man with deflated lungs were cut short by ammo being discharged by the intense heat.

The creature took no notice of its triumph, its attention fixed entirely on its next target. A stomp of its foot missed Dore by less than a yard. The sergeant, yelling maniacally, kept running for his life, giving no thought to Lergee who had tripped over a broken branch.

Black eyes zeroed in on the screaming human. Lergee was on his back, pushing with his heels and palms to scurry away.

He cleared a total of eight inches before its foot elevated over him.

"No! Noooo!"

Down it came.

SPLAT!

The beast lifted its foot, strands of Lergee dangling from its toes. Its black eyes turned to Bergis.

His heart fluttered. The burst of adrenaline failed to jumpstart his senses. He began to push himself off the ground, only to collapse.

Boom! Boom! Boom!

Three consecutive explosions sent the creature staggering. It turned on its heel, setting its sights on Honda and the grenade turret.

Another shot hit it square in the chest. Like the other weapons, it failed to inflict anything more than a few scratches.

The beast charged.

Honda was quick to abandon the vehicle and make a run for it. It did him no good, for the beast tucked its head down and rammed the Boar like a freight train. It tumbled off the tree trunk right onto Honda, pancaking him against the earth.

"Go! Run!" Galloway shouted to Dyson. The carefree security operative had won his bet, and lived just long enough to regret it. He joined Galloway in a retreat, squealing in hysterics when the pounding footsteps closed in behind him. The last thing he heard was a gravely roar, then a *snap* of its teeth intertwining.

For Bergis, the soundtrack of carnage continued with a sound of splintering bones and the spraying of blood.

The beast kept moving, proceeding to munch on Dyson's corpse while it went after Galloway.

The sergeant was cut off by a large fire which had spawned from a piece of burning fuselage. Covered with fuel, it easily ignited everything around it, resulting in towering flames he could not penetrate. He attempted to circle left of it, only to be cut off by a line of thick thorn bushes.

"Shit!"

The earth shook beneath his feet.

Galloway turned around, his back against the wall of vegetation as the sail-back reptilian closed in. It took its time, as though deliberate in its ability to strike fear into its victims.

The sergeant was not immune to fear, but he did not allow himself to be crippled by it. Like Bergis, he had served in the North African Campaign and had seen more than enough carnage to last a lifetime.

Not even a raging dinosaur standing in front of him would make Galloway break his rule of not succumbing to fear. He did not scream, nor did he even quiver.

He lifted his weapon and unloaded his magazine into the enemy.

The creature went for the kill.

"No!"

Bergis pushed himself to his knees, pointed his rifle, and sprayed bullets at the creature. Wobbly arms barely managed to keep the weapon steady, the recoil shifting its muzzle all over the place.

The creature stopped and turned its huge, narrow head over its shoulder. It located Bergis with its eyes, then as though shrugging off his entire existence, returned its attention to Galloway.

The sergeant fired the last rounds of his magazine before switching to his sidearm. Those drooling jaws yawned open and shifted over him.

Galloway fired.

"Do your worst, motherf—"

SNAP!

Bits of Galloway shot out of the creature's mouth, as did a thick pink cloud.

Bergis dropped his weapon and fell forward. Resting on his palms, he watched the reptile turn around. Dripping blood from its jaws, it came his way, its black eyes conveying an ancient bloodlust.

He waited. His energy was gone and his team was dead. All except him. All he asked for was a quick end.

Droning sounds from high above gave the creature pause. It looked skyward and searched the treetops before laying eyes on the Dragonfly squadron hovering from west.

A downdraft from their rotors swept through the jungle, kicking up ash from the wreckage.

The carnivore bellowed a challenge to the dragonflies. They responded in kind, unleashing a slew of rockets in its direction. Black clouds of uprooted dirt kicked up around the beast. It staggered backwards, evading the detonation of several more rockets in front of it.

Charred dirt and gunpowder rained down on Bergis. He coughed and gagged, then laid his head down. Feeling the vibrations of a retreating giant, his mind faded to black.

CHAPTER 5

The darkness split open and made way for blinding white lights. A world of senses came to life in a heartbeat, spiking blood pressure the firing of synapses.

Through the confusion came one concrete image: elongated jaws armed with huge thick teeth.

Bergis shot up with a yell. His hand went for his sidearm, finding an absence of nylon fabric and instead a thin polyester gown.

"Whoa! Guess who came back to us!" someone exclaimed.

Bergis raised a hand over his eyes. Over the next few moments, his vision adjusted and his mind cleared. That blinding white light over his face was an overhead LED. The clothes he wore were grey patient gowns.

He was in Command Central. More precisely, he was in the infirmary. Other patients—some wearing the same dull attire, others still in their fatigues—rested on bunks.

Hurried footsteps tapped the floor behind him.

"It's alright, Corporal," a female voice said. "You're alright. You're at Command Central—the infirmary."

It was a voice that quickly managed to calm Bergis from his rush. He leaned back in his hospital bed, his vision fully adjusting to normal while Dr. Riley McKeon reconnected a cord that had been yanked from his monitor.

Having been called to duty during her day off, she didn't bother with tying her strawberry blonde hair back per regulation. Being one of the best, and few, doctors on the island, nobody was going to throw a fuss. Not even the colonel, most likely. Not at a time like this.

She came over to the right side of his bed. "Sit up, please." As Bergis did so, the doctor checked a bandage on his shoulder. "You lucked out."

"Pardon?"

"You took a hell of a hit," she explained. "Going by the report of the unit that picked you up, you had been hit by one of the Boars."

"Not in the traditional hit-and-run sense," Bergis said. "More like it was a bowling ball and I was one of the pins."

"I guess that answers my next question," McKeon said. "You remember what happened?"

Now Bergis was feeling the pain. Like lightning strikes in his mind, he saw the blazing Dragonfly, the smashed Boars, the fleeing team... the titanic beast coming after them. Gunshots, footsteps, and screams echoed from the depths of his memory.

The surreal nature of the sensations sparked a desperate hope that everything he experienced was nothing more than a crazy dream.

That hope was squandered at the sight of other wounded staff throughout the infirmary. The entire wing of the station had been converted into an emergency room, with staff working tirelessly to treat many severe injuries.

Those injuries ranged from contusions to third degree burns.

Bergis laid back, taking in the final snippet of reliving the horrors of his encounter. The memory was not brief, but rather took its time in excruciating detail.

There stood Sergeant Galloway, the last man standing, defiantly emptying his rifle into the reptilian. Then those mighty jaws shut over him, bringing his war to an end.

"Corporal?... Lon?" McKeon gently tapped his face.

Bergis returned to reality and remembered her question which he had yet to answer.

"I remember." He took a breath. "You call me lucky. But am I deserving? That *thing* butchered my team. Seven men just chopped to pieces. Torched. Crushed." His teeth clenched. "Eaten."

"Lon, you're alive. That's all that matters right now," Riley said. "And yes, you are deserving. Just because you got knocked on your ass doesn't make you a coward."

Bergis felt a new ping of regret for breaking his rule about not drinking alcohol. One slip up, thanks to stupid poor judgement, forced him to disclose his biggest secret to her.

It was two months ago at a birthday gathering in the mess hall for one of the other security guys. The guest of honor, known for his love of booze and carelessness with his finances, bought rounds for everyone in the room. It was essentially an open bar.

For Bergis, it was a gateway towards trouble. One 'innocent' drink turned into two, two to four, and so forth. The result was a more than tipsy security operative whose mind was very susceptible to manipulation, intentional or happenstance. In the case of that day, it was the latter.

Next thing he knew, he heard the popping of firecrackers outside the door. Flares and sparks put the compromised brain back into North Africa.

He ducked for cover behind a table and pulled his sidearm out, accidentally putting a round in the ceiling in the process.

In the blink of an eye, the festivities came to an awkward pause. Following regulation, Bergis was confined to a holding cell for negligibly discharging a weapon inside the premises. What followed was a psychiatric examination conducted by Dr. Riley McKeon. With his job on the line, the truth had to come out.

It was then Riley learned about the ambush in Algiers.

It was the last days of the war. Word had spread that all sides were at the negotiating table and were making great progress towards a peace treaty. Updates came hourly, each crumb of news better than the last. After a while, it became a near-certainty that the war was almost over.

But war, like everything else, was not over until it was over.

It was the day before the signing that the battalion Bergis' Scorpion unit joined with was ambushed by Russo-Chinese forces. Having evaded detection, they stormed the camp, guns a-blazing.

Bergis was away from his Scorpion at the time. In the chaos and fear, a single lucid thought took over his mind. His great-grandfather had served in the Pacific Theater during World War Two. He was a fighter pilot with fourteen confirmed kills under his belt. He was shot down above Tokyo, four days before Japan announced its surrender. It was a cruel twist of fate that haunted his family ever since. Lieutenant Wade Bergis, decorated pilot and war hero, had survived countless battles throughout the entirety of the war, only to die in the closing days.

During the attack in Algiers, Lon Bergis found himself staring at an all too similar fate. His courage and determination which carried him through the continent was swept away and replaced by the simple will to survive. The war was essentially over. Why die now?

An explosion a few yards from him sealed the debate. Flaming hot shrapnel nicked his thigh and back, putting his fear into overdrive. It was his first true injury of the war. In the eighteen months leading up to now, he suffered little more than a few skin infections on his arms and cramps in his legs. Aside from that, he was one of the lucky ones.

Now it was different. Blood was drawn, metal was in his body, and more bombs and shrapnel were coming down all around him.

Bergis ducked behind cover, pistol in hand, and waited for the madness to end.

Through the deafening mess of explosions, gunfire, and shouting, three words reached his ears.

"Lon! Get on the laser!"

It was Captain Bruce Kingsley, the recently promoted commander of his unit. He shouted to Bergis three times before the corporal mustered the strength to peek.

Kingsley was taking cover inside an impact crater. The enemy had employed long range artillery before launching the ground troops. Hunkered down with him were Wingman, Woods, Marston, and Bogdanovich.

All five men were part of Bergis' Scorpion unit. Bergis served as the main pilot, Marston and Woods as the support crew who replaced thermal batteries and reloaded rocket pods. Bogdanovich was the lead mechanic, and Kingsley the commanding officer. He was a lieutenant up until a week before the attack in Algiers.

Beyond them was a bazooka squad of Beijing commandos. Rifle fire kept the Scorpion squad pinned down while the artillery men got into position. Though in a perfect position to strike, they were unaware they were a prime target for the Scorpion's tail laser. All it needed was a pilot who was willing to sprint to the cockpit and operate it.

Gunfire from the rest of the conflict kept Bergis from committing to that run. It proved to be a decision that would forever haunt his memory. The next *boom* he heard cemented Lon Bergis as the sole survivor of Scorpion Unit Bravo-Eight-Echo.

The fate he so badly wanted to avoid for himself became a reality for his five teammates.

When the dust settled, Bergis was awarded a West Alliance Merit Badge for his injuries. No action was taken against him for his inaction, for the investigators had assumed the shockwave from the explosion and the shrapnel injuries had knocked the wind out of him. He arrived home a month later to a hero's welcome. Another few months passed until his discharge and the start of his employment with Globus.

Riley was kind enough to keep the details of his story to herself. She wrote the incident up as a case of PTSD triggered by alcohol and an unsanctioned use of firecrackers in the mess hall. As a result, Bergis was able to keep his job and avoid any penalties.

Bergis took another glance into the infirmary. The fact they were treating people out in the lobby and hallways meant all the rooms and hospital beds were full.

"How many casualties?"

Riley sighed. "Too many to count."

"Have you heard any word on where that thing came from?" Bergis asked.

"No." She held up her hands and the fresh pair of rubber gloves she wore. "I've been a little busy, in case you haven't noticed."

"How could he?" someone said. "He's been snoring up till a minute ago."

It was the same voice he'd heard when he'd first woken up. Bergis looked over his left shoulder at a security operative sitting on a hospital bed. He was still wearing his uniform and gear. His addition from the staff in the infirmary was a white bandage on his forehead and left arm.

None of it was enough to make Gavin Hoover unrecognizable. Like the late Lergee, he was a green hire. There was a smidge more experience on Hoover's résumé. Prior to signing on with Globus, he worked at a typical contract security company, who assigned him as a door guard at a bank in Toledo. How the guy got through the interviews at Globus without being thrown out the third-floor window was beyond Bergis.

The better question was how he managed to survive an encounter with the monster out there when tougher men did not.

Of all the guys to avoid getting stepped on...

Bergis hated himself for having that pessimistic attitude. Worse yet, he despised himself for not feeling guilty about his thoughts about Hoover. There were more deserving guys, many of them on this island as a matter of fact. Hoover just happened to be the most annoying. He was one of those guys who thought himself a comedian. Every other sentence was something snarky or sarcastic.

And for some reason, he always ended up in Bergis' proximity.

"Where is it?" Bergis asked through clenched teeth.

Hoover made a pained smirk. "You know, the growling voice isn't so intimidating when you're wearing *that* outfit."

Bergis looked down at his stupid gown, then over at Riley.

"Why am I in this crap?"

"We thought you were in more critical condition," she answered. "Your stuff is in the locker room."

Bergis swung himself off the bed and marched in that direction. He groaned after hearing the sound of boots tapping the floor behind him.

"Go away."

"Just answering your question," Hoover said. "Echo Squadron tracked the thing eastward. Lost it somewhere near the Blooming Lake."

Bergis entered the locker room. "So, it's still alive."

"As are we," Hoover said. The corporal opened his locker and glimpsed at the talkative soldier wannabe, waiting for him to clarify his point. "You and I have something special in common."

Bergis raised an eyebrow. "And that is...?"

"We both saw the thing in the flesh and lived to tell the tale. More importantly, we're able to get right back into the fight." Hoover waited for a response, but got silence and a hint of annoyance. "It attacked the east helipad. Tore through it like a kid with Legos. Not a pretty sight."

Bergis grabbed his clothes from his locker and started getting dressed.

"Since you're intent on staying by my side like a yapping puppy, I might as well get some useful info out of you. Has there been any explanation on what that thing is and where it came from?"

Hoover shrugged. "Not to my knowledge."

Bergis squeezed his shirt as though to strangle it. "Figures."

"Dr. Dietz has an explanation," a voice boomed from the hallway.

Bergis knew that voice. He looked to the entryway as Godfrey Parr entered the locker room. Six-foot-three, broad-shouldered, square-jawed, he was practically a walking stereotype of the gruff mercenary type. His deep voice and meat-headed attitude fed into the image.

Accompanying him into the locker room was Munro and Sagara. They were both a couple inches shorter than Godfrey, but shared the same meat-headed demeanor and shady mercenary background. The fact that they were hired into a 'regular' company like Globus meant one of two things: either they were tired of being shot at on a regular basis and wanted steady employment, or Globus had some dealings that were off the books.

The former certainly did not seem plausible. Especially not with the added spring to their step. It was subtle, but noticeable to someone like Bergis. A new challenge had been presented, by nature of all things, and they were looking forward to meeting it head-on.

If they were paying any attention to a nobody like Bergis, it was because they believed he would prove useful in their endeavor.

"Nice to see you up and moving, Corporal," Godfrey said. "Looks like that little bruise on your shoulder served you well. Shame the rest of your guys suffered far worse while you were incapacitated. Seems you've got a knack for coming out as the last man standing."

Bergis stood quietly, not giving Godfrey the satisfaction of a heated response. He was the only other person aware of the truth of what happened in Algiers. He was not there, but Munro was. He was delivering some kind of supplies to the battalion leader on the day of the attack, and got caught up in the fighting. One to remember familiar faces, he was sure to inform Godfrey the truth of the lone survivor of Scorpion Unit Bravo-Three-Echo.

"Fortunately, in this case, it might've worked out to our advantage," Godfrey continued. "With all our technology, aerial surveillance, and visual monitoring, we've only managed to obtain a few short bits of footage of the creature. You two are pretty much the leading authority when it comes to it."

"What does Dr. Dietz think?" Hoover asked.

"We'll hear the whole spiel at the briefing," Godfrey said. "All he's saying right now is that it's a dinosaur. As if that was hard to figure out. I guess I should've gotten myself a doctorate in geology. Then I could state the obvious and be paid six figures."

"He said something about it possibly being a Spinosaurus," Munro said. "Makes sense, I suppose."

Hoover shook his head. "No, I don't think so. I mean, it's similar, but it's different. For one, it's bigger than all fossil specimens. It's fully bipedal, and more importantly…"

"…I doubt Spinosauruses were capable of withstanding direct hits from machine gun and impact grenades," Bergis added.

The trio cracked smiles, more interested in Hoover's apparent knowledge of dinosaurs than the relevant tactical information provided by the Scorpion operator.

"How would you know this?" Godfrey said to him.

Hoover tilted his head and made a face. "What can I say? I never outgrew dinosaurs. I like to read about them."

"You use the correct colors when drawing between the lines?" Bergis muttered.

"Hey! Not nice!" Hoover said. "And no, these are full textbooks written by distinguished names in the field."

"Fascinating," Godfrey said. "Alright then, genius, what would you call the thing if it's not a Spino?"

"I don't know," Hoover said. "I don't claim to know everything. I just know it is not a Spinosaurus. Similar, yes, but different. Maybe it's a newly evolved version. A… I don't know, a *Sailsaur,* or something."

"Hmm!" Sagara turned to his two pals. "Suits me."

"Sailsaur, huh?" Munro said. "Yeeaaah, no. It's a big lizard with a sail on its back. I'm calling it a Spinosaurus. I doubt your proposed name will catch on. Maybe you're hoping to find yourself in one of those paleontology books."

"That'd be nice," Hoover said, rolling with the sarcasm.

"Just hope it isn't in the list of unlucky bastards squashed by the big lizard," Godfrey added. "Especially if you end up coming with us."

Bergis perked up at that last statement. "Beg your pardon?"

"Colonel's holding a briefing in twenty minutes," Godfrey said. "I think he expects to have a word with the two of you after. We're going after it. By the end of today, I'll add *my* name to the book as the guy who killed the mighty Spinosaurus!"

Pleased with his declaration, he and his two companions turned around and exited the locker room.

Bergis leaned against his locker. "I suppose there's worse news to be had."

"You *want* to go after it?" Hoover exclaimed.

"It killed the one man I considered a friend," Bergis said. "Damn right I'm going after it."

"I'm sorry about Sergeant Galloway," Hoover immediately replied. "I've met him a few times. He seemed to be a cool guy. Kicked my ass in poker."

That managed to get a small grin from Bergis. As it turned out, he and Hoover had another thing in common other than surviving the Spinosaurus' rampage.

His smile faded away, the good memories sparking more anger. Never again would he share games, meals, and other enjoyable moments with the sergeant. All thanks to that beast out there, and Bergis' foolish insistence they would be able to take it down.

That, and his inability to step up to the task when things got rough.

Fueled by a rising thirst for vengeance, he moved past Hoover.

"Report to the briefing room. Colonel's orders. You took this job wanting to be a discount soldier. Now's your chance to see some real action. Or you can request guard duty here… which is honestly what I'd recommend for you. Maybe you can think of a title for your book while we kill the Spino."

As he went through the hall into the infirmary, he heard a half-comical murmur from Hoover.

"Ouch."

CHAPTER 6

Colonel Merian C. Tarsus was not a man to be trifled with. He wore his twenty-four years in the Marine Corps not in the form of medals or ribbons, but creases of the face, powder burns in the skin, shrapnel in his left leg, and a low tolerance for failure.

He stood at the front of the briefing room, hands crossed behind his back, heels touching while he waited for everyone to assemble. His hair was white, not from age, but extreme stress. He was only in his early fifties and aside from his hair color, he appeared healthy and extremely fit.

The consistent story about the hair color was that it occurred during his infantry days. Being on the ground in areas the West was not officially supposed to be operating in, with no air support or pickup available, Tarsus knew what it was like to live on the edge. It was in the years leading up to countries forming their alliances. The world was changing, but government figures were still intent on their schemes, whether they be regime changes, assassinations, sabotage, or otherwise. Anything to keep their sponsors happy. Tarsus was just another pawn in the system back then.

Today, he was a rook.

Lon Bergis took a seat near the back of the room, making sure to not stare at the colonel. He had collected a new rifle and sidearm from the armory. While ineffective against the reptilian's tough hide, there was always the hope for a lucky hit through the eye socket. Furthermore, given the mood he was in, Bergis simply felt more comfortable having a weapon in his possession.

He shut his eyes and made sure to keep his finger far from the trigger. Hoover arrived and took a seat beside him. Bergis kept looking straight ahead and reminded himself that falling to temptation and blasting the annoying operative would only result in a lifetime behind electrified prison bars.

"Hoping he won't notice you sitting all the way back here?"

Bergis shook his head. As usual, he hoped his silence would make the guy go away. It didn't.

Hoover admired his own rifle. "I've never shot one of these babies outside the range."

"That's the *only* place you want to find yourself shooting them," Bergis said. He kept his eyes on the front of the room. Another man joined Colonel Tarsus. He did not wear the black tactical pants and black shirt sported by the colonel and the security operatives under his command. His attire was business-like, a button-down shirt, tie, and grey slacks.

Dr. Xavier Dietz was well known for being a legend in his own mind. He was not considered the type of guy most people would want to have a beer with. From what Bergis heard through the grapevine, Dietz generally treated anyone below him on the totem pole like crap. Those who were above him, he kissed up to. Those considered equal, he generally butted heads with.

That third dynamic was the case with him and Colonel Tarsus. They were men of vastly different backgrounds, both equally ambitious in their individual fields.

Tarsus was the war fighter, not one to turn his back on an adversary. It was not a well-kept secret that he was controversially adamant in his stance against the peace treaty. He believed in victory either through attrition or surrender, not settling a fight with signatures on a piece of paper that could have been signed before hundreds of thousands of soldiers lost their lives. His well publicized remarks lost his already dwindling favor with the bureaucrats, and as a result, he was forced to retire.

If his attitude made an impression on anybody, it was the heads at Globus.

Then there was Dr. Dietz. A graduate of the Central European University of Vienna, it was rumored he was shunned for his theories of harvesting new elements from space rock. For many years, he tried to work with various space agencies to land a spacecraft on the asteroid Ceres. While it was largely believed many asteroids contained nickel, copper, gold, and other metals and minerals, it wasn't considered a cost-effective investment. Things got even worse for Dietz when he published his theories regarding undiscovered heavy metals inside some asteroids, similar to uranium, that could potentially hold the secret to new clean energy.

Only Globus, a multinational conglomerate who specialized in goods and services ranging from pharmaceuticals to home appliances, to military technology and weaponry, gave Dr. Dietz the time of day. Granted, they were more interested in using him to find actual uranium deposits, but they were smart enough to hook him with proposals of funding future research.

Bergis had to give credit where it was due. Dietz made sure to exploit the resources of Globus to his advantage while searching for uranium deposits. His search uncovered some strange readings of radioactivity levels on the island of Delta-5 Caprona.

It was enough to get the company overlords interested. With the most advanced underground scanning equipment at his disposal, Dietz confirmed the presence of a massive asteroid buried underneath the ground. He theorized it had broken up into several meteorite fragments upon entering the atmosphere, hitting the Earth like pellets from a giant shotgun blast. Not enough to cause mass extinction, but certainly enough to make a very bad day for probably hundreds if not thousands of prehistoric creatures.

Most importantly, samples of one of the smaller fragments confirmed Dietz' theory about a new element. Like uranium, it appeared to have properties similar to radioactivity. Further tests confirmed it was unlike any heavy metal on Earth, and more importantly, was wholly capable of producing vast amounts of energy through fusion.

It was a game-changing discovery, one that was bound to attract powerful forces and even throw the world back into chaos as those forces vied for control of it. Globus was able to make promises of eastern superpowers with buying opportunities. It was enough to keep their military from coming uncomfortably close to the island.

That did not mean they could be trusted. Nor did it mean independent entities were not looking to sabotage Globus' operation.

That led to the hiring of Colonel Tarsus and the militarization of their security forces. Dietz did not hide his displeasure of Tarsus' oversight. The man had a mind for guns, not rocks.

Here, for once, Bergis suspected the two men saw eye-to-eye for once. Generally, they never stood closer than six feet apart unless in a meeting. Today, they were side by side.

I guess having a giant dinosaur ruining your day tends to help with getting priorities straightened out.

"Listen up, gentlemen," Tarsus said to the room. All idle chatter ceased. When the colonel was ready to get down to business, only the dumbest of the dumb would not be paying attention. He eyed the dead-silent room, then began slowly walking down the aisle between the two columns of benches. "If we learned something today, it's that we can never be too prepared. Every patrol, every lookout, every man on this island has a purpose. That purpose can mean the difference between life and death." He stopped at the back of the aisle and turned around. His eyes settled on Bergis and Hoover, their gaze cutting into both men like surgical instruments. He proceeded walking back to the front of the room, hands behind his back.

"Gentlemen, something has arrived on this island," he continued. "When I took the job, I was certain that if trouble would rear its ugly head, it would be in the form of Iranian infiltrators, Russo-Chinese, a few others. Maybe even the Lightning Corporation." He reached the front of the aisle and pivoted again to face the crowd. "I certainly did not expect a dinosaur."

It was one of few instances in which he allowed some verbal reactions from his men. Knowing the colonel's type of personality, he was probably reeling from the fact he said the word 'dinosaur' in relation to his operations.

Bergis broke the pause with, "What's the plan, sir?"

Tarsus seemed to like that, based on the barely noticeable smirk.

"Dragonflies tracked the creature down to Blooming Lake. Seismic readers indicate it has not left that area. For us, that's both good and bad. Good because we know where it is, bad because the rough terrain will make it nearly impossible for us to engage it with heavy weapons."

From out of the crowd came Godfrey's voice. "Why not just have the dragonflies pepper that whole area with cluster bombs? They can pummel the whole side of the island all month long."

"That's a good question, soldier," Tarsus said. He pivoted in Dietz' direction. "Perhaps I should leave that one to the academic to explain."

Dietz did not appear to appreciate that. Perhaps their united front was not as concrete as Bergis anticipated.

After a scornful glance, Dietz addressed the group. "We cannot drop heavy ordinances because we cannot risk damaging the new mine in that area. Scans reveal possible shallow ore, and should we just drop bombs in that region, we risk destroying a billion-plus dollars worth of product."

"You all get that?" Tarsus said. "To protect the doctor's bottom line, we're left with no choice but to send a response team into that area."

Dietz crossed his arms. "Remember, gentlemen, that bottom line puts money in your bank accounts."

"Just make sure you live to spend it," Tarsus added. "The objective is simple: locate and destroy it. As we won't be able to utilize our tanks, we will deploy our mechs to support the strike team."

Hoover raised his hand. Tarsus pointed at him and nodded in acknowledgment.

"Pardon me for pointing out the obvious, but this is a real-life dinosaur we're going after, right?"

Tarsus stared for a moment. "You're very observant."

"Has there been any word on where it came from?" Hoover asked. "I mean, it appeared out of nowhere. And given its size and attitude, I think it's safe to say it was not in hiding all this time."

"Dr. Dietz has a couple of theories, but we can't know for certain until we investigate further," Tarsus said. "We can't investigate until we blow that thing's head off. It's responsible for over twenty-five fatalities and many more critical injuries. And the casualties will continue to rise until we neutralize the threat.

"So, here's the deal; we're going to set up security perimeters over all major sites. All ground units not part of the strike team will be centered around Command Central, the flight deck, the docks, and garage. All dig sites will be unoccupied until the situation is under control. I want all boat units to patrol the east shore. If we can drive the thing to the beach, they can hit it with their guns. As mentioned before, our mech units will assist the strike team, as they are the only vehicles that can traverse that part of the island. You will all receive notifications on your PRO devices at the close of this meeting, giving your assignments. Report to your station in fifteen minutes. Any questions?"

One soldier raised his hand.

"What is it, Freiver?" Tarsus said.

"Pardon me, sir, but aren't we allowing ourselves to get a little too cautious?" the soldier named Freiver said. "Don't get me wrong, it's a dangerous animal. But it's *still* just an animal. I imagine a few direct hits from some impact grenades or our .50 cals should get the job done easily."

"The better question is where did all that fire come from?" Bergis added.

The whole room turned in his direction. Tarsus began another walk down the aisle.

"Corporal Lon Bergis. I was going to consult you in private, but I guess for the sake of transparency and time, why not do it here?"

Bergis stood up.

"To answer the guy's question about the method of killing the creature, its skin is proven to be resilient to light explosives and high-caliber weaponry."

The room broke into a series of murmurs. From within the mess of confused and nervous chatter were the words "bullshit!" and "no freaking way!"

"You witnessed this?" Tarsus asked.

"It was right in front of us," Bergis explained. "Both dig teams hit it with everything they had, including the grenade launcher. The thing came out with only a few scratches."

More murmurs.

Several rows away stood Godfrey. "Ah, yes. The twice-lone survivor speaks. Don't know about you, Colonel, but it almost sounds like the corporal is trying to prevent a response."

"Think what you want," Bergis said. "I'm just providing the facts as I know them. And your dumb argument holds no water.

For all I know, I've been assigned to greenhouse gardening duty."
He looked to the colonel. "On that note, I'm more than eager to see
the thing dead."

His words appeared to have little impact on the colonel. Tarsus
looked at him with that piercing gaze, probing every facet of
Bergis' character he could detect in that moment. It was clear by
his speculative expression that Godfrey had spilled the beans on
Algiers, and used the story to cast doubt on the encounter with the
Spinosaurus.

"Hoover!" Tarsus barked. "Can you verify the corporal's
claim?"

Hoover looked at Bergis, then back at Tarsus, equally nervous
about upsetting either of them. In the end, all he could do was state
the truth.

"It hit the flight station hard," he explained. "We did not land
any heavy machine gun fire or any explosive on it. Just stray rifle
fire, and frankly, everything was so chaotic, I can't tell you if it
hurt the thing or not."

"Understood," Tarsus said. He began walking to the front of the
room again. "In that case, we will gladly test Bergis' theory."

"But sir, what about the fires?" Bergis said.

Tarsus stopped. "Around the Dragonfly crash areas? What
about them?"

"I'm not sure if they were a result of the crashes," Bergis said.
"At Dig Site Four, their thermal detonators went off without
explanation."

Tarsus turned around. "You suggesting the lizard set them off?"

"I…" Bergis' newfound aggression slipped away when faced
with the colonel's impatience. "I don't know."

"You were in the infirmary, Corporal. You saw what that beast
is capable of. We can't sit and wait for it to reemerge from hiding
and attack again. It's too dangerous to send small reconnaissance
teams out there. We need to strike hard and fast."

It was the winning attitude Tarsus was notorious for. The
creature had drawn first blood. Now he wanted payback.

Yet, something still felt off. Bergis knew the colonel was a
professional. Yet, it seemed he was eager to rush headfirst into this
situation for a quick result.

Pressure from headquarters, maybe?

Bergis didn't buy that. Tarsus was the type of guy to tell his superiors to stick it where the sun don't shine if they presented dumb ideas.

"Unless there are no further questions, gentlemen, this briefing is over. Report to your stations in fifteen minutes."

Right then, a series of pings rang out from everyone's devices. All operatives stood up and began hustling to their assignments.

Bergis checked his.

Strike team. Mech Unit Three.

He got his wish. He was going after the Spinosaurus.

Hopefully, the armaments on his mech would be enough to put the thing out of its misery.

CHAPTER 7

The Model S-4 Battle Mechs were undergoing their inspection by the dock crew when Lon Bergis arrived. Standing at twenty-two feet in height, they were one of the latest advancements in military engineering.

Granted, it was not military personnel who invented the mechs, but private citizens. It was not war they were originally designed for, at least not in the literal sense, but sporting events. As the 21st Century pushed on, humans required new avenues of entertainment. With the world tiring of the digital age, mankind's collective consciousness took a liking to robotics. What better entertainment could one get than the new sport of robot fighting?

It did not take long for someone in the military to take notice. A new model of battle mechs were rushed into production, and within two years, they became the primary heavy armor, replacing the M1 Abrams tank as the centerpiece. Humanoid in shape, they moved on two legs as opposed to treads, earning them the nickname marchers.

They were capable of much more than marching. Their right forearms were equipped with a Bushmaster autocannon, their left with a miniaturized L30A3 tank gun, capable of firing 120mm shells.

Though Bergis spent most of his Army days behind the controls of the M3 Scorpion, he was plenty experienced with the S-4s. Unlike tanks of yesteryear and the Scorpion mechs that came later, the S-4s were operated by one pilot.

Three of them stood in their bays, retrieving a full battery charge from the grounds crew. A fourth one was held up by cables. It almost resembled a giant string puppet, its arms barely attached to the partially imploded torso. Its armor plating looked like crumpled paper, the wire guts hanging from the abdomen and hips.

"Looks like a five-million-dollar chew toy."

Bergis looked to his left. Approaching from behind him was Louis Boyka, a mech pilot who joined the service after a few bouts in the Chicago stadium. Confident after his victories bashing other mechs, he thought it would be fun to take it to the next level and operate one with heavy weaponry.

He stood a head taller than Bergis and had forearms marked with tattoos from his ringside days.

"It's been a while since I've seen one mangled like that," he continued. "I messed one up pretty good in Illinois one time. It was a good thirty-minute bout." He pointed at the ravaged mech. "They say the pilot didn't even know what hit him. The machine went down in under two minutes. I guess he tried to respond to the flight deck attack. Wasn't prepared for what was in store for him."

Bergis nodded. Going by what Boyka said, 'they' was actually a 'he', and that 'he' was Hoover.

"I'm assuming the pilot wasn't able to get a shot off."

Boyka shook his head. "Nothing that hit its mark. Thing supposedly was gone when he arrived. Jumped him from the tree line. Now we're down to three. That, and your Scorpion. Where is it, by the way?"

"Down by the dig site," Bergis said. "A little too far out of the way. Not to mention a tad big for where we're going."

Boyka made a face. "I keep hoping we'll get word that the Spinosaurus has vacated the area and moved to the central hills. It's almost as though it knows we're coming after it and is baiting us into a trap." He glanced around to make sure he wasn't being overheard. "And the colonel's walking us right into it."

"It's a big lizard. How hard could it be to kill?"

Bergis had a feeling Stacy Ward was going to be the third mech operator assigned to this mission. Her cockiness was on full display, from the strut of her entrance into the garage to the hotshot tone in her voice. Her brunette hair was tied back, soon to be covered with her pilot's helmet.

"My first thought would be you weren't paying attention during briefing," Bergis replied.

Stacy sported a white-toothed smile. "Oh, trust me, I heard every word."

"Which leads me to my second thought," Bergis said. "You've got your head up your ass."

That smile went away.

"Geez, you're testy."

"Whoa!" Boyka, knowing the corporal well enough to understand the kind of fire Stacy was lighting, stepped between them. He faced the latter. "You do realize he lost pals out there, right?"

"I'm as well aware as everyone," she said. "Just as we're aware he was the only one who walked out. With only some bruising. Funny how he keeps getting lucky that way."

Bergis suddenly became aware of the many eyes on him. He recognized the body language of people talking amongst each other, trying not to be heard by the one they were speculating about.

He looked to the two crewmen by his S-4. "How much longer until it's charged?"

One of them checked a reader. "Close. About five minutes."

Enough time for Bergis to get a breath of fresh air.

He exited the garage and made a left, keeping outside the gathering of the response team. Roughly thirty security operatives, all fully armed, made up the group. Some sat in Boars, ready to get started. The turrets were already manned. Everyone and their brother wanted dibs on shooting the dinosaur. There hardly appeared to be a sense of retribution for the fallen or a desire to prevent further casualties. No, they just wanted to be the first to claim they shot and killed a dinosaur.

At the front of the line of Boars was Colonel Tarsus and Dr. Dietz. The former, like the men he commanded, was fully equipped from head to toe and held a Ravager M4 battle rifle. His rank never made him soft. He was a fighter at heart, and no insignia on his arm would ever change that.

Hoover was with them, nodding along while the colonel spoke. Bergis exhaled slowly. Go figure the guy was selected for the response effort. Odds were the colonel wanted to use him for intelligence on the creature.

The fact he was not consulted after the briefing spoke volumes. Either Colonel Tarsus did not believe Bergis, or he did not like what he heard. It did seem a little uncharacteristic for Tarsus to move with such haste and to disregard important information. Maybe he believed killing a big reptilian did not require extensive planning. Most people seemed to believe the L30A3 guns on the S-4s would be enough to do the trick.

Bergis could not necessarily hold that reasoning against them. After all, he leaned on the same logic when he first heard about the counterattack. Even after what he witnessed, it was hard to imagine the Spinosaurus could withstand too much punishment.

The more he thought about it, the more he questioned his memory. He was in fact dazed through most of the event, and the battle with the rest of his squad was a considerable distance from where he lay. Maybe the thing did take more damage than he thought. It would explain why it went into the thickest part of the jungle.

"Lon? You okay?"

Only one individual on the entire island referred to Bergis by his first name. Dr. Riley McKeon practically materialized out of nowhere. She emerged from the crowd, looking entirely different than their meeting in the infirmary. Her white coat, trousers, and blouse were traded in for black tactical pants, boots, and a long sleeve shirt and vest. Her hair was tied back into a bun, and on her hip was a 9mm Shipley pistol. Some of the non security staff were given the opportunity for weapons training by the company in case of wartime emergencies. Looking at that semiautomatic on her thigh, she took advantage of it.

"I'm good," he said. "Shouldn't you be in the infirmary?"

"Colonel Tarsus asked for a medic," she replied. "I guess you aren't aware—several of the EMTs were injured or killed by the thing. Others are still out with the firefighters."

"You volunteered?" Bergis exclaimed.

Riley scowled. "That offends you? Weren't you foaming at the mouth to join the convoy? If they didn't assign you, I'm certain you'd be poking at the colonel's shoulder, nagging him to let you tag along."

"I have a score to settle."

"A score to settle?" She stepped closer to him. "Or something to prove?"

Bergis stood quietly for a moment. It was as though Riley had a probe in his brain feeding her every thought in his head, even the subconscious ones. There was no beating around the bush with her. She had a read on his every action, including his desire to take the job, his persistence in getting Globus to salvage the Scorpion mech, and his friendship with Galloway.

"You're not a coward," she continued. "Even if you think you are. You don't need to gun a dinosaur down in order to prove otherwise."

Bergis shrugged. "As much as I appreciate that, my orders say otherwise. What about you? Why are you so eager to tag along? Got a death wish? Or are *you* the one trying to prove something?"

With a break in eye contact and a derisive smile, Riley stepped back.

"You're just mad I beat you at the arcade," she said.

It was a successful method of breaking Bergis' icy exterior, even if slightly. A few days after he arrived on the island, he was making a few extra bucks beating all of his buddies at a *Street Fighter* arcade in the rec center. When asking for any new challengers willing to go for his accumulated six hundred dollars, only one voice came out of the crowd.

He, nor anyone else on base, expected the charming lady doctor to have the digital skill set of Bruce Lee, Chuck Norris, and Georges St-Pierre combined, but she did.

She was nice enough to buy him a drink with the money.

"Well.., we all know you cheated," he remarked.

Riley made a few 'tisk' sounds. "Tell you what: let's get through our dinosaur hunt in one piece. And when we get back, we'll honor your buddy with a rematch. You know him better than I, but I do recall him saying something about him wanting his funeral to be a party with lots of betting on fights."

Bergis snorted. That sounded like something Galloway would say when off duty, especially when being treated in the infirmary. Being on an island near Asia, there were plenty of tropical infections going around which required medical attention. Often, soldiers would make light of their ailments by acting as though their rash or sores were fatal.

Loud beeps from the towing vehicle made Bergis look at the garage. It was time to load the S-4s onto the towing trailer.

"Saddle up!" Tarsus announced. "Get your game faces on, people. We've got ourselves a lizard to hunt."

Riley picked up her bag and gave Bergis a nod. It was her way of wishing him the best of luck, both in the physical battle, and the internal one fueling it.

As of right now, Bergis only gave a damn about the former. He spun on his heel and marched to his mech.

CHAPTER 8

The final three Dragonfly aircrafts, designated Drago Unit, passed overhead in the initiation of their patrols. The boat units checked in through the radio, confirming that they were near the west beaches. All around the flight deck, garage, and Command Central, foot patrols were constant. Nobody was off duty, and until the threat was eradicated, that was how things would remain.

Colonel Tarsus was in the lead vehicle with Dr. Dietz and Godfrey. Two Boars traveled behind them, then the personnel carrier, and the towing vehicle with the three S-4 'marcher' mechs. They exited the east gate and took a left to travel around the north perimeter fence.

Bergis sat in the backseat of the towing vehicle, in-between Boyka and Stacy Ward. There, he was subjected to their endless trash talk and jokes. He kept his eyes forward, his mind switching from the Spinosaurus, the attack that claimed Galloway's life, and trying to spot Riley in the personnel carrier.

The start of the trip took them past the front of Command Central. Even after several months on the island, it was still a hell of a sight. Globus spared no expense with their fortress.

A perimeter fence separated the five-acre lot from the rest of the island. A service drive led through a check-in station and gate at the northern side. Guard towers were manned by two operatives. Like everything else on the island, they were thought to be overkill by most of the staff, until today.

On the other side of that gate was a small gathering of buildings, the largest being Command Central itself. Similar to the White House design, it had an east and west wing, and a center executive station. The west wing contained the labs and infirmary, the east holding the mess hall, galley, crew quarters, the lounge, and a few offices. All of the really important administrative functions took place in the central part of the building.

Other structures inside the perimeter included a water treatment plant, a workout center, warehouse, greenhouse, and generator building. The garage was on the easternmost side of the settlement, with its own gate allowing for patrols to come and go.

Before long, the fortress was out of sight, and the convoy was surrounded by bright green vegetation. They followed the trail northwest in the direction of Blooming Lake.

A mile and a half into the journey, they came to a clearing that was Dig Site Eight. It was the third largest of the digs, and over twice as wide as the one Bergis was assigned to. Heaps of metal that were once jeeps and construction vehicles lay around the gaping mine. Based on the information shared through the personnel tablets, Site Eight was hit not too long after Teams Three and Five encountered the beast.

"All units, halt," Colonel Tarsus ordered. The five vehicles in the convoy were quick to obey. Several men filed out of the carrier, rifles shouldered and ready to shoot anything that moved while the colonel, Dietz, and Godfrey moved to inspect the mine.

"Wonder what's on the colonel's mind," Boyka said.

"I thought he was in a hurry to kill a lizard," Stacy replied. "I guess he'd rather stare into a hole."

Bergis shook his head. "Colonel's not the type to waste time. Something's got his attention."

Right then, Tarsus spoke through the radio. *"Bergis, Hoover, join me at the mine."*

"On my way." Bergis tapped his fellow mech pilots on the shoulder. "Case and point."

He exited the towing vehicle and made his way to the mine. Hoover was already ahead of him. The anxious rookie wore sunglasses and a stone-faced expression, the look of every person who wanted to appear tough and serious.

The veil came to a quick and clumsy end when the knucklehead tripped on a charred helmet on the ground. Hoover hopped on one foot and did a complete spin before regaining his balance. Saving face, he gave a thumbs up to the guys on the carrier.

"All good! All good!"

Bergis bumped him with his shoulder. "How about you take those damn things off?"

Hoover removed the glasses and walked with him. "In my defense... eh, who am I kidding? These things are cheap crap." He tossed the shades aside. "I know a guy who is selling some nice aviators. Maybe I'll hit him up after we're done."

"Thanks for sharing," a disinterested Bergis said.

"Don't mock a man's choice in sunglasses," Godfrey said. He proudly sported his own aviators after overhearing the two approaching operatives. Somehow, Bergis could sense the mercenary was trying to get a response.

Colonel Tarsus had his hands behind his back while relentlessly studying the pit.

"Gentlemen, you both saw the creature... this Spinosaurus... or Sailsaur, as I heard someone refer to it."

Hoover leaned over to Bergis. "Damn! Maybe that name *will* catch on! Wonder if it can be copyrighted..."

Bergis shut him up by elbowing him.

"Its claws," Tarsus continued, "how large were they?"

As he spoke, he directed their eyes to markings in the crater walls.

Bergis immediately understood the purpose of the question after spotting the marks. They were made by three-digit instruments.

Claws.

There were dozens of them. Hundreds, even, originating from the bottom of the hundred-foot pit all the way up to the edges. They were widespread, with some trails directly across from where he stood, and others on the west and east sides.

Whatever had made them was numerous and large, hence the colonel's question. He needed to know if he was going to war against one reptilian beast or many.

Bergis shook his head. "Whatever made these was smaller. The Spinosaurus has hefty claws. Its talons are almost as long as a man. These markings were made by something big, but not *that* big."

"I agree," Hoover added. "That said, I think it's safe to say we have a new development in the situation. There's a new player in the game." He gestured at the wide spread of claw marks. "Or *players.*"

"More lizards?" Godfrey asked. "Offspring, maybe? Hence the smaller size. Our Spinosaurus might have some pesky kids running around. Good thing we packed some heavy weapons."

Bergis shook his head. "No, these don't look right. The Spinosaurus' claws were like hooks. If it was climbing out of the pit, it would have dug in deeper. Even a smaller one would have. These markings are all shallow, and more importantly, they're singular. Double at most. Not three-fingered markings like what the reptilian would have left."

Hoover leaned over the ledge for a better look into the depths of the pit. The sediment and gravel at the bottom had a strange violet color where the meteorite minerals were harvested. It was a sight many people hardly got used to, and it was a substance requiring heavy equipment and specialized suits for extracting.

"You guys see what I'm seeing?" He pointed at two dark spots in the pit.

Tarsus took a look through his binocs. "Good eyes, Hoover." He passed the glasses to Dietz. "You were wrong, Doctor. Whatever made the markings did not fall down the pit. They emerged from under the ground."

Dietz took a quick look then dismissingly passed the glasses back to the colonel.

"Impossible. This is the third-largest deposit. Nothing could survive down there with all of that Element X material."

"So you say," Tarsus replied. "But it doesn't take a scientist to know those holes were not there before. And I don't know about you, but I'd say those tunnels run deep."

"Irrelevant," Dietz said. "We've discovered nothing but bone fragments down there. No signs of life."

Hoover raised his hand. "Excuse me? *Bone* fragments? Not *fossil* fragments?"

Dietz had a deer in the headlights look on his face. He was used to talking down to everyone else about science matters without getting substantive questions.

Bergis found himself making the gruff, tough guy face. It was all he could do to make sure he did not reveal how impressed he was. Maybe Hoover's nerdy reading and documentary watching was actually proving useful.

Not only that, no matter how much he wanted to deny it, he could not unsee the similarities he had with the soldier wannabe. Who was Bergis to poke fun of Hoover's fascination with science? Just that morning, he was being made fun of by Galloway for his supposed knowledge in meteorite density and geology.

One thing he was *not* knowledgeable on, though, was prehistoric predators.

Dietz cleared his throat. "Well, there was a deal of calcium mixed with sediment…"

"But what about the collagen levels?" Hoover said.

Everyone stared at him, Dietz being the most perplexed of them all.

"Fossilized bone is mostly made up of calcium carbonate which replaces the original organic matter. Organic bones are mostly made up of materials like collagen. So, I'll ask again: what were the collagen levels in the bones?"

Bergis rubbed his chin, then pointed his thumb at Hoover. "Yeah, Doc. What he said… What were the Callahan levels?"

"Collagen," Hoover whispered.

"Yeah, collagen," Bergis said.

Now even Tarsus was interested. His piercing stare was enough to get the ambitious geologist to spit out the truth.

"The bones—they were not fossilized."

Hoover perked up. "They were preserved in their organic state?"

"It's possible they were not dinosaur bones," Dietz said. "Further analysis is needed, but…"

"Yeah, sure," Bergis said, shaking his head. "It's perfectly reasonable a giant crocodile dug its way down there and died."

"Doc, you think I'm an idiot?" Tarsus said. It was a change in tone that struck everyone around him. Tarsus' matter-of-fact and calculated demeanor had momentarily lifted, and in its place was the hint of a dangerous force of nature ready to unleash its wrath. "Two months ago, you were practically bragging about the preserved skeletons you discovered… or rather, *my men* discovered, and you identified. You had said they were the most intact theropod specimens ever found. Now, you're actually trying to tell me they aren't dinosaurs? I've seen the bones, Dietz. I urge you to rethink your explanation and preferably come up with something that doesn't involve me being a moron. I might not understand the calcium-preservation-fossilization crap, but I damn well know what a dinosaur skeleton looks like."

Dietz made careful use of a period of silence before giving his reply. He was notorious for butting heads with the colonel over trivial things like procedures and decision of resources. Tarsus generally was laid back and diplomatic with the geologist. This time, however, the colonel looked and sounded as though he would turn Dietz into minced meat if he said the wrong thing.

"Okay, we've found preserved dinosaurian remains, among other species," Dietz said. "We've been a little busy with Element X to perform proper analysis…"

"And didn't want to send samples out and risk someone else claiming any kind of credit for the discovery," Bergis said.

"It doesn't matter," Dietz said. "As I said before, it's irrelevant because it's unrelated to the current situation."

"Right, sure," Bergis said.

"Nothing could survive prolonged contact with the element," Dietz insisted.

Tarsus was done listening to him, as was Godfrey.

"If the element could preserve ancient remains, perhaps it could do much more," the latter said. "Can't believe I'm suggesting this with a straight face, but what if the meteorite managed to preserve more than just bones?"

Dietz laughed. "You're suggesting a dinosaur has been kept in suspended animation for a hundred million years?"

Godfrey shrugged. "Oh, gee. Since we've got a—what do you call it? A *dinosaur* running around wrecking shit, I'm willing to consider any explanation."

"Sir?" Hoover said to Tarsus. "Maybe we should consider holding off on attacking the creature until we have more information. We don't know what else might be out here in addition to the Spinosaurus. God only knows what crawled out of this pit. I don't even see any tracks outside of the edges. It's as though they crawled out and just vanished."

Bergis looked at the ground around the mine and instantly felt stupid for not noticing that little detail himself.

"He might have a point." It was painful to acknowledge, but facts were facts.

Tarsus shook his head. "Negative. We have a lead on the reptile. We need to destroy it quickly before it causes any more problems."

"Sir, going after it might be the problem," Bergis suggested.

"Your concern has been noted," Tarsus said. His tone was teetering on harsh, being just intense enough to deter the corporal from persisting. "Return to your vehicles. We're carrying on."

Hoover gave a look of concern to Bergis, hoping one of them would have the stones to talk the colonel out of committing to the attack. Neither of them did.

Following a unanimous "Yes air," they returned to their rides.

Bergis climbed into the towing vehicle and took a seat between Boyka and Stacy. The infantrymen returned to the carrier. After an order from the colonel through the radio, the convoy resumed its course.

"What was all that about?" Boyka asked. "What was down there?"

Bergis gave one last look at the mine before it was out of sight.

"That's what I'm still trying to figure out."

CHAPTER 9

The Blooming Lake was a gorgeous invention of Mother Nature. Equivalent to three acres, it was a regular area of outdoor recreation for the Globus personnel on the island. A large rock wall overlooked its northwest side. After a large rainstorm, a waterfall would trickle into the lake from the top ledge, often lasting for days.

It was at this point the vehicles became useless. The higher elevation and thicker jungle on this side of the island made passage incredibly difficult, if not impossible.

The convoy came to a stop near the southeast corner of the lake. First to set foot on the ground was Colonel Tarsus. A true war fighter, he had his weapon firmly grasped and pointed low, ready to be pointed at anything even resembling a threat.

"Hope you enjoyed the ride, boys and girls. We walk from here."

"Suits us just fine," Stacy Ward said. She disembarked from the towing vehicle and went straight to the trailer to board her mech.

Bergis and Boyka set foot on the ground. The latter of the two scraped his boot against the rough gravel.

"I'm with her. It's rough terrain out there. Them guys are sure to get blisters on their feet. I guess we should count ourselves as the lucky ones."

"I'm not sure lucky is the word," Bergis said. "Given the size of the mechs, we'll be the very first thing the beast will notice. Ergo, it'll attack us first." He gave a look to the thick forest in front of them. The more he looked at it, the more he opposed the colonel's plan of flushing the Spinosaurus out. "I don't like this. Using our cannons will be difficult. We'll have obstacles every few feet. We're more likely to blow ourselves up than that thing."

"The chain guns should do the trick," Boyka said.

"Not based on what I saw," Bergis said.

"What you saw." Boyka sported a sardonic grin. "Your face was pretty much kissing the ground when they found you. You had your bell rung pretty good. You sure you saw what you saw? I mean, you really think the thing took all that punishment without getting hurt? No offense, but I find that a little hard to believe."

Bergis was not sure how he wanted to respond. Part of him was ready with a sly remark. Another part urged him to say nothing. He decided to follow that strategy.

His attention went to the rest of the platoon. The thirty soldiers were gathering on the north side of the lake. Tarsus was in another debate with Dr. Dietz, this time regarding whether the geologist should wait here with the vehicles rather than risk himself unnecessarily in the hunt. Dietz, based on his body language and tone, clearly intended to tag along, probably to ensure his precious meteorite sites would not be damaged. According to his research, they were shallower than the other fragments, meaning they were more vulnerable to explosives.

Bergis scanned the crowd with his eyes, spotting Dr. Riley McKeon.

"You coming, Corporal?" Boyka asked, waving him towards the mechs.

"In a minute," Bergis replied. He jogged over to where Riley stood. Go figure, Hoover was standing right by her.

The guy's like a cockroach. Always turning up wherever I go.

Two men strutted in front of them. Zackery and Howell, two former airmen from Seattle. They were visibly irritated, not bothering to maintain the veneer of discipline.

Howell stopped to look at Bergis. "Wanna trade?"

Suddenly, it became clear why they were moody.

"Stuck with guarding the vehicles, huh?" Bergis said.

"Yeeeep!" Zackery said. "Don't know why he didn't assign you to the role. I hear you're pretty talented at waiting on the sidelines while other people do the fighting."

Bergis held his breath. Zackery was well known for being a provocateur. He was already on thin ice with the company. In all likelihood, it was probably why the colonel assigned him to guarding the vehicles. The last thing he needed during the hunt was trouble from his personnel, and this was the area where Zackery was least likely to cause any.

In the crowd behind the grumpy operative was Godfrey's tagalong, Munro. He was watching the interaction, having obviously spread word of Bergis' secret from Algiers.

Riley, sensing the tension, stepped over. "Guys, this is not the time. And Zackery, learn to shut up. I've treated you twice in the infirmary after you've gotten your ass kicked. I'm going to be too busy out here to scrape you off the ground if you get on someone's bad side."

Zackery gave her a bitter glance, then looked to Howell for support. The older, less amused security operative simply walked off, desiring not to deal with his colleague's antics.

"Hope you know what you're getting yourself into," he said to Riley. "For all we know, he might use you for bait so he can get away if things go south."

"Says the guy who got busted to E-1 because he was caught with vodka while on duty and tried to pin it on one of his fellow airmen," Bergis said.

"At least everyone I served with came back alive," Zackery hissed. He rested his rifle over his shoulder and moved to the lake. There was nothing else for him to do around here. The view was all he had going for him.

Hoover brushed his hands against his pants. "Nice to see you're good at making friends."

"I guess I have a natural talent for being a shit magnet," Bergis said. Hoover leaned away from him, stung by the pointed delivery of those words.

"Wow. You're mean." Hoover pointed at the mechs. "Aren't you supposed to be manning one of those things? We're gonna be heading out in a minute."

"I am. I wanted to have a word with the doctor first."

A look of concern came over the doctor's face. "Are you okay? Need painkillers for your shoulder?"

"No, no, I—" Bergis smiled. Something about her natural caregiving personality warmed him. Even now, on the verge of beginning a tense trek through thick jungle, the wellbeing of her fellow staff was forefront on her mind. It was a quality that furthered his motivation for speaking with her. "I'm okay, thanks. Actually, I wanted to ask if you're going to be armed with anything more than that Shipley."

Riley looked down at her sidearm. "This not enough?"

"Against that thing? Absolutely not," Bergis said. "More importantly, we don't know what else might be out there. So…" He unslung his rifle and extended it toward her.

Riley almost recoiled from the prospect of handling such an intimidating looking weapon.

"Oh!"

"Don't worry, it won't bite you," Bergis said.

"I'll be with a bunch of people who'll be armed with the same thing," she said.

"True." Bergis pointed at her sidearm. "Then why bother having that?"

"As a precaution," she replied.

"Precisely. Consider this a better, more effective precaution."

Riley smiled and gently accepted the weapon. He showed her how to properly hold it and placed its strap over her shoulder.

"You sure you won't need it?" she asked.

"I'll be cramped inside a mech," Bergis said. "It won't do me much good while I'm in there. And if I have to bail out quickly, I might not be able to grab ahold of the gun anyway. See, it's stored on an overhead rack in the cockpit. Can't have it on our person or else it would be digging into our body the whole time. Trust me, it's safer in your hands."

"Okay." Riley rocked the weapon in her grasp and got used to the weight. She looked over its thick barrel and frame, then put her eyes to the iron sights. "Mind giving me a crash course in using this thing?"

"That was part of my plan," Bergis said. "Don't worry, it's not as complex as it might look. And if you have more questions while we're out, Hoover will be able to help you." He turned his eyes to the inexperienced, but probably most trustworthy security operative.

Hoover recognized the look he was receiving and the meaning behind it.

"I'll stay close to her. I'll watch her six. Won't take my eyes off it." Hoover swallowed, instantly realizing how that sounded. He cleared his throat. "I mean, not watching her behind, but everything *that is* behind her."

"Hoover, sometimes a simple 'yes' will do," Bergis said.

Hoover gave a thumbs up. "Understood. And… agreed."

Bergis put his hand on Riley's shoulder and led her to the lake.

"Okay, what you've got here is a T-4 Python assault rifle. It's armed with standard light armor piercing rounds, forty to a mag. You see the switch on the frame? That has four settings: safety, semiautomatic, three-round burst, and fully automatic. I recommend you either use semi or burst. Conserve your ammo."

Riley pushed the switch with her thumb.

"Okay. Understood."

"When you are ready to use the weapon, hold it so the stock is against your shoulder," Bergis helped her position the weapon, keeping its rifle pointed out at the lake.

"How heavy is the kick?" she asked.

"Not too bad as long as you keep a good stance. Make sure you don't square up like you do with basic handgun training. Keep your feet and shoulders at a forty-five-degree angle. Make sure your weight is on the balls of your feet and not the heels. Otherwise, you'll be more likely to lose your balance when it recoils."

Riley got a feel for the weapon. She swept its muzzle across the lake.

"I guess I have a new toy to play with at the shooting range," she said. "You ever consider a career as a firearms instructor?"

"Ha." Bergis shook his head. "I'm not much of a people person."

Riley turned to look at him. "I don't think that's as true as you think."

Bergis knew the meaning behind her reply. What he didn't know was whether he wanted to acknowledge it as the truth. Aside from his hangouts with Galloway, he avoided most social gatherings since Algiers. Since then, though he rarely spoke about it, he was on the go, staying away from home where his family and those of his friends lived. Somehow, Riley could sense he was avoiding them, and how it was not out of a desire to be alone.

"Corporal Bergis!" Godfrey shouted. "Quit flirting with the doc and get aboard your mech! The colonel wants to move out, and you're dicking around and holding us up."

"Yeah, dickhead!" Zackery said. The grouchy guard was standing at the shoreline, idly attempting to skip stones across the lake. "What's the holdup? Trying to avoid another firefight? Figure if you hold back long enough, you can slip away and let everyone else shoot the thing?" He laughed and tossed another stone.

Bergis gave a hardened glare at the jerk. Part of him was ready to oblige Zackery's thirst for confrontation. He was a bully, and Bergis was a firm believer that a good ass whooping was the best cure for their behavior.

His gaze went to the spot where Zackery's last stone disappeared. The ripples were wide and moving fast. He had seen the pebble Zackery had tossed, and it definitely did not look as though it weighed as much as a bowling ball.

"Corporal!" Godfrey shouted.

"You deaf?" Munro joined in. "The captain is talking to you, dummy."

Their voices were nothing but background noises to Bergis' laser-focused mind. He hook notice of some unrelated ripples farther out in the water. To his knowledge, nothing lived in this lake. No fish, no amphibians, nothing. There were not even any birds, which was even more strange. Being the only source of natural freshwater for miles, it was a popular spot for the island's indigenous species to gather. Only now did he notice the platoon was literally alone.

The presence of men and vehicles would not stop local and migrating birds from making their usual rounds at Blooming Lake.

No, something else had scared them off. And *scared* was the accurate term. Only fear and the instinct of self-preservation would keep the feathered travelers from this waterhole.

Fear of something *in* that waterhole.

"Zackery…"

"He speaks!" the guard said.

"…get away from the water."

Zackery smirked. He was expecting a one-liner or a snide remark from the corporal. Instead, he was getting a random warning about the lake.

"The hell's the matter with the water?"

"There's something in it."

Zackery laughed. "The Spino's way too big to hide in there without being seen." He picked up a nice round stone. "I think it's safe to assume you've lost your marbles."

He tossed the stone in the water.

Splash.

Bergis took his rifle from Riley and pointed it at the lake. "Move!"

Even though the instruction was directed at Zackery, Riley backpedaled as though he was speaking to her. Hoover took her place, rifle at the ready.

Behind them, the entire platoon was watching. They made a lane for Colonel Tarsus and Godfrey, who were quickly joined by Munro and Sagara.

"Uh-oh! See what you did? You pissed off the colonel." Zackery picked up another stone. "Can't wait to see you explain to him your crusade against the monster of Blooming Lake."

"The hell's going on over here?" Tarsus barked.

Bergis did not break his stance. He kept his weapon trained on the water.

"Zackery..."

"Take a chill pill," Zackery said. He idly tossed the stone a few inches into the air and caught it. "You're a certified nut. There's nothing in the lake. Except this stone."

He tossed it.

It touched down twenty feet out.

SPLASH!!!

The water rose like fire and ejecta matter from an asteroid impact. From the epicenter of crashing water emerged a rounded mass with green leathery skin and two black eyes. Its body was over fifteen feet from its ugly face to the fin on the back of its mantle.

From below those eyes was a gathering of serpentine arms. Without hesitation, they lashed out like striking rattlesnakes.

Zackery's condescending sneer transformed into an open-mouthed look of horror and disbelief. Two of the arms, dripping lake water and slime, snagged the guard and plucked him off the shoreline.

His rifle strap slid off his shoulders and hit the dirt. Reaching with both arms, Zackery pleaded to the very soldier he mocked.

"Help me!—BLECH!"

The two tentacles pulled him in half.

All at once, the platoon went into disarray at the sight of blood and guts raining into the once beautiful lake.

"Whoa!" an astonished Howell exclaimed. It was simultaneously a gasp from witnessing his buddy's fate and a cry of terror as one of those slimy limbs came at him. Its underside was lined with large pores. From those pores, curved teeth protruded, like those of a tiger shark.

The tentacle wrapped tightly around his abdomen, driving those teeth deep into his flesh.

As it lifted him, other arms stretched in the direction of the other humans. They came over the shoreline, revealing lengths exceeding fifty feet.

Bergis fired off a few bursts. Large holes erupted in the nearest tentacle. Jetting black fluid, it retracted to the main body.

"Holy—" Hoover fired off a few bursts, managing to hit one of the tentacles.

Colonel Tarsus got right down to business barking orders to his platoon.

"Squads one, two, and three, take the right flank! Stay out of the reach of that thing. Four and five, move left. The rest of us will keep its attention while you create a crossfire. And get the mechs off the trailer, damn it!"

He joined Bergis and Hoover in batting the swarm of tentacles. The guard, Howell, was in the water near the umbrella-like series of joints where the arms connected with the mantle.

A final gargling cry left the man's throat before his abdomen was compressed all the way down to his spinal cord. His body perforated, letting loose fountains of blood and crushed organs.

Bergis took aim at its head and squeezed the trigger. At the same time, one of the arms slashed at him like a whip. He fell backwards, avoiding its constricting grasp around his body. The tentacle wasted no time moving down with him.

He felt the wetness of its skin around his ankle and shin, then the prodding of those weird teeth on the verge of cutting down to the bone.

"Hold still!" Hoover shouted. He moved to Bergis' foot and shot the arm point blank. Strands of tissue stretched between the tentacle stub and its severed end as it retracted into the lake.

Bergis scooted back, dragging three feet of tentacle from his ankle. Tarsus grabbed him by the shoulder strap of his vest and pulled him off the ground.

The beast slapped the water, its meaty stub jetting fluid like water from a garden hose. Its body shifted back and forth, pushing hundreds of gallons over the shoreline in large swells.

It pulled its hefty mass to the edge of the leg. Bergis, Tarsus, and Hoover formed a firing line and pumped lead into its face. Large holes popped under those big eyes. It reared back, exposing the jaws under its mantle. It was not a beak like normal cephalopods, but rather resembled the mouth of a lamprey, with teeth arranged in concentric circles.

"Light her up," Godfrey said through the radio.

The two teams initiated the crossfire. More holes popped open across the creature's body. Its tentacles slashed the air with increased ferocity, each one searching for the strange source of the seemingly invisible stingers entering its body.

Mechanical gears whined and heavy footsteps rocked the earth.

Behind Bergis, Tarsus, and Hoover was Stacy Ward piloting her three-ton mech.

"Let's get out of the way," the colonel said.

The three men moved behind the mech.

Stacy aimed its right arm at the beast and armed the Bushmaster.

"Sayonara, sucker."

The autocannon fired off a stream of 25mm rounds. In a matter of moments, the already tattered mantle lost all semblance of its original shape.

Shreds of tissue flew in all directions. The natural bluish-green color of the water turned into an oily brown. Bits of muscle and internal organs drifted across the lake. The arms ceased their slashing and sank like drowning worms tossed from a fisherman's bucket.

Boyka arrived in his mech, only to lower his cannon after seeing that the threat was already dealt with.

"Awe!"

"That's what happens when you're slow," Stacy said through the comm.

The platoon gathered around the colonel. A soundtrack of questions and concern replaced the stunned silence.

"The hell was that thing?"

"Two of our guys are already dead!"

"Where'd it come from?"

"What else is out here?"

"It was a freaking octopus!"

"Octopuses live in saltwater. This lake only has freshwater."

"Isn't it octopi?"

"You're seriously worried about proper octopus terminology right now?"

Tarsus waved a hand. "Everybody, calm down."

As the group settled into silence, Bergis took a look at Riley. She was just as rattled as everyone else, her eyes still frozen on the drifting mass of body parts.

"You alright?"

"Y-yeah." She caught her breath. "I think I'm a little more open to taking your rifle, if the offer is still on the table."

He loaded a fresh magazine and handed the weapon to her. "Didn't expect to give you a demonstration so soon."

She flipped the switch to semi-automatic.

"Shit happens, I guess."

The sound of Dr. Dietz' jittery voice redirected their minds to the situation at hand.

"I don't know what the thing was! How the hell should I know?" he shouted. "Do I look like a marine biologist to you?"

"I think you know more than you're letting on," Tarsus said.

"Whatever it was, it came from one of the dig sites," Hoover said. "Sir, I think it's safe to assume we've awoken some kind of dormant ecosystem."

Tarsus kept his eyes on Dietz as he listened to the young operative.

"Maybe I should've brought him along as my science adviser."

Dietz spat on the ground. "He's a kid who's watched too much television."

"Maybe we should pull back," one of the sergeants said. "We just lost two men, sir. We don't know what else might be out here. If we can take the time to plan out a new strategy—"

"Can that crap right now, soldier!"

The sergeant was quick to shut up at the unusual occurrence of the colonel's unveiled anger.

"Jesus!" a chuckling Godfrey said. "Bunch of wussies here. You all do realize the Spinosaurus is probably aware of our position. It could be watching us right now. Given what just occurred, it's safe to assume it's interpreting our presence as a treat. If we head back, it might follow us right to Command Central."

"That's why he's paid the big bucks," Tarsus said. "He's smart."

"Excuse me, sir," the sergeant said. "We can move to a different location."

"Saddle up!" Tarsus said. "Last known sighting was half a klick from here. Let's move. Ward, good shooting. You get to take point."

"Thanks a lot, Colonel."

Stacy steered the S-4 to the front of the platoon.

"What are you waiting for, Corporal?" Godfrey said.

Bergis nodded. Before going to his mech, he looked at Hoover.

"Stay by her side."

Hoover puffed his chest out. "I'll protect her as if she was my girlfriend." He withered after getting a different facial reaction than what he was going for. "Or yours."

That choice of wording switched Bergis' body language from impatient to plain uncomfortable.

"No, we're not... Just keep an eye on her, okay?"

"Bergis! Mech! Now!" Godfrey called to him.

Bergis maintained his stare.

Hoover nodded. "You've got my word. All I ask in return is that you drop the act and buy her a drink when you get back. Let's face it, you're not fooling anyone."

That statement sparked a tiny, but noticeable smile on the doctor's face. Even after witnessing two men get massacred and a raging sea monster appear out of nowhere, the idea of a date with Bergis still warmed her.

Unfortunately, it failed to have the same effect on him. On any other occasion, it would have. But Bergis knew what was lurking inside the jungle. It had already cost the life of his friend. They were willfully going through hell to fight the baddest demon to ever show its ugly face. It was no place for a non-combatant like Riley.

"Let's survive this first."

There was no more to be said. The corporal turned around and walked to his mech.

The hunt was officially underway.

CHAPTER 10

It was like riding a bike.

Bergis shifted the two joysticks and rolled the foot gears strapped to his boots to get the S-4 through a tight space between two trees. The steel hull scraped against their trunks, removing shards of bark and wood.

He was at the rear of the platoon, assigned to watch their six. Even from the cockpit of the twenty-five-foot-tall machine, he could still sense the uneasiness within the group. Some of the troops were on edge, responding to every sound heard from the distance. Others were unaffected by the deaths of Zackery and Howell. More than that, they were exhilarated by the successful takedown of the cephalopod. For them, as well as the colonel, it boosted their confidence that the Spinosaurus could be taken down.

In its passage through the thick jungle, the Spinosaurus had left a trail of debris in its wake. The footprints were fresh, as were the markings on the trees. The three Dragonfly units reported no movement in the area, meaning the creature was still somewhere in this part of the island.

Bergis was appreciative of being assigned to the back of the group. It allowed him a good vantage point of the whole platoon. More specifically, it enabled him to keep an eye on Riley and Hoover.

From what he could see, the doctor was keeping up with her squad. She held his rifle exactly how he showed her, keeping its muzzle pointed down and her finger off the trigger. Hoover assisted in carrying her medical gear. How she was expected to haul two bags on foot out here, Bergis would never know.

Every so often, she looked back at him. She could not see him through the tinted glass of the cockpit, yet whenever she looked at the mech, her eyes were pointed right at him.

Bergis wanted to chastise her for willingly coming on this mission. He wasn't buying into the idea she was being a dedicated employee and physician. There was something else driving her. Something personal. He could feel it.

"Less than one mile until we arrive at the shoreline," Boyka reported.

"The target must be close," Tarsus said. *"Boat units, be ready. We will attempt to force it to the shoreline. If we're successful, you'll be able to hit it from the water."*

"Copy that, sir."

They continued onward. At the front of the line, Stacy was using her mech to carve a path for the rest of the platoon. A circular saw extended from the stub of her mech's left arm, shredding undergrowth and low-hanging branches.

Boyka's mech was right behind her, its Bushmaster cannon sweeping the jungle in search of a target. Colonel Tarsus, Godfrey, Munro, and Sagara led the ground forces.

"Drago-Three to all units! I've got something!"

All units came to a halt.

"Is it the reptilian?" Colonel Tarsus said.

"Negative! It's something else! It's—whoa!"

Drago-Three's transmission ended abruptly. There was a sharp whining sound of dying engines, followed by the sound of a massive object penetrating the thick canopy.

BOOM!

Sensors picked up readings of shockwaves coming from the northwest. Bergis could not see any fire or smoke from his position. Not that it mattered. It was obvious what the Dragonfly's fate was.

Right away, the ground troops were visibly uneasy. Rifles were pointed in every direction. Those in the group who were already on edge began backing away, unsure if they were willing to commit to the objective.

"Drago-One and Two, report!" Tarsus said.

"Drago-Two here. I'm closing in on the crash area right now."

"Any visual on the creature?" Tarsus asked.

"Negative. It's unclear what happened, sir. Drago-Three was fifty feet above the treetops."

"Distance from my GPS?" the colonel asked.

"Two hundred meters. The fuel cells ignited on impact. There's no way anyone survived—Contact! I've got con—"

A *CRASH* burst through the frequency. Tarsus attempted to regain contact with the pilot, giving up after the sound of thunder in the west.

"Boat Two here. We've got a visual on Drago-Two. It came down on the shoreline."

"Boat One here. I see it. Moving towards you, Two."

"Boat Three heading your way as well."

"Any of you see what happened?" Tarsus asked.

All three boat units replied with *"Negative."*

"Drago One awaiting instructions."

"Drago One, take your bird out over water. Whatever brought our guys down is clearly targeting our aircraft."

"Copy that. Heading over water."

Now Bergis was the one feeling uneasy. His lust for vengeance was overshadowed by a razor-sharp anxiety. This was not the work of the Spinosaurus. The two dragonflies were hit in completely different locations. The reptile may have been stealthy for its size, but there was no way it could cross a couple hundred yards without being heard.

"Colonel, I must suggest we pull back," he said.

"I'm losing my patience with you, Corporal," Tarsus said.

"Sir, we've got at least two bogeys out here. It was one thing when we believed the Spinosaurus was the only hostile. But it's clear we are unprepared and at a disadvantage."

His warning went plainly ignored by the colonel.

"Ward, Boyka, push forward. Get us to the shoreline."

"Aye-Aye, sir," Ward said.

She and Boyka resumed leading the platoon westward.

With no other choice, Bergis followed. Now, he wasn't just watching his surroundings, but also the sky.

CHAPTER 11

As they made their way to the coast, Tarsus had to navigate a path around the fires resulting from Drago-Three. There was no point in investigating the crash, as nothing could have survived the detonation of the fuel cells and armaments. The firefighting teams at Command Central had been put on standby, but were ordered to hold back until the Spinosaurus was dead or confirmed to no longer be in the area.

The instruction was interpreted by many to be out of concern for the lives of the fire rescue team.

Bergis felt otherwise. Following the colonel's odd haste and uncharacteristic hostility, he could not help but suspect the fires were allowed to spread in hope of driving the target out into the open. A steady flame, as long as there were no explosive detonations, would not affect the Element X deposits, so there would be no pushback from Dietz.

After seven hundred meters, the jungle began to thin. Breakers could be heard hitting the shore, and the smell of charred metal made its way through the ventilation system.

The platoon arrived on the shoreline. Even without the wrecked Dragonfly, the view was not easy on the eyes. The whole western shoreline was not comprised of beautiful white-tan beaches, but sulfur deposits and black volcanic sands.

Drago-Two had settled on its starboard side thirty feet from the water line. It came down aft-first, shattering its back rotors on impact, then rolled at least twice before ending up in its current position. The main rotors decorated the beach area, along with pieces of windscreen glass, fiberglass fragments, and rockets which had come free of their pods.

Tarsus' voice came through everyone's receiver. *"Fan out. Teams One, Two, and Three, cover the south end. Four and Five, cover the north. Mech units, form up on the wreckage. Maintain a ten-meter distance. Doctor McKeon, you're with me."*

Everyone moved to their assigned locations. The mechs formed a perimeter around the wreckage, Stacy taking the south side, Boyka the north, and Bergis taking position between it and the shoreline.

Before turning to face the Dragonfly and the island interior, he took a glance at the water. The three boat units had gathered five hundred feet from the shore. They were twenty-two-foot gunboats, each crewed by three security operatives and armed with an M60 machine gun in addition to grenade launchers and small arms. They maintained fifty feet of distance from one another, their total of nine men watching the activity on the beach.

Bergis turned around and opened the windscreen to listen in on the investigation. Tarsus, Dietz, Riley, and Godfrey were gathered at the cockpit.

"I don't understand," Dietz said. "Do you believe he escaped?"

"And gone where?" Godfrey said. "He'd have to be stupid-incarnate to leave this spot."

"There's nothing to suggest the reptilian tracked him over here," Dietz said. "There're no tracks, no damage to the trees aside from the path in which the Dragonfly came down, nothing."

"There's damage to the interior of the cockpit," Riley said. "The instrument panel has damage inconsistent with what the impact would have caused. It appears an edged weapon was used. Not conical, like the creature's claws and teeth would be. No, this is something similar to a blade of sorts. The pilot's seat shows evidence of this as well."

Her words confirmed to Bergis that they were speaking about the disappearance of the pilot.

"Same marks as what we saw in that pit, wouldn't you say, Colonel?" Godfrey said.

"I'd say so," Tarsus replied.

"It's awfully small," Dietz said.

"Big enough to haul the pilot out of there," Godfrey said with a sardonic laugh. "And apparently big enough to bring this thing down."

The geologist groaned. "The reptilian could have done that."

"Yeah? How?" Godfrey said. "Bow and arrow? Cannonball? Atomic breath?"

"Anyway!" Dietz said in a raised voice. "What I meant was whatever did this was small in comparison to the Dragonfly and the Spinosaurus."

Tarsus shrugged. "Your point being?"

Dietz was visibly nervous. More than that, he had the look of a man who was second-guessing his decision to come out here. In addition, Bergis detected a smidge of guilt. Not the kind from somebody whose conscience was bothering him, but that of someone who had a secret on the verge of being exposed.

Tarsus was picking up on those little details as well. He stepped in front of the geologist, his brow furrowed.

"There something you need to share, Doctor?"

Dietz broke eye contact. "I, uh…"

SPLASH!

CRUNCH!

All eyes went to the water. Large waves shot to the sky with explosive force, carrying pieces of one of the patrol boats with it. At the epicenter, the main body had caved in on itself, its occupants lost in the frothing sea.

A heavy motion beneath the surface intensified the swirling of ocean, causing the remains to twist and turn as though caught in a maelstrom.

"Boat Two is down!" One's helmsman announced in a frantic voice. *"I repeat: Boat Two is down! We are under attack!"*

"Three to One, we've got a visual of the bogey. It's huge! It's coming up on your seven o'clock!"

SPLASH!

A wall of water lifted thirty feet high and split apart, unveiling the long muscular neck and crocodilian jaws. The Spinosaurus raised its massive claws and drove them down into the aft deck of Boat One.

Its machine gunner swiveled his weapon one-hundred-and-eighty degrees and opened fire on the beast. The creature flinched from the series of annoying stings. It shook its head and voiced its anger with a booming roar.

Small arms fire joined the sounds of madness, as did the panicked screams of the three men when the boat began to tilt backwards. The bow lifted and the transom plunged into the ocean, allowing seawater to surge onto its deck and through the breaches.

The gunner kept up the punishment, much to the aggravation of the dinosaur. It cocked its head back like a giant rattlesnake, then lunged.

The *crunch* of the machine gun and its handler's body was heard all the way from the shoreline.

Dripping blood from its teeth, the Spinosaurus raised one of its huge claws. A vicious swipe sent the second security operative off the deck like a golf ball from a tee. His body separated at the waist and shoulders, the three parts splashing down in a perfectly straight line.

The third operative aboard Boat One made a defiant last stand from the tip of the bow. He put his rifle on full-auto and sprayed the contents of its magazine at the creature's face. It closed its eyes and turned its head away, raising its arm to block the tiny projectiles.

Pissed off, it sank its claws into the sides of the vessel. With a deathly grip secured, it rotated to its left, capsizing Boat One. Still holding on to the boat, it continued to roll in a rapid motion. It was the exact same tactic crocodiles used with their kill. And like their victims, Boat One's structure could not take the abuse. The hull split until there was nothing holding the vehicle together. After one final *crack*, it came apart.

Dozens of pieces drifted from the frothing water. In the middle of it all was the operative, swimming for dear life. It was a notable effort, even if it only lasted for a moment.

The Spinosaurus cut through the wreckage and scooped him up in its jaws, which promptly slammed shut, ejecting red mist from between those teeth.

It looked to the shore and locked eyes with the large mechanical humanoid standing there. Bergis tensed. With the windscreen up, the beast was able to look directly at him. And there was no doubt it was looking at *him*.

"That's right," he growled. "You recognize me, don't ya?"

Given its distance from the shore, it must have been gifted with binocular vision to study the puny human inside the steel titan.

It maintained eye contact, ignoring all of the other movement taking place on the beach.

Colonel Tarsus marched to the shoreline, radio in hand. "Boat Three, light it up."

The machine gun and grenade launchers sounded off.

Bergis' stare-down with the beast came to an explosive end. Roaring and thrashing, the beast fell to its side while a series of explosions rocked its left shoulder, ribcage, and neck. The ocean was quick to swallow its enormous mass and conceal it from view.

Little by little, the waves calmed.

Colonel Tarsus watched intently. "Boat Three, any visual?"

"Nothing yet, sir."

Somewhere behind Bergis, Munro was laughing loudly. "So much for the Dino being invincible."

"Shut up," Tarsus said. He watched the water with unblinking eyes, combing over every inch of the sea. Suddenly, he cursed and lifted his radio. "On your nine. Thirty feet. Closing in fast!"

Bergis could barely see it. The swells were tiny, but concentrated, clearly the result of a large mass moving beneath the water. The men on Boat Three took aim with their weapons and stabbed the water with lead. Grenades plunged into the swells and detonated, creating brief mushroom formations where the water lifted.

It all culminated in one final burst, not from an explosive, but from ten tons of mass lifting out of the water.

Two grenades struck it square in the middle of its breast, knocking it back a couple of feet, but failing to cause any severe damage.

Realizing the futility of their efforts, the helmsman tried putting the boat in full throttle. It cleared no more than ten feet before it was set upon by the beast.

It put all of its weight into a devastating body slam. The top of the vessel collapsed in on the rest of it. Sparks flared, igniting spilt fuel.

A fiery blast erased any recognizable form of the patrol boat and its occupants. Pieces of metal, wood, fiberglass, and body parts arched in midair and splashed down in all directions, each one trailing smoke like burning meteors.

In the middle of it all was the Spinosaurus. Surrounded by a literal sea of fire, it resumed its challenging stare at the humans on land. Not a single drop of blood was spilled from its body. As far as everyone could see, it had not suffered any grave injury.

In this moment, Bergis' statement about the creature's ability to withstand heavy weapons was substantiated.

Tarsus was backing up. "Mech units, form up. When it moves in, I want you to hit it with everything you've got."

Stacy and Boyka brought their mechs to the shoreline.

"Let's do this!" the latter proudly exclaimed. Soldiers took position behind the firing line, with the non-combatants placed at the uppermost part of the beach.

The beast held position, watching the metal opponents and their small human companions.

For a painfully long minute, the standoff persisted.

"The hell is it waiting for?" Stacy said.

"I think we've got it scared," Boyka replied.

Bergis shook his head. "No. I don't think so."

The creature's head shifted ever so slightly in an upward motion. Its eyes were no longer on the platoon, but on the trees.

"You hear that?" one of the soldiers said.

Bergis listened. Branches were shuddering and leaves were being ripped from the canopy. A strange collection of droning sounds joined the soundtrack of minor destruction.

"What the hell is that?" someone else said.

Bergis turned his mech around and looked to the canopy. From the veil of green vegetation came a swarm of grotesque shapes. Fluttering X-shaped wings carried segmented multi-limbed bodies over the platoon.

Six legs coiled under the middle segment, their tips pointed like ice picks. As deadly as they appeared, they were nothing compared to the two crab-like arms attached to the upper torso. With serrated edges, they were designed for ripping and tearing. Behind the assortment of deadly limbs was a segmented tail, similar to that of a scorpion. Tipped with a jagged stinger, they maintained a half-coiled position under their bodies.

On the other end of their bodies were two huge red eye sacks. Beneath them were a series of razor-sharp mandibles, whose sole purpose was to rip and tear flesh.

There were dozens of them, all arriving to carry out one single goal: Kill.

"Whoa!" Godfrey exclaimed. He was the first to squeeze the trigger. "Light em up!"

Next to fire was Tarsus, who barked into his mic, "All units: weapons free! Weapons free! Drago-One, we need air support."

"Drago-One en route."

A volley of rifle fire tore into the swarm. Lead projectiles punched through insectoid bodies, raining streams of yellow blood. The bugs, with little concern for their own safety, dove at the platoon.

In the blink of an eye, all sense of organization and strategy was gone. Men were running every which way, each one trying desperately to avoid the clutches of those serrated pincers.

Bergis shut his cockpit windscreen. The rounded barrier slammed shut, right as one of those ugly bastards made a run at him. The six-foot dragonfly shape faceplanted hard against the glass with enough force to dislodge one of its mandibles. It clawed at the windscreen, hissing in protest at the strange see-through barrier between it and its prey.

Its tail rose behind its thorax, the stinger dripping green fluid. One did not need to have a degree in insect studies to know what that was. Venom.

The stinger jabbed uselessly against the rigid shell of the mech, smearing its front with the green crap.

After a few failed attempts, the bug fluttered its wings and hovered in front of the mech in search of a weak spot.

Bergis twisted the right joystick, raising the arm on the same side.

"Buzz off."

He swung the arm, smacking the creature out of the air. It landed on its back, its legs and tail thrashing.

Bergis turned the mech to the left, approached the thing, and finished the job by bringing a giant metal foot down on it.

SPLAT!

One down, around two hundred more to go.

All around him, things were going from bad to worse. The platoon was in total disarray. Soldiers could barely get any shots off at this point. Most of them ran around the beach trying desperately to avoid being seized by the horrifying things.

For good reason, too.

Several yards ahead of him, one helpless soldier was boxed in by a group of bugs. He swiveled on his feet, looking for an escape route.

One of the bugs moved in for the kill. It shifted its body vertically, jabbing its victim with its stinger. The soldier yelled, then hit the sand, arching his back and frothing at the mouth while the venom shut down his vital organs.

His killer seized him with its powerful arms and lifted him to the sky. Joining it were three of its brethren, all carrying casualties of the platoon.

Bergis swiveled his mech to get a visual on Riley. She was using his rifle precisely how he showed her, and to his relief and pride, proved to be a good shot. The falling body of a bug demonstrated her deadly accuracy. It hit the ground, its head and thorax spewing blood from three bullet hits.

Hoover was right by her, staying true to his promise of protecting her. All remnants of his usual snarky demeanor had vanished in this hectic moment, leaving the fierce look of a man fighting for survival.

Above them, six more bugs gathered. They fixed their ugly red eyes on the pair and readied their stingers.

Bergis pointed his autocannon and put it to work. Orange streaks cut across the air and into the horde. One-by-one, the six bugs were cut to pieces.

Hoover looked up just in time to witness the gory rainfall coming down on him. Plastered in insect guts, he looked to Bergis.

"Thanks a lot for that!"

"You're welcome," Bergis quipped.

"Heads up. We've got incoming from the water," Tarsus announced.

Bergis looked at the water. The Spinosaurus was shallowing, effortlessly tearing through the pesky insects with its claws and teeth. A cunning predator, it gladly took advantage of the mayhem to eliminate its human foes.

"Sir, I strongly suggest we fall back."

"All mechs, prepare to engage!" Tarsus ordered.

"Sir, I'm a little preoccupied!" Stacy said.

Bergis blasted another few bugs out of the sky before getting a look at his fellow mechs. Stacy's was swinging its arms as though in a fit of rage. He counted seven insects perched all over the machine. Two of them clung to the windscreen, blinding the pilot. Tails jabbed at the strong metal, failing to penetrate, but making it impossible for the mech to perform its task.

Behind her, Boyka was blasting his autocannon at a group of insects circling around the north side. Splotches of yellow blood burst from those caught in the horizontal storm of 25mm rounds.

Bergis flicked a switch above his left shoulder. From the "wrist' of his mech's right arm came a five-foot blade. When the S-4s were crafted, they were fitted for all kinds of combat, including going mano a mano with other mechs. It was a scenario he always dreaded. Shooting at other soldiers and their machines was hell enough. Being face to face with another S-4 was nightmare fuel.

That is, until Bergis found himself on an island with bulletproof dinosaurs and giant bugs. Compared to them, enemy mechs were a breeze.

He approached Stacy. "Hold still."

"You better not miss, Corporal!"

"I won't, as long as you don't move."

Stacy ceased all movement.

Bergis closed in on her, stopping momentarily to cut down a bug which decided to hover in front of him. The blade passed through its body with little effort, sending both halves tumbling to the sand.

The same fate befell its brethren perched on Stacy's mech. A series of carefully angled slashes removed the blinding problem from her windscreen.

"Make sure you get my back," Stacy jokingly said. She turned around and let Bergis slice a few bugs clinging to the shoulders and hips.

"Mech units!" an impatient Tarsus shouted through their comms. *"Target is closing in. Engage!"*

The three humanoid machines simultaneously turned to the shoreline and pointed their autocannons. The Spinosaurus was only thirty feet out, the water barely covering its ankles.

All three of them opened fire. The combined might of three automatic cannons firing 25mm rounds brought a swift halt to the creature's approach. It took a few steps back, snarling and slashing at the painful bombardment.

"Good God! It's not dying!" Boyka said. *"Is this thing related to the Hulk or something?"*

"Depends," Stacy aimed her L30A3 at the creature. *"Let's see how it handles THIS."*

BANG!

The shell struck the reptilian right below the neck. A flash of fire and metal expanded with a deafening *boom.* The Spinosaurus reeled backwards, roaring in distress until the ocean drowned out its voice.

Bergis and Boyka joined in. 120mm shells made explosive impacts against the writhing mass, kicking up strange mixtures of hot flame, smoke, and water.

Their assault was interrupted by a horde of tenacious insects. The gnarly fates of the others who went up against the machines meant nothing to them. A hive mind, they threw themselves at the steel opponents, clawing with their pincers and stabbing with their tails.

"My gosh!" Boyka said. He swatted one of the things out of the air. *"These things are really starting to BUG me!"*

"Very original," Stacy remarked.

Behind the haze of flying insects, the three pilots noticed the swirling of water. The Spinosaurus' tail raised high like a huge kraken tentacle and smacked back down. Its feet clawed the air, gaining momentum for the creature to roll off its side.

The angular head rose, jetting mist from its nostrils.

"You've GOT to be kidding me!" Boyka said. *"How is that possible? Nothing can take that kind of abuse!"*

"That's not a dinosaur," Stacy said. *"That's a demon!"*

Bergis could not bring himself to say anything. What was there to say? The creature had taken several hits from weapons designed to destroy enemy armor, and it was rising to its feet like a boxer in a ring ready to carry on to the next round.

A shadow swept over the battlefield.

Drago-One made a few passes, forward guns blazing, reducing the bug population that hovered over the platoon.

After thinning the herd, the pilot took position near the Spinosaurus.

"Hot damn! That's a big bastard!"

"Tough one too," Bergis said. "Be careful. It has taken hits from our artillery guns and it's still moving! God knows what other tricks it has up its sleeve."

"I appreciate the concern, but I'm well out of reach," Drago-One said. The cover panel retracted from the front of his missile pods. *"Here's a trick. Voila!"*

Six missiles streamed at the creature, striking it along the back. Buried under fire, smoke, and tremendous concussive force, it fell forward.

"Boom. Take that," Drago-One said.

"Nice shooting, ace," Tarsus said.

The water settled around the creature, submerging everything except its mighty sail. There was no movement so far, but no sign of blood either.

Bergis took advantage of the lull to get a gauge on the situation with the bugs. Most of the platoon was still standing, much to his relief and surprise. It was not all good, though. A few mangled corpses littered the beach, and based on the number of men he saw, at least seven were carried off by the swarm.

Riley was tending to one of the casualties. She hooked up an IV and got to work performing field surgery. Hoover was right there with her, serving as an assistant in the procedure. Oddly enough, he looked more nervous assisting with surgery than he was battling giant bugs.

The remains of the swarm had moved to the trees. Clouds of black smoke from the artillery explosions turned out to work in the platoon's favor, as it appeared to act as a repellent against the bugs.

"Are you for real?" Drago-One exclaimed.

Bergis looked to the water. "Geez…"

The Spinosaurus rose to its feet. Its body was perfectly intact, aside from some scar damage and flaking on its torso where the explosives had struck.

"Colonel, are you seeing this?" Drago-One asked.

"Affirmative," Tarsus replied. *"I also see you sitting there doing nothing. Hit it again, damn it. You too, mech units. Fire everything you've got. It may be a tough bastard, but even it can only take so much. It's a mathematical certainty."*

The only certainty Bergis was aware of was the *uncertainty* surrounding this mission. But orders were given and he had to follow them, and pray the colonel was right.

Drago-One banked fifteen degrees towards the shore to line his rockets up with the same area he had struck previously.

The Spinosaurus remained in place. Its head was down and its back was hunched, bobbing with what appeared to be deep breathing movements. Furthermore, the coloration in its sail altered. They were bizarre changes, like drops of ink shifting in a jug of water.

"Maybe we did more damage than we thought. Fella looks like he's about to upchuck something big and hot," Drago-One said. He steadied his Dragonfly and prepared to fire. *"Sayonara, sucker."*

The Spinosaurus spun on its heels and pointed its snout at the aircraft. Those jaws parted ninety degrees, ejecting a puff of jet-black smoke.

From the back of its throat came a torrent of dark orange rippling light.

Bergis and the rest of the platoon shared a collective gasp of shock and disbelief. Not only was the Spinosaurus twice as large as normal and bulletproof, but it had a secret weapon in its arsenal. It was an ability associated only with ancient dragons in fantasy worlds.

The Spinosaurus could breathe fire.

Hotter than molten lava, the stream of flame struck Drago-One. The pilot's screams filled the radio channel before the heat shorted out the transmitter.

"It spits fire!" Boyka yelled in a panic.

Drago-One descended into a tailspin. Completely encased in flame, it spiraled towards the beach... right at the center of the group.

"Incoming!" Tarsus warned.

The platoon split apart, the personnel running in all directions to avoid the steel meteorite with burning missiles coming at them.

It came down near the tree line. Its armament and fuel tank detonated into a gigantic fireball. Displaced air moved from the crash at hurricane speeds, carrying smoke and debris. Traveling even faster was the blast wave. It traveled through the air and ground, bending trees and kicking up soil.

The swarm of bugs went berserk. They took to the sky and flew in circles, their senses warped by the concussive force and thick smoke.

Below, the platoon was in equal disarray. Fire clung to a few unlucky soldiers, who darted across the beach in agony.

Colonel Tarsus, bleeding from his forehead and chin, barked orders at everyone in sight. Dietz, escorted by the mercenary trio, was led back into the jungle.

A hundred or so feet left from the burning wreckage was a group of bodies. One of them was a strawberry blonde, laying face-down, motionless.

Bergis' heart jumped into his throat.

"Hoover?" he shouted into the radio. "Hoover, where are you?"

"I see her," Hoover replied between coughs. Bergis failed to locate him in the crowd and smoke.

Heavy footsteps from the water forced him to focus on the main threat.

The Spinosaurus' pace had doubled. Pissed off and covered in scars, it was twice as dangerous as before.

The force of the Dragonfly explosion had knocked his fellow mech units closer to the shoreline, right in the creature's path.

Boyka saw the thing coming at them and put himself between it and Stacy.

"Bring it, Dino!"

His mech extended its right arm to put the autocannon in the Spino's face. The dinosaur lunged and slammed its jaws shut over the barrel. Like a canine in a game of tug of war, it turned its body and swung the machine. Boyka staggered in a circle, the hydraulics in the legs groaning as they tried to keep up with the irregular motion.

The cannon fired wide, hitting nothing but dirt and the left knee of Stacy's mech.

"Crap!" Boyka ceased fire. *"Get this thing off me!"*

With Stacy's mech dropped to one knee, Bergis was the only hope. He moved in and extended his blade to slash the creature's face.

It rotated on its heel to swing Boyka again. Its tail lashed with the motion, striking Bergis' mech across the cockpit. The twenty-five-foot battle mech fell on its back with a heavy *crash* that kicked up a fresh new cloud of ash, smoke, and dust.

"Shit!"

"Damn it! I can't shake him off!" All sense of confidence and cockiness was completely erased from Boyka's tone. The pilot was in utter panic. For the first time in his life, even at the control of a powerful military vehicle, he was not the biggest badass on the block. Uniformed armies and their machines proved no match for him in the Eastern European front. Yet, nature had produced something surpassing mankind's inventions.

Boyka pounded the creature with his mech's other arm, rattling the gun attached to it. The Spino retaliated by slashing with its mighty claws.

The cockpit windscreen shattered, revealing the flustered pilot inside. He cursed at the theropod and struck again with his free arm, the hand shuddering against its skull.

The Spinosaurus maintained its grip on the gun barrel. With a twist and a yank, it tore the weapon free from the arm. It spat it free and threw all of its weight into its foe. Boyka was tackled to the ground, helpless to do anything except witness his machine get disemboweled right in front of his eyes.

Claws and teeth tore mechanical guts from the mech's midsection, spilling its fuel supply and shutting down its systems.

After spitting out a mouthful of inorganic material, the creature slowed down and peered directly into the cockpit. Boyka's reaction was not one of defiance, but terror.

The Spinosaurus cocked its head back.

Boyka's screams could be heard even through Bergis' closed windscreen.

"No-no-no-no-NO!"

It brought its jaws down.

CRUNCH!

The Spinosaurus raised its snout from the crater that was once the cockpit. Dangling from its teeth was a mesh of electronics, steel, and flesh.

It tossed the mouthful aside in a way that could only be interpreted as scornful. Its eyes turned to Stacy's mech.

"Not happening!" she shouted.

Still down on one knee, her mech pointed both arms and blasted the autocannon and tank gun. The Spinosaurus came at her, gladly absorbing the impacts in pursuit of the reward of tearing through its adversaries.

It closed in on Stacy and put its foot against her cockpit. The front of her mech imploded on impact, the force of the kick putting it on its back.

Stacy was still alive, her transmission garbled by static and failing equipment.

Sweat soaked Bergis' hair as he attempted to right his mech. "Hang on!"

His words carried no weight. The Spinosaurus stood over her, watching the activity inside the smashed cockpit, savoring the experience of the kill. It raised its foot one more time.

Stacy's defiance came through in broken transmission. *"—ck you!"*

The foot came down with all of the creature's weight above it, burying Stacy inside her cherished weapon.

"No!" Bergis pounded a fist against his dashboard. He had finally gotten his mech to its feet, only to witness his fellow pilot get brutally killed.

It was a circumstance that cursed his existence today. Twice now, he had been temporarily incapacitated while his fellow soldiers were slain.

He listened to the shouting coming from behind him.

"Move! Move! Let's go!"

He glanced at his rear-view monitors. At least twenty men were still regrouping, many of them working desperately to gather the injured.

Between them and a furious, fire-breathing dinosaur was Bergis. He steadied his mind and forced aside his sorrow. There was no room for vengeance or even anger, whether it be at the beast or himself. There was only duty.

He had failed to save his Scorpion crew back in Algiers. He was doomed to witness his friend Galloway and the rest of his dig team get massacred.

He would *not* stand for letting Riley and Hoover, as well as the rest of the response team, suffer the same fate.

The Spinosaurus looked at him and bellowed.

Bergis had to think fast. Artillery and bullets were not effective. The creature was superior in both strength and mass, and was fueled by an anger surpassing his own.

He glanced at one of the rear-view monitors again in hopes of seeing Riley getting up. She was still face-down on the ground. Hoover was kneeling at her side, waving at some other soldiers for help.

Three of them ran his way. Before reaching the fallen doctor, they were forced to stop and shoot high at a group of insects. Despite the smoke, they were attempting to make a run at the bodies on the beach before departing with the rest of their swarm. Their attention turned to the three soldiers. One of them was quickly cut down by bullets. The others darted at the troops and jabbed with their tails.

One of the soldiers caught a stinger to the belly. He dropped to his knees, baring teeth as he tried to use willpower against the venom. It was a battle that could not be won; a fact demonstrated by his final collapse.

A thought crossed Bergis' mind.

The venom!

He learned forward and put his head to the glass to get a look at the mech's front. As he hoped, a river of the insect venom from the drone that tried to sting him was still on the exoskeleton.

The Spinosaurus roared and began stomping his way.

Bergis maneuvered his blade to rub the tip in the venom.

The Spinosaurus extended its jaws and came in for a bite.

Bergis jabbed.

The tip of the blade grazed the soft tissue on the roof of its mouth. Yelping, the Spino lurched back, recoiling from the unexpected pain. It was only a momentary reprieve in aggression which ended in the blink of an eye.

It came at him again.

Bergis braced for another head-on attack, positioning his blade for a fatal plunge into the back of its throat.

With the agility of an expert martial artist, the Spinosaurus pivoted on its feet and swung its body. Its tail came around hard, bashing the cockpit and knocking Bergis on his back a second time.

"Damn it!"

He found himself staring at the sky. Twisting his joysticks, he began to get the machine back upright. It leaned up into a seated position with the support of its right arm.

The Spinosaurus hissed and rammed its foot into the mech. Bergis was back on the ground, pinned by the weight of the Spinosaurus.

It leaned down close enough to get a look at the man inside. That big eye came within a couple of inches of the glass.

Bergis swallowed. He shut his eyes and braced for the end.

He felt a shift in his mech as the weight came off. When he opened his eyes, the Spino was staggering backwards to the water. It appeared to be gasping for breath, its mouth hung open.

There was a sluggishness in its movements and stiffness in its posture. Saliva drizzled from its mouth in thick globs.

Bergis took a breath.

It worked. The venom was in its bloodstream and giving its insides hell. The effects appeared to be limited, as only a small amount had gotten through. While it was stiff and lethargic, the Spino did not look to be fully succumbing to the invading molecules.

Still, much of the fight had left it.

Coughing up spew, it turned around and waded back into the ocean. It turned northwards and wallowed until only its sail was visible. Cleaving the water, it maintained its northern path until it was out of sight.

More rifle shots and shouting cut short the corporal's feeling of victory. He leaned the mech upward and took a look at the chaos behind him.

Hoover had just barely managed to gun down one of the bugs, dropping its dead body right on top of himself. Flattened on his back, he yelled "No!"

Bergis found himself doing the same.

The rest of the drones took to the sky. In the clutches of one of them was Riley McKeon.

An electric shock of anguish surged through Bergis' veins. He pointed his autocannon at the retreating swarm and rested his finger on the trigger. A sliver of self-control prevented him from firing. He could not risk hitting Riley.

He got his mech on its feet and immediately moved over to Hoover. The windscreen came up, making way for the sounds of mayhem and agony.

Hoover stood up and looked up at the mech. He ran a sleeve over his blackened face, smearing smoke, tar, and sweat.

"I tried.. I…"

"What's her condition?" Bergis said.

Hoover stammered, then realized what he was getting at. "She was knocked unconscious by the blast. The bug didn't sting her. Not that I saw, at least. They were trying to collect some of the bodies to take back… wherever they came from."

A ping of relief hit Bergis. Riley was still alive. Considering the nature of her abductors, that could change at any moment.

"I'm going after her," he said.

"How will you find them?" Hoover asked.

Bergis raised his PRO device. On its screen was a map with a bleep moving steadily inland.

Hoover connected the dots.

"That rifle you gave her—it has a GPS in it." He chuckled. "Smart son of a bitch. Alright, I'm going with you."

"Nobody's going anywhere until we come up with a strategy," Colonel Tarsus yelled out from the burning wreckage. "Corporal,

I'm going to need you on point while we make our way back to Command Central."

"Oh, *now* you want to head back," Bergis said. "You were in a hurry to come out here against all logic, but now all of a sudden you're worried about the wellbeing of your men?"

"Watch your tone, Corporal. I need that mech."

"So does Dr. McKeon," Bergis said. He looked at Hoover. There was no time to argue and convince him to stay behind. "Try and keep up."

Hoover sprinted alongside the mech, quickly moving northwards in pursuit of the horde.

CHAPTER 12

"I said keep up!"

"Easy for you to say!" Hoover tore through a batch of thick ferns, spitting out leaves as he yelled back at the mech pilot. "In case you haven't noticed, some of us actually have to move on our own two feet! Probably hard for you to consider up there, with your wrists aching from jerking your sticks!"

Bergis probably would have chuckled at that if it were not for the drastic situation at hand. His two fellow pilots had been killed right in front of him, the last Dragonfly gunship had been blasted out of the sky, several troops had been stung to death by giant insects, and the one person aside from Galloway who had ever shown him kindness had been captured.

It was not a day for laughs.

However, Bergis knew Hoover had a point. He slowed his mech down enough for the operative to keep up.

Operative.

Bergis still struggled with thinking of Hoover as a soldier. To the naked eye, he looked like one. He had the wardrobe and gear. But his bias continued to keep Hoover from reaching that level in his mind, even after he had experienced the firefight at the beach. Sure, the guy had done his duty, but that did not change the corporal's perception of him as someone 'playing soldier' without having to make the proper commitment.

"So, what's the story with you and the doctor?" Hoover asked.

Bergis gave thought to shutting his windscreen. Then again, Hoover would just continue the conversation through the radio, for everyone to hear.

"You think just because I'm trying to save her life there has to be something going on between us?"

Hoover laughed. "I'll answer your question with a question: if I was carried off to what is likely a hive of bugs and you thought I was still alive, would you go after me?"

Bergis made the mistake of giving the scenario a fair amount of thought before forcing out the word "yes."

"Oh, wow! That was totally convincing!" a sarcastic Hoover replied.

"I needed to focus on cutting through some branches," Bergis said defensively.

"Uh-huh! I'm sure you would've planted a GPS chip in my weapon as well."

Bergis stopped his mech and looked down at his fellow operative.

"I already had it installed in my gun. In case you've forgotten, there's a strict penalty for misplacing your weapon."

Hoover shook his head. "Right. I didn't take you as someone with a habit of misplacing your gun."

Bergis groaned. "Is this seriously what you're focused on right now?"

"We've got a bit of a walk ahead of us," Hoover said. "Might as well pass the time with chit chat."

"Chit chat? After what you've just been through, you want to chit chat?" Bergis said. "You just watched a dozen people die. Nearly got yourself added to the body count. And you want to go on with this high school gossip crap?"

Hoover kicked a batch of leaves on the ground.

"Don't you think that might be *why* I could use some casual conversation? Yes, everything you listed just freaking happened. And here I am, going after a bunch of big-ass bugs with only an assault rifle and a battered mech whose pilot has a stick up his ass. No downtime, no chance to mentally recover. So, yeah, I could use some small talk; something to feel semi-normal and prevent myself from rethinking being out here."

Bergis thought about that. For the first real time, he saw something more than a naïve and overly eager soldier wannabe. Hoover was a person with a heart and soul, who hoped to get back to his life outside of the job.

The guy was scared. He was right to be scared. Only the biggest moron would not be scared right now. Yet, here he was, putting his ass on the line, and for what? There were no medals to gain, no special veterans holiday, or any other special accolades. If anything, he was risking a reprimand for defying Colonel Tarsus' orders.

He was doing the right thing.

Exactly what Bergis failed to do in Algiers.

Perhaps he's more of a soldier than I'll ever be.

Bergis turned the mech northeast and continued the trek. "There's no official thing between us."

"As in, neither of you have made a move yet," Hoover said.

"I'm not particularly looking for anything," Bergis replied.

"I believe you," Hoover said. "Here's the thing: you don't have to be looking to find something you really need. When you find that something, you naturally want to protect it."

Bergis maneuvered through a pair of trees, holding some low-hanging branches up so Hoover could pass below.

"Pretty insightful. I'd almost assume you were speaking from experience."

Hoover made a sardonic laugh. "What makes you think I wasn't?"

Bergis released the limbs and inspected the jungle ahead of him. The trees were better spaced out here, allowing them to walk in more of a straight path.

"Got yourself a lady back home?"

Hoover made the same snarky sound, increasing the corporal's curiosity.

"More or less," he said. "Her father is not my biggest fan."

"They never are," Bergis remarked.

"Well, there's a little more to it than just being protective of his daughter," Hoover said. "He was serving in the Eastern Pacific Region during the war. When he returned home and met me, he took major issue with the fact that I never enlisted. Funny enough, I always wanted to join throughout middle school and high school. Then I met Grace during senior year, we fell in love, and I didn't want to leave. The war went on, I did not enlist and I didn't get drafted."

"He make her dump you?"

"Not exactly. He demanded I prove myself as a man and enlist. Problem was, the Navy or Army did not want me due to a little hiccup from my youth."

Bergis was able to do the math. There weren't many things that would disqualify someone from the military these days. One such thing was a juvenile record.

"What'd you do?"

Hoover bit his lip, having not expected the conversation to go in this direction.

"I was sixteen. I stole a car for a buddy—for someone I thought was a buddy—who sold it for drug money. He got caught and I got looped in as an accomplice. Not exactly something Grace's dad was happy to learn. So, he knew someone at Globus and rang him up. Got me a job." He gave a small laugh, the kind one made to cover up embarrassment. "I'm not stupid. He was just trying to get me away from Grace under the guise of..." he made air quotes, "...making me worthy."

"Huh!" Bergis cringed at letting his surprise be known.

Hoover stopped and smirked at the cockpit. "'Huh' what?"

"Just, uh..." Bergis tried to think of a reasonable lie. After a short while, he decided it was better to just come out with the truth.

"I didn't realize that was why you had taken the job. I kinda just assumed—this might come out sounding a little mean..."

"You? Mean?!" Hoover mimicked a look of shock. "And let me guess: you thought I was just some guy who wanted to play soldier without actually serving?"

Bergis again tried to think of a lie, but ultimately settled on the truth. "Yes."

"You one of those veterans with a stick up your butt towards those who didn't serve?" Hoover asked.

"Only the ones in these kinds of jobs," Bergis said. "I just figure they want to put on a tough looking outfit, carry a gun, and look cool without having any real commitment. 'Playing soldier' as I call it. Plus there's the fact that a lot of them get handed the job. Usually someone makes a call on their behalf. I guess it tends to bother me because these security careers make good work for veterans."

"I get that," Hoover said. "Trust me, I'd rather be on the mainland watching documentaries about dinosaurs."

"Beats nearly getting eaten by them," Bergis remarked.

The two men shared a laugh.

Interrupting their levity were cracks of gunfire coming from somewhere to the northeast.

"The hell?" Hoover muttered.

"Nobody else is supposed to be out this way," Bergis said. "Colonel made that clear."

Hoover tried his radio. "Anyone north of Blooming Lake, please respond to this transmission if you can hear it."

"Thank God. We need help! We're pinned down by an excavator! This THING is trying to get at us."

A snarl followed his statement.

"We're coming. Hang tight," Hoover said. He looked at Bergis. "Any chance you wanna trade?"

Bergis gave a "ha-ha" and a "Nope!" before moving on.

Hoover shrugged. "Worth a shot."

CHAPTER 13

"You sure you don't wanna trade?"

"I'm good."

Hoover bumped the mech's heel with his boot. They watched from a gap in the trees, studying the reptilian creature as it circled the personnel carrier. The driver's side was crumpled inward after sideswiping a tree.

The predator was a theropod with skin covered with spines. It was much smaller than the Spinosaurus, only twenty feet from its nose to the tip of its tail. Large sickle-shaped claws protruded from its feet.

"You're the expert," Bergis said to Hoover. "What is this thing?"

"I'm no expert," Hoover sharply whispered. "I read a lot of books and watch a bunch of documentaries. There's a reason I was never a very popular kid. Or adult."

"Okay, great. So, you saved yourself a bunch of money by not going to college," Bergis replied. "You're the expert today. So, I ask again: what is this thing?"

Hoover watched the creature. It was nudging the vehicle's cracked windshield, eyeballing the fresh meat on the other side.

"Some kind of large raptor," he whispered. "Based on its size, I would say maybe a Utahraptor, but there are no feathers. Then again, I wouldn't call the Spinosaurus normal either."

"How do we kill it?" Bergis asked.

Hoover held his hands to the side. "It's not like I've lived on safari with these freaking things! Books and TV, remember? None of which mentioned anything about dinosaurs withstanding missiles and breathing fire!"

The Utahraptor lifted its head and looked in their direction. Both men froze, Hoover moving behind the mech's leg.

"Shit, it heard us," he whispered through clenched teeth.

Bergis kept his autocannon pointed. He gladly would have blasted it right now, except doing so would possibly kill the men in that carrier.

The creature took a step closer to them, bobbing its head like a turkey. It sniffed a few times, then turned around, its curiosity cast aside in favor of the meat literally at its feet.

Bergis exhaled. The thing was not going to give up. At any moment, it would try and tear through that truck and kill the men inside.

"We don't have a lot of time."

A yellow button flashed on the right of the console. Hoover had discovered the lever for the cockpit ladder, located behind the machine's left ankle. Reluctantly, he pressed the button and lowered the expandable set of bars.

Hoover climbed the height of the mech, coming over the shoulder. "All this time, you had me talking from down there?"

"I like my solitude," Bergis replied.

"I could've held on to this while we were moving through the jungle!"

The corporal shrugged, "I was worried you'd fall off."

"Oh, so you were being considerate of my wellbeing. How noble of you." Hoover looked at the raptor. "Surprised it didn't smell us."

"There's fuel leaking from the vehicle," Bergis said.

"Ah. That would do it," Hoover replied. "Now we just need to get it to move away from those guys so you can blast it. And yes, that's my amateur-expert opinion: shoot the thing and hope it's not bulletproof."

Bergis nodded. "Good enough for me."

Hoover rested his chin on his arm. "Now, to get it to move…" He looked at Bergis and cringed after seeing the look on his face. "Why are you smiling? Guys who smile in moments like this are never up to any good."

Bergis looked up at the trees. "You good at climbing?"

Hoover's jaw dropped. "You're a real bastard, you know that? Using me as *bait!* Is that part of your consideration for my wellbeing?"

Bergis sported a grin. "At least I can use the mech to lift you up there. That way you won't have to do much climbing."

"Imagine my gratitude." Hoover groaned. "Alright, what's the plan? I'm sure there's more to having me up there than making my life miserable. And possibly shortened."

"Simple. I get you up there, then I get into firing position. Once I'm set, you fire off a few shots from up high and lure the thing over to you. When it gets to the tree, I send it to hell. Easy peasy."

Hoover glared at him. "Easy peasy? Says the guy *not* being used as a worm on a hook."

"You've got nothing to worry about," Bergis said. "I mean, aside from getting eaten alive, torn apart, plucked off the tree by a passing bug, falling down and breaking multiple bones, getting caught in the blast…"

"Your sales pitch needs work." Hoover took another look at the tree and cursed under his breath. "Alright, fine! You better not miss and—wait, what did you mean by 'blast?' You're not planning to use the big tank gun thing, are you?" The look on Bergis' face was all the answer he needed. "Ohhh."

"Come on, worm," Bergis replied. "You'll be fine. I calculate a sixty-five percent chance that you'll pull through this."

Hoover climbed to the mech's left hand, stopping midway to flip the bird at the corporal.

"Again, sales pitch."

Bergis carefully lifted him onto a large branch. With his rifle hanging off his shoulder by its strap, he hoisted himself off the metallic limb onto the wooden one. Not satisfied with being only twenty-five feet off the ground, he grabbed ahold of another branch and moved farther up.

Bergis backed away twenty meters then aimed his tank gun. He could no longer see the raptor from his location. Hoover was barely visible in the tree branches, the spade-shaped leaves doing a good job of concealing him.

"Ready whenever you are," he said into his radio mic.

"Is that a way of telling me to hurry up?" Hoover said.

"You're catching on quick."

"Ugh. Yes, I'm ready. Ish!"

Bergis watched the shirt in the leaves as Hoover readied himself.

Bang! Bang! Bang! Bang!

"Oh, dear Lord! It worked. It's coming right at me. And it's pissed!"

The evidence to that statement came crashing through the jungle. Feral and moving at cheetah speed, the raptor was at the base of the tree in no time.

It circled the tree, staring up at the human in the tall branches. After completing a couple of passes, it stopped and barked to the northwest.

"Anytime now, Bergis."

"Hang on."

"Hang on? Hang on for what? It's right there. Just blast it. Look! It's not even moving."

The raptor turned around and lifted its head, perplexed at the sight of the huge mechanical humanoid standing nearby.

Bergis kept the mech completely still. The windscreen was down, preventing it from seeing him through the tinted glass. Without making even a slight movement, he was just another obstacle in the jungle.

The raptor turned its attention back to Hoover. Growling, it began raking its front claws at the tree trunk.

"Beeeergis?"

"Take a chill pill. I'm curious about something."

"Are you for real?"

The creature started making its way up the tree. Hoover pointed his rifle down and hit it with a couple of bursts. The raptor slipped off the trunk and whipped itself into a frenzy. Spinning in a circle, it kicked up dirt as it brushed its hands over the scratches on its snout resulting from the bullet hits.

Its skin was thick, but not impenetrable. The available guns ought to be enough for the job. Bergis just needed another moment to confirm a certain hunch that was nagging at him.

The raptor ran another circle around the tree, then initiated another attempt to get at Hoover.

"Bergis! If this is some sort of joke you're playing, it's not funny!"

"Just wait a few more seconds."

"Wait for what?"

Bergis jittered at the sight of shifting undergrowth beyond the tree. From the northwest, where the raptor was directing its calls, came another one. It was a crest of equal size; possibly a sibling or a mate. Decorated with the same type of denticles as the other, it gave a look at the motionless mech, then fixed its eyes on Hoover.

"What the??

"That's what I was waiting for," Bergis said. He adjusted his aim. "Cover your ears."

The two raptors detected his movement. They pivoted in a simultaneous motion, lowering their heads and raising their tails. Drool slipped off their snarling jaws as they challenged the foe.

Bergis answered with a single shot from his tank gun. The projectile struck the one on the left. Head, arms, legs, and tail went in different directions, their speed matched only by the shock and sound waves of an artillery explosion.

A flash of flame and smoke consumed the raptor's body. Nothing was left intact. Its bodily components were either vaporized, mangled, or charred beyond any hope of identification.

The blast knocked the other one to the ground. Its right leg was barely attacked, its body and face charred and bleeding.

Even so, it was digging at the ground to pull itself closer to the mech. Even against all odds, it was determined to kill.

Bergis fired the autocannon and put the creature out of its misery. It slumped against the forest floor, its head and neck imploded by the punishing hits.

He lowered the guns.

"Okay, you can come down now, Hoover."

The operative slowly started working his way down to the branch Bergis had lifted him to.

"Mind lending a hand?"

"Oh." Bergis moved to the tree. "Certainly."

He raised an arm to the branch. Hoover eased himself onto it and held on until he was lowered to the ground.

As soon as his boots touched down, he kicked the mech's foot.

Bergis opened his cockpit windscreen. "What was that for?"

"'What was that for?'" Hoover mocked. "Like you don't know."

"I shot the lizards," Bergis said. "You're fine. Got all your fingers and toes."

Hoover grunted and waved his arms at the second raptor. "Quit playing dumb. How'd you know there was a second one?"

Bergis sniggered, amused by his partner's agitation. "I didn't know for sure until the second one showed up. The thing made a particular noise and motion that made me suspect it was trying to communicate. So, instead of blasting the first one right away and potentially driving away the other, creating the possibility of it stalking us while we look for Riley, I decided to let it put itself in firing range. Two birds, one stone. Boom."

"Ya could've said something," Hoover said.

"Yeah, but listening to you freak out was more fun," Bergis replied.

Hoover looked at the sky, a half-smirk on his face. "Interestingly, this is probably the nicest you've ever been to me. That said, you owe me a beer if we make it back to Command Central."

"I suppose I can live with that," Bergis said.

They moved to the overturned personnel carrier. Three men crawled out from the cab. One of them wore a brown dust jacket and utility gloves. While his two partners pulled themselves out from the vehicle, he approached the two security operatives.

"Thank God for you two. I thought we were goners for sure." He touched his thumb to his chest. "My name is Irrfan Kaushal." He gestured at the others. "The one in the khaki shorts and stupid choice of shoes is Blake Layne. The dark one with the goat pee is Colin Sermon."

The latter facepalmed. "GoaTEE! And I appreciate the remark about my skin tone."

"What?" Irrfan asked. "Is it not true? You are the darkest one, yes?"

"Oh gosh," the one named Blake Layne remarked.

"Anyone else?" Bergis asked.

"No, just the three of us," Irrfan said.

Bergis climbed out of his mech and joined the men at ground level. He looked at the vehicle and the dirt trail it was riding on. From what he could see at this point, it was a crude job, with only the underbrush cleared out without bothering to smooth the ground out. Those who made trails this way were either lazy, or were only planning for extremely limited use.

He then studied the faces of Irrfan, Blake, and Colin. They were not part of the Globus personnel on the island.

"Who are you guys? What are you doing out here? When was this trail carved out? I don't recall it being on the roster at any point."

"As I said, I am Irrfan Kaushal. This is Blake Layne and Colin—"

"No, no, no," Bergis said. "I mean, *who* are you? You're not part of this colony."

"Oh!" Irrfan exclaimed. He laughed openly at his mistake, completely at ease as if he was not almost eaten alive by a carnivorous dinosaur five minutes ago. "Goodness me. I'm so silly."

"In other words, it's another day that ends with Y," Colin said.

"We came in by boat," Blake said. "We were given orders to deliver this truck to the main dig site."

"Given orders?" Hoover said. "Given by whom?"

"Dr. Xavier Dietz," Irrfan said. "We got a call this morning. He instructed us to bring a payload to a vehicle left near the dock he had constructed for us."

Bergis winced and waved both hands, overwhelmed with the bizarreness of what he was being told.

"Wait, back up a sec—we'll come back to the 'payload' thing you just mentioned—but first, why the hell do you guys have a special dock and trail?"

"The dock was built two months ago," Hoover said. "They said it was for the boat patrol units in case they had an emergency while on the northwest corner of the island. This trail, though, is new."

"Even this rough of a job would have a hard time going unnoticed," Bergis said. "We would have heard the branch cutters and haulers."

"Unless!" Hoover raised a finger. "Unless it was done while everyone was confined to Command Central."

"Just over a month ago," Bergis added. The two men had the same realization.

Thirty-five days ago, Colonel Tarsus had received word of an offshore freighter that had suffered a major chemical leak. The Dragonfly units were dispatched to airlift the crew and take them to the Western Alliance base in New Zealand. There, they would wait overnight and be checked out for any symptoms of the leaked chemicals believed to have been released into the air.

During that time, all personnel on the island were confined to Command Central to limit exposure. The quarantine lasted precisely two days before the spill was contained.

"The freighter!" Bergis and Hoover both exclaimed.

"Oh, that?" Irrfan said with a chuckle.

"You know about the chemical spill?" Hoover said.

"Everyone knows about that," Irrfan replied.

"Everyone also knows it was an inside job," Blake added. "Normally, I would ask why somebody would want to unleash a chemical plume in the middle of the Pacific. Then we received our instructions, and it became very clear very quickly the staff working here weren't supposed to know about this trail, and what was being hauled out through it."

"What was Deitz having you guys haul out?" Bergis asked.

"Monsters!" Irrfan exclaimed.

Colin shook his head and walked over to his overly enthusiastic fellow smuggler.

"More or less. In the digs, Dietz discovered perfectly preserved skeletons of prehistoric animals. Not fossils, you see. I'm talking actual bones of dinosaurs and other crazy things. Looking at them, you'd think they died fifty years ago at most."

"That's just the tip of the iceberg," Blake said. "After a while, the doctor discovered eggs. Real preserved eggs in one of the digs. Soon enough, he discovered evidence of living specimens, somehow contained and preserved by the super meteor minerals you guys are digging up here. And today, he wanted us to blow up the reservoir. Kill everything down there and bury it all. All in one big explosion."

Bergis and Hoover looked at each other.

"That son of a bitch," the corporal said. "He knew these creatures were on the island all along."

"He engineered a plot to get the specimens off the island without anyone from Globus finding out," Hoover said.

"Maybe he was selling them to a competitor," Bergis suggested.

Hoover nodded in agreement. "Fast-forward to today, everything goes tits up. He knew he'd be found out in the investigation, so he called these guys in for a Hail Mary attempt to destroy the evidence. If Colonel Tarsus were to find out he knew there were living organisms in the mines, he'd string him up and use him as a piñata."

"The colonel guy can be my guest. Last time I'm taking a job for that jerk," Colin remarked. "Guy said nothing about killer dinosaurs running around. He just told us to blow up the mine."

Bergis raised an eyebrow. "Blow up an entire mine?"

Colin shrugged and pointed at the carrier. "See for yourself. I don't care at this point."

Bergis and Hoover moved to the back of the carrier. The back door had come loose when the vehicle turned over, providing a direct view to the contents inside.

Those contents turned out to be multiple cases labeled QMT.

"Whoa!" Hoover exclaimed.

"You guys weren't kidding," Bergis said.

"I guess, being soldiers, you two are familiar with those explosives," Irrfan said.

"Well..." Hoover chuckled nervously. "I'm not actually a soldier. I'm just a lowly security guy. But I know what QMT is."

"Wait," Irrfan stammered. "You are not a soldier? I thought the company liked to hire—"

"Uh, Irrfan? Not now," Colin said. He looked at the operatives. "He gets obsessed over inconsequential stuff like this."

Bergis paid no mind to the subject. His attention was on the explosives in the back of the carrier and how he could use them for the objective at hand.

"There're enough explosives here to open another deep, dark hole in this island." He looked at Hoover. "I'd say we've been rewarded for our act of kindness."

Hoover smiled. "Gosh, I would hate to see all those cases go to waste." Slowly, that smile fell as his mind began to ponder the practicality of their idea. "Then again, getting it there and planting it might be tricky."

Bergis laughed and tapped his shoulder. Hoover forced a nervous smile, unsure if there was a purpose to Bergis' display of humor or if this was the calm before an angry outburst. When the corporal pointed northwest, Hoover realized it was the former.

Farther up the trail was a four-wheeler with a large cargo trunk sufficient enough for transporting three cases. When the raptors had attacked, they must have ripped the door open and let the small vehicle fall out before the carrier fishtailed and flipped. It made sense, as the vehicle would be needed to get the crates down the corkscrew path leading to the bottom of the large mine.

They moved to the four-wheeler and righted it. The engine came on without any problems.

"Let's load it up," Bergis said. "We'll figure out a plan of attack when we get there."

"Works for me," Hoover said. "I'm just happy to give my feet a break."

"Wait, you guys are going to war?" Irrfan asked. "I thought you, or at least that one..." He gestured at Hoover, "...was not a soldier."

"Where's the rest of your security forces?" Colin asked.

"Regrouping," Bergis said. "We kinda got our asses kicked by a swarm of big bugs and a super Spinosaurus that forgot to audition for a Japanese takoyishi film... whatever the word for guys in suits is."

"Tokusatsu," Hoover corrected him.

Bergis looked over at him. "Learn that from one of those documentaries?"

"No, I'm just a nerd," Hoover said. "I grew up on all that stuff, even the obscure ones like *Yongary, The Last Dinosaur*..."

"Good lord. No wonder Grace's dad wanted to get rid of you."

Meanwhile, the three smugglers were still struggling with the new information they had just heard.

"Bugs?" Blake croaked.

"A Spinosaurus?" Colin struggled to get the question out.

"It gets better!" Hoover said. "It breathes fire like a freaking dragon. And it's impervious to our weaponry."

The three men looked at each other. All three sets of eyes simultaneously went to the four-wheeler.

"Sorry, we're gonna need that," Blake said.

Bergis put his hand out. "Before you think about escaping on your boat, just know the Spino was last seen swimming in the water on this side of the island. It already sank all three of our patrol units. If it sees you, it won't be pleasant."

"You think we're just gonna let you take our only means of getting to the dock?" Colin said.

Bergis tapped the four-wheeler. "Yep!"

Colin scraped his boot against the ground, tempted to challenge the operative. The presence of the firearms quickly put that temptation to rest.

"Nothing's stopping you from getting the carrier back on its wheels and limping to the dock," Hoover said. "That said, you guys can make yourselves useful and help us save this guy's girlfriend."

Bergis shifted to look at him. "She's not—"

"He has a woman?" Irrfan said.

Bergis waved his hands. "No, no, no."

"What happened to her?" Colin asked.

Hoover grimaced. "Those giant bugs we mentioned... she was taken by them. Presumably to be eaten."

Irrfan put a hand over his mouth. "That is horrible! We cannot stand by and let the love of this soldier's life get murdered."

Bergis shook his head. "She's not—"

"And you are heroically coming to her rescue!" Irrfan continued. "Young love is beautiful. So is old love, but it is not as easy on the eyes."

A moment of awkward silence followed that statement.

"You're suggesting we let these guys screw us over?" Colin said.

"It's not screwing," Irrfan replied. "The soldier's woman is in trouble. If it was my wife, rest her soul, I'd stop at nothing to save her."

Colin looked away. "If it were mine, I'd tell the bugs 'bon appetite. Here's my mother-in-law as a bonus'."

"Where is she?" Blake asked the operatives.

"We have a tracker showing her location," Bergis said. "Signal is barely over a mile north of here. If you help us, we can have this done in just over a half hour."

"A large number of them were killed in the battle," Hoover added. "There probably won't be too many of them left. Who knows? Rescuing Riley might be a piece of cake."

"We have the mech and I saw some firearms in the carrier," Bergis said. "The advantage is ours. Like Hoover said, piece of cake."

The three smugglers shared glimpses, ultimately succumbing to their better nature.

"I like cake," Irrfan said.

CHAPTER 14

"Piece of cake, my ass!"

This time, Bergis felt a ping of intimidation from Colin's growly tone. He could not blame the guy for getting worked up; he was feeling a little agitated himself after laying eyes on the insect nest.

Watching from a hillside under the cover of brush, they beheld the sight of a honeycomb formation encompassing a small indentation in the jungle. Comprised of a light brown shell, it towered to a height of approximately two hundred feet. From what the group could see, it appeared to have a relatively smooth texture with ribbed linings spaced roughly ten feet apart.

It was a shape easily identified by people regardless of nationality. A hive.

It was incomplete in its construction, the southeast side wide open. The shape of the opening brought to mind an old ceramic vase Bergis' grandmother owned and never got rid of. The opening in the hive had large jagged edges, revealing the two-meter thickness of the walls. Bugs crawled near the ledges on both sides, slowly applying saliva and resin to close the thirty-foot gap.

Their numbers far surpassed Bergis' estimation. Flyers patrolled the skies like Air Force choppers circling a military installation. Ground units crawled around the base, protecting it from any intruders that wanted to sneak in from the forest floor.

"Yeah, your girlfriend's dead," Blake said.

"We don't know that," Irrfan yelped.

Colin cupped a hand over his shipmate's mouth. "First of all, keep your voice down. Second of all, yeah, we know it. She's dead." He looked at Bergis. "Sorry, man."

Bergis stayed low, binocs pressed to his eyes. He checked his PRO device. The GPS reading on the screen showed Riley, or at least her rifle, inside the hive. He zoomed in and confirmed the signal was originating forty feet above ground level and on the northeastern-most side of the structure.

"We need to move and get a better look," he said.

Colin wheezed. "Alright, sure. Knock yourself out."

The corporal lowered the binocs and looked into the jungle behind him where the mech was parked. Even with that firepower, there was no hope of getting anywhere close to that nest before getting overpowered.

Hoover was next to him, his face looking as if it would turn green at any moment as he watched the nest. He too was caught off guard by the vibrant activity around the nest.

He lowered his own set of binocs and took a breath.

"You alright?" Bergis asked.

Hoover bit his lip, then scooted to the right to make way for the corporal.

"No. Look through the gap. You'll have to look in from my angle to see what I'm referring to."

Bergis crossed the fifteen feet of distance and took a peek through his glasses. He could only catch a few glimpses of the monstrosity inside, but even without a clear line of sight, it was obvious what it was.

"Oh, shit."

"What?" Blake asked.

Bergis closed his eyes and scowled. "I'm so stupid. I should have suspected. It was obvious these bugs were working as one colony. And most insect colonies are centered around a..." he took a breath, not wanting to mutter the word.

"A *what*?" Colin said.

Bergis exhaled.

"A queen."

Colin let himself slide down the tiny hill. "Yeah, she's dead."

Blake was skidding down with him. "Nice meeting you, Corporal. But I think I'll be on my merry way. You know how only an idiot would stick his head into a hornet nest? Well, it would take a really really really big idiot to stick his head in a *monster* hornet nest!"

"What about the Spinosaurus?" Hoover asked. "You go out on that boat, you might be in for a rude awakening."

Colin did not hesitate to respond with, "I'll take my chances." He looked at Irrfan. "You coming?"

Irrfan kept his eyes on the huge, horrible nest in the distance. "These guys saved us. Least we can do is stick around and make sure the Army man's girlfriend is alive."

Bergis opened his mouth to argue that technically wasn't true regarding Riley, but decided now was not the time.

"Even if she is alive, how would we get her out of there?" Blake asked.

"We'll cross that bridge when we come to it," Irrfan replied. "For now, I don't want to willingly abandon a woman to this horrible fate. Not good on my conscience."

Bergis stared blankly, his focus on Riley interrupted like a radio signal caught in static.

This guy's the most interesting smuggler I've ever seen.

"What about her radio?" Hoover said. "Does she have one?"

Bergis snapped back to reality. *Damn!* He felt like a horse's ass for not thinking of that himself.

"She dropped the two-way radio the security guys gave to her. *But* she has her PRO." He dug his own out and brought up her contact information.

"If she's still unconscious, it might not matter," Colin said.

"It's our best shot at finding out if she's alive," Bergis said. He sent out a call and put the receiver to his ear. The first round of generic ringtone sounds came through. Usually there were five before the call went to voicemail.

"Anything?" Irrfan asked.

Bergis put his face in his palm. "Yeah, sure. I always make phone calls where I don't say anything."

Irrfan thought about that. "Hmm. Tushy."

"Oh, Lord." Colin threw his head back, closing his eyes as though in pain. "It's *touché.*"

Bergis listened to the second ring. The third followed. His stomach ached with feelings of anxiety and helplessness.

The fourth ring began, then stopped abruptly.

"Oh, God. Please help, whoever this is."

Bergis lifted his head. "Riley? You okay, Doc?"

The others scurried near him to listen in on the call, each one astonished that the doctor was still alive.

"Corporal? Lon? Is that you? Where are you? Are you alright? The Spino..."

Bergis felt paralyzed for a moment. Here she was, trapped in the worst nightmare imaginable, and five seconds into the conversation she was more concerned about knowing if he came out unscathed from the fight with the Spinosaurus.

"I'm good. Let's focus on you. What's your condition?"

"I'm wedged into a narrow crevice in the wall. There are bugs everywhere. Lon, you won't believe this, but there's a..."

"A queen. Yeah, I see it."

"You see it? You're close?"

"Very close. You're inside a giant hive. It's unfinished, by the looks of it. There's a big breach in the side."

"I thought so. There's sunlight and wind coming through. Are you able to get close?"

"Eh... My crew and I are trying to work something out."

"Don't risk your own safety, Lon. I've got fifteen in the mag, one in the chamber. At the moment, the bugs are focused on the dead bodies and tending to the queen. They don't seem too interested in dragging me out of this little hideout. If it comes to that, I'll make sure to end it quickly."

"Riley, uh, Doctor McKeon; you stay exactly where you are. I'm working out a plan as we speak. I'll keep you updated."

"Oh, Lon. Don't get yourself hurt."

"Relax. I know that's easier said than done, but try your best. Leave the work to me and my new friends."

"O-Okay."

"Okay. Preserve your battery. I'll call you when we're ready."

"Thank you, Lon."

"Don't mention it." He ended the call, at once relieved and overwhelmed. It was an impossible situation, one that probably had a ninety-five-percent chance of certain death.

"She's alive!" Irrfan exclaimed with glee.

"Ooo, yay!" Colin mocked. "We're treating this as if it's a good thing. All we're doing is giving her false hope. And getting ourselves killed in the process."

"We won't let that happen," Hoover said. He was looking at the hive as he said that. "On that note, how *do* we pull this off without getting ourselves killed?"

Bergis sighed. "Before we do anything, we need to inform the others of this thing." He switched frequencies. "Command Central? This is Lon Bergis, Site Three M3 Scorpion operator. There's been a new development in the situation."

It was not the dispatcher who responded, but a furious Colonel Tarsus.

"Corporal! Where the hell are you?"

"Colonel, everyone listening, the bugs have constructed a nest roughly one-half mile west of Site Two. They are numerous and well-fortified. We need to order an evacuation immediately."

"You don't give the orders around here, Corporal. You're on notice for abandoning your unit. Our scouts have spotted the Spinosaurus swimming south. You could have finished the job had you stuck around. But you had to waste your time on a rescue effort for someone we all know is dead."

"I just spoke with her, Colonel. She's alive. And what the hell are you thinking sending scouts along the shoreline? Even without the knowledge of these bugs, you should have ordered an evacuation an hour ago. We have no air support, no patrol boats, God knows how many casualties…"

"Don't tell me how to do my job, Bergis. Not that I owe a grunt like you an explanation, but I contacted Globus and demanded reinforcements be sent."

"ETA?"

"Between two and three hours. They're redirecting a Battle Freighter that was en route to resupplying Globus' facility in New Zealand. We'll have more mechs, more troops, more gunships, and more firepower coming our way."

"A battle freighter," Colin muttered. "The Globus corporation practically is its own branch of the military."

"Helps when you make most of the toys," Blake added.

"That's all fine and good, Colonel, but what about an evacuation?" Bergis said. "We can have two Lockheed C-150s flown in from New Zealand in less than ninety minutes. Hell, we'd only have to wait twenty by now had we called after the fiasco on the beach."

"No, we're not running away like scared puppies. I'm ordering you to regroup at Command Central. You'll want to anyway, because my scout has informed me that the Spino has come ashore and is heading inland."

"Where?"

"A mile and a half north of where we fought it. That's enough chatter. Now bring my mech back to Command Central."

"Will do." Bergis switched off the radio. "After I get Riley out of there."

Colin and Blake's faces were turning green. All they took away from the conversation was the fact the Spino was coming in their direction.

"It's coming from the west," Blake said. "Our boat is northwest. We might be able to pass it by without the thing even noticing."

"That's assuming it's gonna walk in a straight line," Hoover said. "What do you think, Corporal?"

Bergis watched the nest again, studying the patterns in how the bugs moved. His mind went to the encounter at the beach. Several of the flyers had gone after the Spinosaurus. He didn't think much of it at the time, as he was busy trying to keep himself alive. Now, a realization was setting in.

"God might be lending us a hand."

The group, including Hoover, replied with a simultaneous "huh?"

"We'll use the Spinosaurus to our advantage," he said.

Colin stared slack-jawed. "This is why I don't make friends. Because too many people in the world are clinically insane! Thanks for reminding me of that, Corporal."

"The bugs went after the Spinosaurus," Bergis explained. "There's no way they would have been able to transport it to the nest for food. It's far too large. I think they attacked it because they perceived it as a threat. Same with the mechs. Given its temper, I don't think the Spinosaurus has a high opinion of them either."

"I get it," Hoover said. "You're suggesting we lure the Spinosaurus over here."

"Its presence will draw most of the warriors out of the nest," Bergis said. "It is our only chance of getting Riley out of there. I'm not banking on waiting for reinforcements to get her out. They're not going to risk the whole settlement on one person. They'll bomb this nest with her inside of it."

"That sounds accurate," Irrfan said. "Okay, Corporal, how do we get it here? Don't mind my friends; they're willing to help. They just hope not to become lunch in the process."

"Oh, gee!" Colin exclaimed. "You must be a genius, Irrfan! Why don't you tell them what two plus two equals?"

Irrfan shrugged. "Four. Everyone knows that."

Colin closed his eyes. "No, I was being... never mind." He and Blake shared a long look at one another, each one looking for any valid excuse to abandon this cause that would not make them feel like absolute cowards. In fact, they found a hundred different excuses. None of them erased the fact that there was an innocent person trapped in a hellish situation, and only they were the difference between whether or not she would make it out alive.

"Oh, great," Blake muttered in defeat.

Colin looked over at Bergis. "If we pull this off, that lady of yours, she's gonna... she's... she'll owe us big! She's gonna have to..." He waved a finger and clenched his jaw, so flustered by his decision to help that he could barely complete a thought.

"She can buy us pizza," Irrfan said.

Colin dropped his hand and gave a look to his shipmate. *Really?*

"Hmm." Blake's tone was one of 'why not?' "I like pizza."

Colin gave the same look to him, then lowered his head. He was outvoted.

"There better be double cheese and sausage on mine!"

Bergis smiled.

"I think she'll be happy to arrange that."

CHAPTER 15

Boom!

The bundle of QMT explosives formed a titanic mushroom cloud five hundred yards to the west where Colin and Blake had set it. A resulting tremor rippled through the side of the island, putting the colony of insects on alert. Flying warriors took to the sky and circled the nest.

Bergis and Hoover stood tensely near the S-4 mech, experiencing a ping of doubt in their plan. Now that it was underway, it felt real. They were officially luring the Spinosaurus in this direction.

Irrfan continued working behind them. The S-4 was put on standby mode, which essentially was a crouched position to allow support crews access to the weaponry. Multiple shells had been removed from the cannon, their gunpowder extracted and placed inside a singular, hollow shell. Its fuse and sensors had been removed, relegating the projectile to a weak dud.

"It's all set," he said. "Shoot this thing into the nest. The shell will crack on impact and dispense the powder. Launch flares at it, and you'll have a nice little bonfire inside the nest."

"Works for me," Bergis said.

The three of them lifted the shell and manually loaded it into the cannon.

"You'll only have one shot," Irrfan added. "Make it count."

"That's the plan." Bergis looked to the west. "As long as I can get close enough."

Another blast rocked the island.

The swarm intensified their activities. Ground-level workers moved into the hive through the incomplete section in the side. The flying drones kept inside the perimeter, each one on guard against anything that may pose a threat.

The radio crackled and Colin's voice came through.

"We're still alive, if anyone cares."

"I was going to ask," Bergis replied. "Glad to know you managed not to blow yourselves up. Any sign of the Spino?"

Colin answered by simply putting his thumb on the transmitter. Through the frequency, Bergis could hear the *thumps* of the massive feet moving their way.

"I guess your tactic of putting venom in its bloodstream had only limited effect," Hoover said.

"It was only a small amount. Probably has a hell of an immune system," Bergis said. "Colin, Blake, work your way back over here."

"Ha ha ha. It's so cute that you think we were gonna wait for your say-so to do that."

Bergis rolled his eyes and looked at Irrfan. "He always this smug?"

Irrfan nodded.

The radio crackled again. This time, it was Riley's voice coming through.

"Lon? I don't know what's going on. It's going nuts in here all of a sudden. I thought I heard some blasting in the distance."

"Doctor, I'm glad you called," he responded.

"Oh, just call her Riley," Irrfan said. "The jig is up, Corporal."

Bergis gave the smuggler a look. "Really? You know there's a forty-ton monster coming our way, right?"

"All the more important to be straightforward with her," Irrfan replied.

"Can't argue with that," Hoover said.

Bergis grumbled. Of course the knucklehead was gonna agree with the smuggler on this issue. A nuclear warhead could be coming their way, and the two of them would be more focused on romantic notions than survival.

He turned his attention back to the radio. "Listen, I'm coming to get you out. Things are going to get hot in that nest. I mean, really hot. Fiery hot, to be precise."

Irrfan and Hoover looked at each other and chuckled.

Bergis' jaw dropped. He could not believe what he was seeing. As fate would have it, he was stuck with the only creatures that were stranger than mutated insects or dinosaurs.

He growled and waved a hand at them, conveying the message of *Get your heads out of the gutter!*

"Anyway, Riley, we've got a plan. The drones will soon vacate the nest. When they do, I'm gonna move in with my mech and fill the place with smoke. The bugs in there will either vacate or move to assist the queen. Either way, they'll be too distracted to notice you making a run for the breach. When you get out, grab onto my leg and..." He cleared his throat loudly after hearing Hoover and Irrfan snickering. "My *mech's* leg, and I'll get you out of there. You think you can do that?"

"Yes. Oh, Lon! Thank you!"

"No problem. Keep your radio on, and be ready to run. And use that rifle if necessary." He clipped the radio to his belt and looked at his two companions. Hoover pretended to be serious and focused. Irrfan, true to his nature, maintained that smile on his face.

"I haven't officially met her yet, but I can tell she's a good woman. You chose well, Corporal Bergis."

Crashing stomps to the west prevented Bergis from giving a sarcastic response. They were too far away from the clearing to be able to see the Spinosaurus, but it did not matter. The first part of the plan was working.

Smaller footsteps gave away the presence of a nervous Colin and Blake. The two of them, gasping for breath, arrived at the hideout and leaned forward. Their brows were sweaty and spit was shooting from their lips.

"Holy crap! That thing is big!" Colin exclaimed.

Bergis moved to the edge of the clearing and knelt at the small hill. The flying drones were acting with haste now. It was more than a general sense of caution. Their attention was on something coming from the left.

More of them emerged through the main entrance at the top. They spread out, their tail stingers coiled underneath their bodies.

A familiar roar echoed from the trees. The Spinosaurus was on approach and, judging by the sound of its roar, was not pleased to see the bugs. It was not a sound of fear, but of hatred. It considered the insects a natural threat, and as far as it was concerned, this island was not big enough for the two species.

"It's working." Bergis ran back to the group and began boarding his mech. He activated the large machine and stood it upright, keeping its cockpit open for the moment so he could speak directly to the men below. "Keep your heads down. At the moment, the bugs couldn't care less about you. They're focused on the dinosaur. That being said, keep your eyes peeled and your guns loaded."

Colin chuckled. "You're only a corporal? They should've promoted you as captain, since you like to state the obvious." He put his rifle over his shoulder, expecting a warmer reception to his joke than the silence he got. "Yes, we'll be careful. You keep yourself and that girlfriend of yours alive."

"Riley is her name," Irrfan said. "Very nice woman. Corporal Bergis is going to be her knight in shining armor. He will rescue her, carry her off into the sunset."

"Make a bunch of little corporals," Blake added.

The group laughed in unison.

Bergis decided not to take the bait. He shut the cockpit windscreen and moved to the edge of the clearing.

It was the moment of truth. He whispered a prayer for his plan to work. He needed it to work. As much as he struggled to admit it to himself, Bergis knew that failure to get Riley out of there was something he could never live with.

Either she dies now from the bugs, or killed in the airstrike. Get over yourself, Bergis. This is her best shot.

And as a bonus, maybe the swarm would kill the Spinosaurus in the process.

He watched the swarm. A thick cloud buzzing ten yards above the hive, they all were faced to the west.

A tree came crashing down as the Spinosaurus came into view. As expected, it had fully recovered from the exposure to venom Bergis had inflicted on it at the beach. Its powerful tail swayed behind its bulk, smashing tree limbs. Those huge feet raked the earth's floor, serving as a warning to the swarm. Crocodilian jaws parted, and from the back of the throat came a defiant roar.

In response, the bugs went on the attack.

The cloud of insects engulfed the Spino, sparking a frenzy of twists, turns, chomps, and slashes. Tails jabbed at its skin. Legs latched to its sail and body, enabling the claws and tails easier access to the thick flesh.

Their assault came with casualties. Every swing of its tail, bite from its jaws, and slash of its talons connected with at least one of its adversaries. Those unfortunate enough to end up in the path of one of those weapons was exploded into a cluster of barely recognizable body parts.

What they lacked in size and strength, they made up for in numbers. Even as dozens of their members were hurtled across the sky, the swarm's density hardly changed. They pressed the assault with no fear for themselves, jabbing and slashing at the Spino in hopes of landing a lucky blow.

Meanwhile, there was hardly anything guarding the hive itself. A few stray flyers buzzing overhead and a few workers on the ground. An S-4 mech would have little trouble with them, especially when given the element of surprise.

Bergis armed the autocannon and sprang from cover. He took aim at the ones in the air and opened fire. Their bodies exploded in spurts of yellow. He aimed the gun low and gave the same treatment to the ground-level workers. The Bushmaster's rounds had no trouble rupturing their exoskeletons and decimating the soft tissue underneath.

SPLAT! SPLAT! SPLAT! SPLAT!

He moved closer to the hive, making sure to keep an eye on the battle taking place to his left.

The Spinosaurus swiveled on its heels, its tail swinging high and batting insects out of the air. The fallen members came down in a gory rainstorm of blood and body parts, many of which twitched and spasmed as the nerves slowly died.

Roaring madly, the dinosaur raised its head, bringing most of its hundred-plus-foot length vertical. Its eyes were closed as the drones gathered near its face in hopes of stinging the soft flesh.

A slash of its right arm knocked two of them out of the air. Their bodies parted at the thorax midway down, spilling organs and yellow blood.

It chomped, imploding another one between its teeth.

Several others moved in under its neck and jabbed their stingers against its throat. Though failing to break the skin, they were successful at inducing minor pain and a sense of urgency.

The Spinosaurus backpedaled.

Others nosedived right into its face, ramming their stingers into its closed eyes. More went for the legs and feet.

The plan worked.

Clumsy and off balance, the Spinosaurus reeled backwards. It hit the ground with the force of a ton of TNT, kicking up a small cloud of dirt and vegetation around it.

"Geez! Look at that!" Hoover exclaimed through the radio.

"Better hurry up, Corporal!" Colin said.

"Look who's stating the obvious now," Bergis replied. "Doc? Hey, Doc, you still there?... Riley?"

"I'm here. My gosh, Lon, it's a real shitshow in here! They're going crazy!"

"Are they coming after you?"

"No, they seem to be focused on the queen."

"Perfect. Do you have a path to run?"

"Somewhat."

"Best we're gonna get. I'm right outside the breach. When I give the word, run as fast as you can. Don't stop unless you need to shoot one of those bastards in the face."

"Alright." She was breathing heavily, psyching herself up for the insane maneuver they were about to pull off.

Bergis found himself starting to do the same.

He squared up with the breach and got a direct look inside. The hive was in chaos, with cockroach-shaped insects scurrying over a large mound.

Bergis exhaled.

Though he could not see it through the workers, it was clear what that 'mound' was. It was something so significant and royal, every member of the colony would not hesitate to give their lives in protection of it.

In this instance, that instinct would benefit Bergis and Riley.

He pointed the cannon and fired the shell.

A black streak went from the muzzle into the interior of the nest. The shell hit the floor of the hive and burst, spreading a thick cloud of gunpowder through the nest.

Bergis lowered the cannon and activated his flare gun from the right shoulder. It fired in five-round bursts, delivering multiple flickering red balls of flame into the nest.

The cloud of gunpowder ignited into a massive ball of flame.

A deafening screech echoed from the hive. The 'mound' went into a whirl, its defenders now encased in flame and driven mad by their literally burning nerves. Fireballs on legs, they moved in multiple directions, partially uncovering Her Highness.

Only thanks to the bright flames and dark smoke did she remain invisible.

"Riley! Go! Go! Go!"

He heard the echo of rifle shots from within the hive. They grew steadily louder, until Bergis was able to witness the body of a worker drone flipping onto its back after taking a shot to the head.

Riley emerged through the opening. Her face and clothes were covered in dirt and goo, but she was in one piece.

Behind her, a squad of insects moved to pursue her.

Bergis aimed the autocannon and sent several shots over Riley's head. The targets disappeared in blobs of yellow.

The doctor reached the leg of the mech and grabbed ahold of a ladder bar. She pulled herself onto the small maintenance ladder and held tight.

"I'm good!"

Bergis reversed his S-4 and made some distance from the hive. In doing so, he gave another look to the Spinosaurus. It had moved back somewhere into the jungle, obscured by the many trees around it. Bergis surmised it was still alive based on the thrashing of several treetops. The tremors on the ground were from a steady hammering of its weight, as though the thing was writhing on its side as opposed to stomping its feet.

He cracked a smile. His plan was working better than anticipated. Riley was out of the hive *and* the Spinosaurus was on the verge of dying.

"That's for Galloway."

SMASH!

His eyes returned to the smoldering hive. The top of the shell broke apart into multiple large shards. From the widened opening came several burning insects, no longer bound by duty, for they were in the final moments of life. Behind them, two crab-like pincers emerged.

They dug into the remaining side of the hive and hoisted the gargantuan body of her royal highness.

Her face was arrow-shaped, with two red orbs that acted as eyes on each back corner. Between them was a pair of antennae stretching five meters out. A dual set of mandibles frolicked. The outer set contained razor-sharp digits like crab legs, the inner set being oddly reptilian in basic shape, with teeth similar to those of a tiger shark lining the upper and lower jaws.

Her exoskeleton was dark brown in color, jet black from where the flames had singed her. In addition to her two forelegs, six segmented legs carried her body. Unlike normal insects, her body was comprised of four segments instead of six. First was her head. Second was her thorax, which resembled the narrow body of a praying mantis. Between the two large arms were four smaller arms designed to help tear apart prey and deliver food to the mouth. After the thorax were the dual abdomens. The first one was fairly small, serving as a base for her six legs to connect.

The fourth abdomen was the strangest aspect of her body. Its base was similar in basic shape to the first abdomen, complete with the ribbed texture of the exoskeleton.

Its rear, however, had a long coil, which Bergis nearly mistook for a sail, much like the Spino's. Only after he noticed the enormous barb tucked in its center did he realize he was mistaken.

Her Highness was armed with a gigantic tail. It had the same general design as a scorpion's, except much more flexible and far longer in comparison to the rest of her body.

Slowly, it uncoiled and lifted its tip high above her head. Mandibles stretched, dripping green saliva.

Bergis stopped. His stomach felt as though it was imploding in on itself. His hands jittered and his mouth went dry. As bad as the Spinosaurus was, this thing was worse.

She truly was a Queen of horror.

"Oh, shit." He backed farther away. "Riley... run!"

"Lon?"

"I'll keep it busy," he said. "Hoover! Get Riley and get the hell out of here."

"Will do, Corporal. Doctor, come this way. I'm waving at ya. You see me?"

"I see you. Coming your way. Lon, be careful!"

Bergis watched his rear-view monitor to make sure she gained some distance. She ran to the dirt ledge on the hill where the others had gathered. Hoover was waving at her. Next to him were the three smugglers, all of whom looked like they might be sick after laying eyes on the Queen.

"Jesus, Mary, and Joseph," Colin exclaimed. *"Corporal, I have a confession: I'm a betting man, and I don't like your odds."*

Bergis rolled his eyes at the vote of incompetence.

"Thanks."

He pointed the Bushmaster autocannon at the giant insect and fired. A barrage of thirty-millimeter projectiles struck her right in the chest.

Hissing frantically, she reared back on her hind legs, arms whipping the air.

Bergis kept up the punishment, planting rounds in her lower thorax and abdomens.

She leveled out, her front feet punching deep craters in the ground. It was the first of many fast motions.

Size was only a minor hinderance to her speed. The Queen moved strikingly fast. Her speed was shy of that of her subordinates, but her ferocity was ten times theirs. And that was when she was in a good mood.

The hits from the autocannon did not deter her. Nor were they able to breach her shell. As large as the Spinosaurus, she had a carapace that was at least as tough as its hide.

"Corporal! Bail out!" Hoover said.

"I thought I told you to get the hell out of here!"

"Corporal—LOOK OUT!"

The Queen leaned her head to the ground and fully uncoiled her tail. It was two hundred feet long at minimum, tipped with a razor-sharp stinger shaped like a serrated kitchen knife.

It moved like a cowboy's lasso. In that same manner, it was hurled at its target.

SMACK!

Cockpit glass shattered on impact.

The mech hit the ground on its back, its pilot juddering in his seat.

Bleeding from his cheek and forehead, Bergis was looking skyward. He wrestled with the controls to get the thing righted. The mech leaned on its right arm and attempted to point its autocannon again, only to be flattened on the ground after the bitch threw her bodyweight at him.

She brought one of her pincers down on the autocannon's barrel. The steel compressed, unable to withstand the vise-like grip of the edged appendage. She moved the claw in a rolling motion, like a plumber with a pipe cutter. After a few motions, the barrel fell free.

The other claw came down on the mech's abdomen, piercing the steel exoskeleton with ease. It twisted deep inside, then came out. Mechanical guts, dripping oil like blood, dangled from the clutches.

Lights flashed inside the cockpit as various systems began to shut down. The arms failed to respond to command. An automated voice blasted warnings about system failure and hull breaches into the corporal's ear.

Through all of it was Hoover's voice yelling through the radio.

"Bergis! Bail out!"

"Damn it, kid! I told you to run! I'm not gonna tell you again! Take Riley with you."

"But Bergis…"

He switched off the radio. There was nothing they could do for him now, and listening to Hoover shouting was not helping matters.

Bergis shifted the pedal, bringing the S-4's knee up.

The Queen rocked from the impact, grabbing hold of the machine to keep herself from falling off. Her tail bent high above her head and came down hard, plunging directly into the mech's center mass.

Right then, all lights switched off.

The fight was officially lost. Bergis was seated inside a useless bucket of bolts, no more battleworthy than the rusted scrap in a junkyard.

The Queen moved forward a few feet, those big red eyes peering into the open cockpit. Only now did she understand the huge silver foe had a smaller lifeform inside of it.

Mandibles twitched and yawned. Saliva fell around Bergis, permeating the cockpit with a vile odor.

Fear transformed into anger. The plan had *almost* worked perfectly. He had mistakenly assumed that the Queen would be some fat, immobile tub of lard laying eggs in the bottom chamber, unable to move herself. In reality, she had a fury only a mother could possess. And Bergis had smoked out her entire home and had murdered many of her offspring. She had plenty reason to be angry.

Even though those eyes were dull and unmoving, Bergis could feel the hatred radiating from them. She was not some dumb bug. She was intelligent, possibly to the point of taking pleasure in the harm she caused.

The jaws opened with intent to bite.

"Bergis!!! Take cover. Fire in the hole!"

It was Hoover, shouting from somewhere behind the mech's head. The creature turned its head to look at the tiny human.

Bergis wanted to yell at the idiot for failing to obey instructions. But those words 'fire in the hole' meant something hot was incoming.

He unstrapped his harness and moved to the back of the cockpit, giving one glance at the creature. A small object, like a bundle of sticks, hurtled up near her neck. Though he could not see it, Bergis was aware of the blinking red light on the detonator. It was the warning light that flashed when the bundle of QMT was ready to burst.

He put his hands over his head.

BOOM!

The Queen lifted off the mech and fell backward, unleashing a sonic wave of a scream. Bergis cupped his ears. They were already ringing from the explosion, but that scream of pain was something else entirely.

It carried on for another several seconds before ceasing. Bergis took his hands off his ears and climbed out of the cockpit. Standing atop the battered chest of his S-4, he saw the Queen thrashing on her back. Her exoskeleton was intact, with some blood leaking through some of the chitin on her right shoulder.

She righted herself and turned to face the humans.

Bergis ran down the arm of his S-4 and found his way to the ground. Hoover was several yards to the south, clearly in pain from the sonic scream. Beyond him was Irrfan, Colin, Blake, and *Riley*.

Bergis grabbed Hoover and began pushing him to the edge of the clearing. "What the hell is wrong with you? I told you guys to run!"

"We couldn't just leave you," Hoover protested.

A large cloud encompassed them, accompanied by the sound of a thousand droning wings.

They looked to the sky at the swarm of warriors. Responding to their mother's scream, they raced to her aid. A few of them landed on her shoulder and immediately began applying saliva to her injuries.

The Queen moved like an enormous tarantula, her forelegs cutting nearly a yard into the earth with each step. Driven by an urge to enact her revenge, she towered over the humans.

Bergis was tempted to grab Hoover by the throat. This whole plan was based around saving Riley. Now, she and everyone else were doomed because he was too stubborn to follow his orders.

STOMP! STOMP! STOMP!

CRASH!

All eyes, human and insectoid, turned to the sound of a tree coming down. Stepping over it was a battered Spinosaurus. Its neck and hide bled from various points where the swarm managed to penetrate the skin with their stingers. Their venom was getting to work, resulting in a very sluggish theropod.

In spite of its illness, it was not ready to give up the fight just yet.

It huffed and puffed, billowing smoke from its mouth. Its sail shifted colors like a moving ink blot.

The reptilian waved its head left and right, generating the energy within itself. Its jaws hyperextended and pointed at the swarm.

Like a firehose from hell, a steady stream of flame spat from the back of its throat. All at once, the swarm was engulfed. Like burning meteorites, they plummeted to the ground one after another.

Their mother staggered back, singed by the hot fire breath. Her offspring rained down around her, their bodies igniting the ground around them.

Letting out another sonic scream of misery, she leaned close to the ground. Her claws went to work in rapid speed, ripping out chunks of dirt and rock.

In a few short moments, she was entirely subterranean. Tremors rippled under the feet of the humans and reptile as she retreated to the depths of the island, intent on resurfacing somewhere else to lick her wounds.

Here in the clearing, her entire colony continued to burn.

The Spinosaurus ceased its fire breath. It took a few heavy breaths, then moved to the hive to make sure the rest of the colony did not live to see another day. It broke down the walls and stomped down any offspring still in there.

Surrounded by smoke, the enormous reptilian lumbered around the clearing. Its breathing was heavier. A swelling became noticeable in its throat and jaw. A more significant amount of venom had entered its system than before, and it showed.

Finally, its legs gave out. The beast collapsed and settled on its side. Drool pooled from its slack jaw. It was still breathing, but incredibly weak.

Bergis glared at the beast.

"Serves you right."

Colin and Irrfan ran up to him and Hoover, the former yelling, "Can we go now?"

Bergis was reluctant to leave without witnessing the Spinosaurus take its last breath, but as he had stated to the others, his first priority was Riley's safety.

"We're going."

Together, they raced into the jungle, leaving the wounded Spinosaurus behind.

CHAPTER 16

It was when they got a quarter mile from the nest that Bergis finally decided to grab Hoover by the collar.

The young operative swallowed and put his hands up in a non-threatening manner. "Use your words, Corporal."

Riley rushed towards him. "Lon!"

"Hey, man!" Colin said. "Are you for real?"

"He saved your life," Irrfan said. "And you're gonna beat him up?"

Bergis blocked out their voices and kept his eyes fixed on Hoover. "I specifically told you to leave. The whole point of us being there was to get Riley out, but you almost pissed that away. And for what?"

He grew more furious with each word, culminating in the balling and pulling back of a fist.

Hoover winced in frightened anticipation. "We—couldn't just leave you behind, man."

"Hey! Hey! Hey!" Irrfan put himself alongside Hoover. He put a finger in Bergis' face and balled his other hand into a fist. "He does not have it coming. You hit him, I hit you."

It was almost a physical shock to receive such harsh words and an equally harsh tone from the overly friendly smuggler.

Riley put a hand on Bergis' arm and went with a gentler approach. "I wasn't going to leave you behind either, Lon. I told the others we needed to do something. Irrfan opened the QMT case and Hoover took the initiative of hitting the Queen with it. I wasn't going to leave. Not even if they went without me. Fortunately, they had the good character to wait with me and help."

Bergis felt himself turning a different shade of red. Anger faded away into the pink shade of humiliation. He released Hoover and backed away. What was there to say in a moment like this?

After a period of awkward silence, he went with, "Sorry. *I'm sorry.* Not sure what else to say, except I should've used the gift of cognitive thought before overreacting."

Hoover gave a nonchalant smile and tapped the corporal on the shoulder. "You're good, man. We're still alive. The plan worked."

Bergis turned to Riley. "Are you alright?"

She answered with a tight hug. "I am now. My God, thank you for coming after me. I thought I was toast."

In an instant, Irrfan was back to his usual cheerful self. "Look how beautiful these two are! They were made for each other! Bergis rescued her from the nest. Now they can live happily ever after."

The corporal groaned. "Here we go again."

"Hey, it's true," Irrfan said.

"Thanks to the big dino," Blake added.

Bergis felt another swell of humiliation. Facing the fact that the Spinosaurus enabled them to escape was nearly as painful as their near-failure in saving Riley. As a matter of fact, it was *more* painful, as it highlighted the reality that Riley would be dead now if the Spinosaurus did not torch the swarm.

"It's not like it was deliberately saving us," he rationalized. "If anything, the dumb lizard should've used its flame sooner. Now it's paying the price. Those bugs managed to get a few stings in. There's a significant amount of venom in its blood now. Probably will die before the end of the day." He found a stone on the ground and kicked it. "Serves the son of a bitch right."

Irrfan raised his eyebrows. "Huh? Purposeful or not, the thing saved us. Why the hate?"

"It's a touchy subject," Riley said.

"It killed my friends," Bergis said. "Guys I've worked with every day for a long time now. Lergee. Walton. Galloway."

The others picked up on the special emphasis on that last name. Each of them understood there was little chance of lifting him out of his hatred of the beast. Furthermore, it provided special insight into why he was determined to rescue Riley.

He had lost everyone who meant anything to him. Except her. Life was short and could be taken away at any moment.

Riley, sensing Bergis' pain, directed them away from the subject.

"We better keep moving."

"Which way?" Colin asked.

Hoover took point. "If we keep pushing east, we'll come to a jeep trail. That'll make our trek back to camp a lot easier."

"I'd rather head back to the boat," Colin said. He looked longingly to the west, rationalizing his odds. "On the other hand, who knows what else is on this island. I guess there's safety in numbers."

With that said, the group pushed on.

CHAPTER 17

Site Ten was said to have been completely excavated. The largest of the sites in addition to One, with a surface diameter of six-hundred yards.

Lon Bergis and his companions stood at the edge of the large pit where the largest portion of the meteorite was supposedly extracted. 'Supposedly' was the key word, for they could easily see the violet color of the Fukuda meteorite minerals encompassing many layers of the earth.

Near where they stood were the remains of the managing trailer for this site. It had completely imploded at its center, its four corners managing to stay upright like light posts. Pieces of siding, drywall, and wood had been scattered everywhere.

Peppered amongst the wreckage were bits of dried blood and shredded clothing.

Next to the trailer was a small crane and an abandoned set of manual digging and drilling tools. The machine had been toppled over and dismantled by brute force. The tracked treads had been ripped as though they were rubber bands, the cab ripped right off the platform.

Three-toed footprints marked the whole southwest side of the pit, creating a mental playback of the Spinosaurus' rampage.

Hoover whistled. "Not hard to guess what went on here."

Bergis explored the remains of the building. "There were at least three, maybe four people here."

"People probably working for Dr. Dietz," Riley suggested. During the walk, she had been brought up to speed by the smugglers. She took a look at the dirt wall on their side of the mine. Multiple grooves, all in groups of three, decorated the granite and dirt. It went all the way from the bottom to the edge. "This is where it emerged. It was preserved here for all of these years."

"But how?" an astonished Colin Sermon asked. "How could something survive for a hundred million years?"

Riley looked at the pit and the violet mineral at the bottom. "An asteroid came to Earth. As it entered the atmosphere, it broke into several meteorite fragments. Came down on a section of land which eventually broke off and became Delta-Five Caprona. For many centuries after the dust cloud wore off, many species came across these deep craters. Some fell in, others may have tried using them for shelter. Somehow or another, some were rendered unconscious and preserved in the subterranean caves. Perfectly preserved by the mineral, until Globus discovered the fragments and dug them up."

Blake scratched the back of his head. "Very astute hypothesis, Doctor. Not sure how that explains how King Lizard back there was able to barf flames like a damn dragon."

"I've treated people who have disregarded safety protocols and had direct contact with the mineral," Riley said. "It's similar to radioactivity in the sense that it can mutate one's chromosome and DNA structure. The Spinosaurus, the insects, the squid creature from the pond, they all ended up in the meteor pits at one point. Those who were not killed were transformed into something else entirely. In the case of the Spinosaurus, it was made larger and given extraordinary abilities. Somewhere in its body, it must possess a reactor of some kind, capable of emitting hot plasma."

"Plasma?" Colin asked.

"Yeah, it *looks* like fire, but it's actually plasma energy. Burns hot. Prolonged exposure can melt the steel of the S-4 mechs."

"Damn!" Hoover said. The geek within him was going nuts right now. "Man, this is insane. I can't believe this is real. The asteroid created a real life, honest-to-God—"

"If you mention that Japanese crap, I'll go bonsai on your ass," Bergis said.

Hoover's enthusiasm did not waver. "It's true though."

"Was," Bergis replied.

That tainted Hoover's gusto. As violent as the Spinosaurus was, it was depressing to think it was dying back at the insect nest.

"You think this stuff was capable of inducing violent behavior?" Blake asked. "I understand the Spino is a predator, but if everything you guys said about its rampage is true, then DAMN! That's not predatory instinct. It's on a killing spree."

"Maybe it's a territorial thing," Bergis suggested. "It probably saw us as competitors. Or maybe it's just evil and didn't have any reason to kill everyone except it wanted to. Some things can't be rationalized."

"This one can be," Irrfan said. He was sorting through the trailer wreckage. In his hand was a briefcase with a computer and several stacks of papers.

"What's that?" Hoover asked.

"When we got our instructions, we were asked to collect all of the data Dietz had in the building." Irrfan took a knee and sorted out some of the papers. Many of them contained photographs of a large Spinosaurus skeleton. More photographs showed subterranean images of the rampaging Spino in the same cave. It was asleep, lying near several spherical objects.

"Oh, my Lord," Riley exclaimed.

"What?" Blake asked nervously.

"These were a mated pair. There was a lack of fossil evidence to suggest the species mated for life, but this completely turns the belief upside down. The dead one was the female. Judging by her left femur, she suffered some kind of catastrophic injury during pregnancy. They took shelter in the pit. It was here she laid her eggs. She did not survive and the male stayed behind with the eggs. During that time, some mineral dust came loose and rendered the creature unconscious. Here, it stayed for many millions of years."

"Eggs?" Bergis growled. "You're telling me there's more of these things wandering around?"

Irrfan shook his head and handed the next set of photographs to Riley. She covered her mouth and responded with a distressed "oh..."

Bergis decided to look for himself. He stood over Riley's shoulder and peered at the photographs.

Dietz had been operating with a private group to excavate the eggs. In doing so, they had accidentally ruptured the shells and killed the young inside.

"Geez!" Hoover's excitement was completely eradicated. Now, he was both sad and sickened by what he was seeing. The diggers left no stone unturned when it came to documenting their findings. They even took images of the dead young inside the eggs. They were miniature versions of their parents, on the verge of hatching, only to be impaled by a drilling machine and an incompetent operator.

Riley placed the photographs down. She had seen enough.

"That's why it's on a rampage. It's not a monster. It views us as a single colony, like insects. They killed its offspring, the only remnant of its mate. It thinks we are all responsible."

"You're suggesting the thing is heartbroken?" Bergis said.

She turned to face him. "You tell me."

Bergis took those words to heart. Here he was, at the end of his own rampage, in hopes of dealing a killing blow to the one who killed his friend and literally stick his head into a hive of giant hornets to save Riley. An inner voice spoke to him about hypocrisy. Why was it okay for *him* to have vengeance based on grievance and not the dinosaur?

The corporal quickly forced the thought from his head. He would not allow sympathy for the creature; not for the one that killed Galloway. Murder was murder. Back home, if one was on trial for such a crime, the judge would not write it off simply because of emotional state. Galloway had nothing to do with the killing of those would-be hatchlings. There was no justification, as far as Bergis was concerned.

Riley could read his thoughts.

"Lon, I'm not discounting your feelings on the matter. Galloway was a good guy. You have every reason to be upset, and I won't try to convince you not to be. All I will say is the truth: the thing, in spite of everything it has done, is not a monster."

"I remember when my wife died," Irrfan said. He looked at the scars on his knuckles. "I got into a barfight two nights later. Nearly killed three men with my bare fists, for no other crime than they had big mouths, and they were in the wrong place at the wrong time. They probably would've choked on their own blood had the medics not gotten there quickly. In jail, same thing happened during yard time. I blamed everybody of a… I'm ashamed to say it now… Latino ethnicity. She was killed by cartel members. I just blamed any criminal of the same race. It was the closest I could get to revenge. Instead, it turned me into a shell of my former self."

The shame was plain in his eyes. He looked at the marks on his hands, wishing he could scrub them off.

Riley, being naturally compassionate, rested a hand on his shoulder in comfort.

Colin turned his eyes southbound down the roadway. "Hey, guys? I hate to break up the melodramatic moment, but I think we've got incoming."

The rest of the group looked in that direction. A pair of Boar vehicles emerged from the bend and approached the dig site.

Bergis hung his head low and groaned after recognizing the men in the leading one.

"Well, well, well!" Godfrey Parr emerged from the front passenger seat. "Look who we have here!"

His two associates, Munro and Sagara, set foot on the dirt road.

"Hot damn!" the former exclaimed. "The cowardly corporal actually managed to rescue the good doctor."

"Credit where it's due," Godfrey said. "I had written her off as literal dead meat. I'd ask how you did it, but first, I gotta ask who these new friends of yours are?"

"That's a question for Dietz," Bergis said. "We have a whole story the colonel will be interested in."

"What are you guys doing out here?" Hoover asked.

"Recon," Godfrey replied. "We were trying to monitor the Spino's trajectory. Then we heard the explosions to the west and saw the big plume of smoke. You don't happen to know anything about that, do you?"

The group members exchanged glances.

"That's a hell of a story," Colin said. "You won't be bored hearing it. Trust me."

CHAPTER 18

Command Central was abuzz with dragonflies, armored vehicles, and troops moving in and out of the perimeter. Reinforcements had beaten their time estimates and immediately launched all of their personnel and equipment intended for New Zealand onto Delta-5 Caprona.

As Bergis was driven through the main gates, he looked at the troops moving about. Almost all of them were in good spirits, leading him to question if they were fully briefed on why they were here to begin with. If they were aware of what lurked on this island, they saw it as a turkey shoot. How tough could a dinosaur be, right?

On the one hand, it did make him feel better to see the additional firepower. It was better to have a bunch of Dragonflies and Boars than nothing at all. He did not have much faith in the tower guns on their own. On the other hand, he knew the best course of action was to get the hell off this island.

But Tarsus, for whatever reason, was damn eager to reign supreme.

Immediately after their arrival at the main compound the debriefing began. Riley went right to work in Med/Lab. One additional bonus to the additional personnel was it allowed quick extraction of injured staff members onto the battle freighter. More medical staff assisted the overwhelmed department, providing emergency aid to those who desperately needed it while the EMS and Fire Rescue departments made runs to the ship and back.

Bergis' testimony was relatively brief. The colonel, initially fuming at the sight of him, took on a whole new demeanor after hearing of the Spinosaurus' condition. The fuming returned when they provided him the explanation as to who Irrfan, Colin, and Blake were and why they were on the island.

They sealed themselves in a conference room for a private meeting, leaving Bergis and Hoover with orders to join up with one of the new units. There was no time for rest. Something was being planned and the colonel intended to implement it very soon.

The pair found themselves waiting in the front yard with Alpha Unit, led by the would-be chief of security for the New Zealand installation, Major Paul Hood. He was maybe eight years younger than Colonel Tarsus, and openly skeptical of why his staff was being mobilized for what appeared to be a field mission.

Regardless of his rank from the West Atlantic Army and his position in the company, he had no problem strategizing with the men under him. This led to a lengthy conversation between him and Bergis, in which the corporal laid out everything that had occurred since that morning.

"So, you're saying the thing is impervious to missiles?" one of the new security operatives exclaimed.

"And it spits fire," another said.

"But it's dead, right? Or, mostly dead?" a third asked.

"Even if it is, there's still Super-bug," a fourth chimed in.

"Settle down, everyone," Major Hood said. He put his hands on his hips and paced back and forth. "I don't like this. We don't know enough about what it is we're dealing with, and yet, Tarsus is getting us ready for war." He looked at Bergis and Hoover. "You said the Spinosaurus torched the swarm and you guys destroyed the nest. Are you positive all of the bug offspring are dead?"

"The ones we saw were," Hoover said. "I can safely confirm that *most* of its colony went up in smoke. That said, there's no telling how many scouts were out foraging for food elsewhere on the island."

"The attack force we encountered at the beach nearly wiped us out," Bergis added. He looked up at the blue sky. "They clearly operate during the daylight hours. I think it's safe to say more could be out there."

Major Hood held his breath. He did not like the situation at all. His eyes went to the compound.

"Some of the drone bodies were delivered to Med/Lab," he said. "I directed my medical personnel to assist that woman you rescued, Dr. McKeon. When the colonel returned with his strike force, they brought back a few dead insect specimens. One of the doctors informed me she was working on some kind of anti-venom."

"Anti-venom?" Bergis said. "Even if she was able to synthesize something, I don't know what good it would do. That stuff acts damn fast; once it's in your system, you're dead in under a minute."

"That's what the colonel said. I guess Dr. McKeon believed she could develop an antivenom that could act as a sort of preemptive vaccine of sorts. That way, if someone got stung, they would already have the antivenom in their system to counteract it. From what I hear, she's making fast progress."

"Wow," Hoover said. "Gotta love medical technology. Just a couple of decades ago, it would've taken months or even years to develop such a thing."

"Yeah, but manufacturing enough for everybody on this island will take an act of God," Bergis replied.

He saw Bravo Unit, fifty yards to the east, making a lane. Moving through the crowd was Godfrey, Munro, and Sagara. In the middle of the trio was a flustered Dr. Dietz, being pushed in the direction of the compound. Godfrey, wearing his sunglasses like a rockstar, spoke into a radio as they went.

Hoover, seeing this as well, switched radio channels to three.

"...bringing him in. You still in Conference Room B?"

"Affirmative. Bring him in now." It was Tarsus on the channel.

Major Hood had his fill of the ambiguity surrounding the colonel's plans. He turned to the Lieutenant in his Unit.

"Hold down the fort. I'm heading inside." He turned around and marched to the main entrance.

Bergis and Hoover started following.

"Pardon me, Major, but it's been a long and exhausting day. I'd like to get to the bottom of this as well," the corporal said.

Hood gave his approval with a wave. "You earned it."

They were ten yards from the doors when Godfrey's crew pushed Dr. Dietz inside the building. The geologist attempted to turn around and berate them, only to be shoved farther.

Bergis put the pieces together. Tarsus was fuming from the revelation of Dietz' coverup. The geologist had spent the last hour or so hiding until the mercenaries flushed him out.

Part of him was glad to see him get exposed. Tarsus was irresponsible in his handling of the situation, but Dietz was the one who set everything in motion with the secret scheme he was running.

They moved to the second floor of the compound, keeping Godfrey's crew in their sights until they arrived at Conference Room B. They reached the double doors before they could latch and pushed their way into the room.

Dietz moved to the corner of the long rectangular table in hopes of getting away from an enraged Colonel Tarsus. Bergis entered the room just in time to see a fist connect with his jaw. Dietz hit the wall and fell to the floor.

"Have yourself a little side hustle, don't ya, Doc?" the colonel bellowed.

Dietz spit out a tooth and glared at the colonel. "Listen, I don't know what those guys told you…" He pointed at the three smugglers on the other side of the room. Irrfan, Colin, and Blake looked nervously in Bergis' direction. With their weapons confiscated, they felt naked, especially in the presence of hot-tempered militaristic maniacs.

"Yeah, sure," Godfrey said with a snigger. "I'm sure the guys were just bored one day and decided this island was fit for a stroll."

"Uh-huh!" Tarsus grabbed Dietz and pinned him against the wall. "And somehow, they just knew to use the secret northwest dock you had built. I wonder if that played any role in delaying deforestation of the west side of the island. So…"

With a sharp pivot, he threw Dietz across the table. A nod to Munro conveyed the instruction of clearing the hallway outside to make sure nobody else was privy to what was happening in here. He would deal with the three bystanders later.

"Whoa!" Hood exclaimed. "Colonel, if I may—"

Tarsus hammered a fist on Dietz' gut, bringing his head and legs up with the shockwave.

"Nobody invited you here," he snarled, shutting the Major up. Grabbing Dietz by the hair, he pulled him over the edge of the table and let him fall on the floor. Planting a boot on his chest, Tarsus looked down at him. "Who are you selling to?"

"Nobody," Dietz coughed. "This is all one big—OHHH!" He spasmed from a stomp to the abdomen.

"You knew there were living creatures in those craters," Tarsus said. He grabbed fistfuls of the doctor's shirt and lifted him to his feet. "You knew those things were out there and tried to cover it up." A punch to the gut served as a break between that point and his next. "You got my men killed."

Hood had had enough. He moved to the other side of the table and put a hand on the colonel's shoulder.

"Sir, it's time to stop this."

"Nobody asked you," Godfrey said. He was picking his fingernail with a knife.

Hood took an instant dislike to the man. Though he did not know Godfrey or his two companions, he instantly sensed they operated outside of the standard Globus security parameters.

Tarsus looked at him. "Get the men ready to roll out. We've got a location of the target. It's incapacitated. All we have to do is finish it off."

"Colonel, there's still the issue of the giant insects," Hood said.

"As Bergis explained, they have been mostly eradicated," Tarsus replied. "Generally, I take issue with people disobeying my orders. But I've got to give credit where it's due. Bergis and his new friends helped solve a major problem."

"It's not solved at all," Bergis said. "The Queen is still out there. And there might be more drones. Yeah, the nest has been destroyed, but that doesn't mean she doesn't have other offspring."

"We'll handle them later," Tarsus said. "First, we'll deal with the sail-back bastard. Once he's dead, we'll focus on the insects. What's the matter, Corporal? This morning, you were foaming at the mouth to go kill that thing. What changed?"

"I might want it dead too. Doesn't mean I'm stupid," Bergis said. "We need to evacuate this island. We're outmatched. We're up against an enemy more ferocious, more ruthless, more determined than anything we've ever fought before. Believe me, we got lucky at the hive. Only their hyper focus on the Spino allowed us to get anywhere near it. If it was an army of us going against an army of them, believe me, it'd be a bloodbath."

"And the Queen sat most of that fight out," Hoover added.

Tarsus snarled and lifted his foot off of Dietz. "The hell are you two doing in here anyway? You're supposed to be on standby with your unit."

"I allowed them to come," Major Hood said.

"And why are *you* here?" Tarsus said. "Last I checked, you have a functioning radio."

"I want to get to the bottom of what's going on," Hood responded. "This is not war. I'm not sacrificing the lives of these men just to kill some animal. We came here to provide backup and medical assistance. Not to initiate some offensive campaign."

Tarsus heard only his words, but missed the point of his statement. "Headquarters approved. I have command of all staff. Mine, and yours."

"They didn't approve a crusade," Hood said.

A fit of laughter interrupted the argument. Everyone in their room turned their eyes to Dr. Dietz. He held his hands over his stomach and cackled as though in a front row seat at a comedy show.

Tarsus balled a fist. "What's so funny?"

Dietz coughed, then stood eye-to-eye with the colonel. "You accuse me of getting everyone killed? What about you? A madman colonel who tried to prolong the West European Campaign despite a declared ceasefire, forced to retire and hired as a Chief of Security on a far-away island, where he led a crusade against a monster out of a personal vendetta. Losing men under your command must be tough. Losing your stepson, whom you leveraged your position with the company to get hired, has got to be worse. Especially when he gets stomped by some oversized lizard."

Tarsus knocked him to the floor with a blow to the left eye.

Hood stepped forward, but was blocked by Sagara.

Dietz continued to laugh. Though Hood did not intend it, he had granted the doctor some leverage by providing an audience who could make a direct call to Headquarters.

"Did I strike a nerve, Colonel? You think I'm not smart enough to tap into the history of every person on this island? Even after I've been performing excavations right under your nose without you even knowing?"

"The hell are you talking about?" Hoover said.

"Colonel Tarsus, retired from the West Atlantic Army, married fourteen years to Cathleen Tarsus, formerly Cathleen Lergee. She brought in two kids from a previous marriage. The older of the two, Dennis Lergee, had a juvenile record of breaking and entering. Spent six months in jail. Struggled to get a job, despite living on the straight and narrow for many years. Stepdad pulls some strings, and voila, Dennis Lergee is part of the security detail on Delta-5 Caprona. Then, when his stepson unexpectedly dies on the job, Colonel Tarsus, emotionally compromised, leads a crusade in an effort to get revenge on the creature, causing the deaths of several other officers in the process."

Bergis watched the colonel's expression as the doctor spoke. The look in his eyes confirmed every word Dietz spoke was true.

"Lergee was your stepson?"

Tarsus did not provide an answer. Again, it only served as further confirmation.

Bergis looked at the equally astonished Hoover. Though he did not personally know Lergee, the guy was very much familiar with the process of having the leverage of respected military relatives to get position in the company.

Hood straightened his collar and took a moment to compose himself.

"Colonel, I'm going to get on the horn with Headquarters. I'm relieving you of your command."

Tarsus pivoted to face him. "I've already had approval…"

"They are unaware of the circumstances. No, sir, we are evacuating this island. We are going to board our vessel and resume course for New Zealand, where we will run thorough recon of this island and properly determine the level of threat."

"It's not going to happen," Tarsus said.

"You heard him," Dietz bellowed. "Don't you all get it? It's bad enough the colonel has to explain to his wife at home her number one boy is dead. Imagine how bad it would be if he isn't able to say he didn't bag the lizard that stepped on him. She'll blame him, leave his sorry ass, and take sixty-percent of his income *and* pension…"

Tarsus drew his revolver, put the muzzle to Dietz' temple, and squeezed the trigger.

Everyone in the room, including the mercenaries, flinched.

Dietz slid down the wall, face frozen in mid-laugh, trailing a line of blood as he went to the floor.

Tarsus inhaled, contemplating what he had just done.

Major Hood slowly stepped back, one hand slowly reaching for his phone, the other cautiously going for his own sidearm.

Tarsus watched him in his peripheral vision. He had crossed the Rubicon and proven Dietz correct. Now, his focus was on covering his own ass… and fulfilling his personal vendetta.

Hood turned on his heel and went for the door.

Tarsus turned and squeezed the trigger.

A deafening *BANG* shook the room.

Hood went down, a large hole burrowed into the back of his neck. Bergis and Hoover jumped in different directions.

For five seconds, Colonel Tarsus had done the impossible: he made them completely forget about the reawakened giant monsters lurking on the island.

Godfrey uncrossed his arms, appearing more mildly annoyed by the escalation in events than shocked.

"Dispatch to Colonel Tarsus. I'm receiving calls of gunshots within the compound, second floor."

"False alarm," Tarsus said. He sucked in a deep breath to compose himself and get his voice sounding calm. "I'm on site. Accidental discharge from a pair of incompetent employees. I've got men apprehending them now."

"Copy that, sir."

"Colonel Tarsus to all units, we're moving out in five. I want mech units to assemble at the main gate. Dragonflies will take point and provide recon and cover."

Bergis' hand tensed. He wanted to go for his pistol, but knew he was outmatched.

Sagara and Godfrey were already on top of the issue. They closed in on Bergis and Hoover and stripped them of their weapons. Pistols were placed at their heads, keeping them in place.

Tarsus looked over at them. "You should've stayed in the yard."

"You son of a bitch," Bergis growled. "You're going to get all of these men killed. And for what? Your own personal vendetta? How many more parents have to lose their sons? You know the feeling as much as anyone."

"Anything we come across, we will destroy," Tarsus said.

"Dude!" Hoover exclaimed. "Have you not learned anything from last time? We hit the Spino with everything we've got, and it still went right through us."

"As you said, it's weak. Probably on the verge of death," Tarsus said.

"And the insects?" Hoover said.

"There's just the big one."

Tarsus' tone was matter-of-fact and lacking in any semblance of concern. He had made up his mind once Bergis' team were killed. He was not thinking like a military strategist. He was a man with one single objective. Maybe in a week, he would feel the guilt of the people he got killed in his pursuit of vengeance. Maybe a month. A year. But right now, he was not the Colonel Tarsus Bergis knew.

He looked at his two henchmen. "You guys have this covered?"

Godfrey twisted the muzzle of his gun against Bergis' temple. "We can do it here or somewhere else. It's gonna cost ya, Colonel."

"Consider it covered," Tarsus said. "Do it in here. These men 'killed' Dietz and Hood. You three 'found' them, they resisted, and you had to kill them."

Bergis could not believe what he was hearing. The once-respected military officer had reduced himself to something equivalent of the lowest crime boss.

Godfrey pushed him hard against the wall. Sagara did the same to Hoover, putting the two framed suspects alongside one another.

Hoover groaned. Much to the corporal's astonishment, he sounded more annoyed than anything else.

"Survived multiple encounters with a mutated dinosaur and avoided getting eaten by a bunch of bugs and a squid-thing—only to get killed by this putz."

Godfrey chuckled. "At least we'll make it quick."

He extended his weapon at Bergis' heart and began squeezing the trigger.

Boom! Boom! Boom!

The sound of roaring explosions started far beyond the perimeter and rapidly approached the compound.

Godfrey and Sagara turned their eyes to the doorway. Munro sprinted inside, pointing behind him at the north window.

"We've got company!"

A frenzy of transmissions filled the radio channel, the words nearly blotted out by gunfire.

"They're coming out of the trees! They're all over the perimeter!"

"Falcon Three's down! Its armament has detonated by the northeast shack!"

"We're being overrun!"

BOOM!

The compound shook.

"There's a big one! It's got a big tail!"

"WHOA!"

A crashing noise filled the channel.

"Falcon Two is hit! It's coming down... Clear the compound!"

BOOM!

The building shook. Like a toy in a child's grasp, the compound tilted backwards and forwards. Alarms rang out and sprinkler systems activated.

All hands in the conference room were forced to their knees. The ceiling broke apart and rained down on the three mercenaries in the middle of the room.

Bergis and Hoover seized their opportunity. The former lunged at Godfrey and put all of his weight behind an elbow to the chin. Godfrey was put on his back, quickly joined by Munro who was sent down by a kick to the chest. Hoover took care of Sagara via use of a chair to the head.

Colonel Tarsus extended his revolver. He fired a shot through the thick dust, his shot passing between Bergis and Hoover. He cocked the hammer and shifted his aim, planting Bergis in the iron sights.

A chair was flung across the room. One of its legs connected with the side of the colonel's head, knocking him to the floor.

Colin Sermon pumped his fist and led the trio of smugglers in a race to the door.

"I better get a 'thank you', Bergis!" he said.

"We're not getting paid by Dietz, that's for damn sure," Blake added.

The five men ran into the hallway right as the compound shook again. A set of window panels on the wall had busted, giving a wide view to the madness taking place inside the north perimeter wall.

"Oh, my God," Hoover muttered.

The bugs were everywhere, in numbers that seemed impossible. They swarmed the ground and the sky, overwhelming the security forces. It was a warzone in the truest sense, with the ground being littered by the bodies of man and insect.

Flying bugs jolted in mid-flight as they were struck by deadly rifle fire. The turrets on the gate towers were unloading everything they had, like Navy gunners repelling Japanese planes in Pearl Harbor.

The garage was completely destroyed, with several Boars and small maintenance trucks up in flames or simply smashed to bits.

Most of the security forces were withdrawing towards the compound. Hysteria and confusion overtook any sense of defensive strategy. Not that it mattered anyway; the bugs had superiority over the air and the ground.

Irrfan was speechless. Between the crazy events back in the conference room and this, he was out of breath and barely able to focus.

"How?"

Assuming he was addressing the number of insects attacking the compound despite the fact most of the nest was torched, Bergis replied with, "I think there was more than one hive."

He was watching the mechs. They had assembled a few yards left of the west tower in compliance with the colonel's orders to move through the main gates, only to get entangled in an all-out melee with the Queen.

She was as agile and pissed as she was at the hive. Her frustrations were taken out on the six S-4 mechs, with the aid of a few flying warriors, and a pair of giant escorts. They were built like rhinoceros beetles, sporting a long, jagged horn from their faces. It was a weapon proven to be lethal, as one of the poor mech pilots learned the hard way.

They were equal in size and nearly identical; the only differentiating feature being a large red scar sported by one of them on the left side of its face.

The two insects double-teamed the humanoid machine, impaling its legs and hips. They took it to the ground and began stomping its cockpit windscreen and penetrating the breastplate.

A slash of the Queen's scorpion-like tail cut through two other mech cockpits. The two machines stumbled backwards, their pilots completely exposed to the elements. Her Highness did not bother giving them any more attention, for her minions were happily willing to take care of them for her. Several warriors crawled through the open barriers and laid waste to the human controllers. The mechs danced in place as their operators were brutally slain, the autocannons firing aimlessly until the deed was complete. Both machines went down hard, guns still firing skyward.

One of the remaining three mechs attempted to fire its tank gun at the Queen. A slash from her tail knocked the machine off balance right as its pilot squeezed the trigger. The round went southwest, connecting with the corner of the main compound.

The five spectators fought to keep balance as the building shuddered.

Another cannon shot went high, arching over the entire settlement and exploding in the distance. The Queen threw herself at the mech, plunging her giant pincers in its hull. Insect and machine tussled for the next few seconds, the pilot attempting to wrestle her into a suitable position for his fellow pilots to get a shot. They understood the drill, having blasted and crushed the few warriors near them. Before they could aim their cannons, they were set upon by the two beetle-like insects.

Charging like the beasts they resembled, they took down the mechs. Both machines had barely hit the ground before their attackers followed up their attacks by raking their horns against their hulls, indenting the thick steel and exposing the insides.

Meanwhile, the Queen overpowered her opponent. Securing her S-4 in a vise-like grip, she headbutted the glass and stuck her face into the cockpit, mandibles flailing.

Bergis cringed, his subconscious forcing him to envision the pilot getting eaten alive.

Another Dragonfly aircraft went down, its cockpit invaded by a pair of warriors. Its armament detonated on impact, shaking the battlefield and spewing hot smoke into the air.

Colin looked over his shoulder at the juncture in the hallway. "Hey guys, not to minimize what's going on out there, but let's not forget there's a bunch of maniacs who want to blow our brains out. Is it possible we can get a move-on?"

"We still have our boat," Blake said. "As long as there are no sea monsters swimming around out there, we have a golden opportunity to say 'bye-bye' to this place and grab Mai Tais in Honolulu."

"I don't see much of a future in this company," Hoover said. "What do you think, Bergis?"

The corporal felt the same. "Let's get down to the infirmary and get Riley."

Irrfan's usual smile returned. "Yes. We cannot leave without the love of his life."

Bergis responded with an 'ugh' sound and led the way to Med/Lab.

CHAPTER 19

To no surprise, the infirmary was in complete disarray, with doctors and nurses scrambling to provide care while figuring out whether or not to evacuate the patients. Multiple soldiers were retreating into the lower levels, many of them taking defensive positions at the windows.

It was the Battle of the Alamo, except with the fort's defenders facing off a siege of insects as opposed to soldiers. All the same, they were overwhelmed and losing the advantage.

Bergis pushed through the crowd in search of Riley. He found her, not in the emergency room, but near the lab where she was applying bandages to an injured soldier.

She saw the corporal approaching and perked up. "Lon!"

"You alright?" he asked.

"All things considered," she replied. "How about you?"

He bit his lip. "All things considered."

"That's a lot of things to consider," Colin chimed in.

"Where the hell did the Queen get all these extra bugs?" Colin asked. "Don't tell me she squeezed them all out in the last couple of hours."

"No, I don't think so," Hoover said.

"I don't recall seeing those two tankers back at the nest," Irrfan said. "Maybe our assumption about there being hunting parties outside the hive was true."

"Not *that* many," Bergis said. He looked at Hoover. "You research random crap. What do you know about insect colonies? These things have to share some sort of characteristics with ants and bees. They have a queen, obviously. Could there be a second hive out there providing, I don't know, reinforcements?"

"To my knowledge, that's not generally how insect colonies operate," Riley said. "Then again, I'm no entomologist."

"And if I may add," Colin said. "Maybe your buddy likes to research random stuff, but do you really think he would one day actually be bored enough to type into a computer 'do separate insect colonies join forces?'. Yeah, given our luck today, I don't think we'd have that kind of convenience."

Hoover cleared his throat.

The others all looked at him.

Colin's brow wrinkled. "Wait, are you serious?"

"It's not common," Hoover said. "But there have been reported instances. There's a super colony of ants in California stretching for over five hundred miles. They have different queens, but they work in unison as though one single group."

"Maybe a princess took flight before we laid waste to the hive," Bergis said. "The Queen escaped and decided to borrow her grandchildren for a grand offensive."

"Oh great!" Colin exclaimed. "*Two* queens? Not to mention those big beetle things."

"The second colony is probably newer," Riley suggested. "New queens go on a wedding flight. It's possible the new big ones served as princes, or escorts, to get the new queen to her nest unharmed. Afterwards, they probably lived out the rest of their lifespans guarding the hive. We didn't see any at the first one, because that colony was initially established millions of years ago, and was preserved inside the meteorite. Not to mention, they're heavily mutated and altered from whatever they were originally."

"Hang on a second." Irrfan raised a finger, his eyes bulging in alarm. "You guys only recently began seeing all of these monsters, right? If they made a second nest this fast, what are the odds they'll make a third? Or a fourth? Fifth? Sixth?"

"Yes, yes, yes, Irrfan," Colin said. "We've all attended first grade. We know how to count."

"We learn by age four in my country," Irrfan replied.

"Oh, yes, right." Colin rolled his eyes. "Dumb Americans. We get it."

"He has a point," Riley said. "They reproduce at an expeditious rate. Not only that, but their young mature within hours of birth. I saw it for myself while I was trapped in the hive. It's possible that, by tomorrow, another queen will be born and initiate a new nest."

Blake gulped. "Are you implying a bug-pocalypse?"

She nodded and turned to Bergis. "We need to do something. Where's the colonel?"

"The colonel's lost his mind," Bergis said. "We'll explain at a more opportune time. Right now, we need to get the hell out of here. These guys have a boat. We can bum a vehicle and make a Hail Mary run for it."

Riley looked at her patient. "We can't leave all of these people. And you heard what we just theorized…"

Bergis tilted his head back, his face pained from what she was suggesting.

"Doc… Riley, there's nothing we can do. We're just a group of people. If we stay, we'll just be killed with the rest of them. They can attempt to get to the freighter if they want. But this place is going to be overrun very quickly."

Riley's eyes swept over the Med/Lab area. The building was rapidly filling with hundreds of frightened personnel who wanted to be anywhere but here. They were all doomed to a horrible fate unless something was done immediately.

"We can't just leave."

"We don't have anything to fight them with," Bergis said. "The mechs are all wrecked. There's only three dragonflies still docked, and they won't be of much use against the swarm. We're beat, Riley. Help won't get here in time. Nobody's coming to save us."

The doctor looked in the direction of the Chem Lab. "Maybe not reinforcements. But there's someone else who might be able to take these things on."

Bergis took a step back. "Huh?"

"Wait… is she addressing what I think she is?" Colin said.

"The Spino!" Irrfan gasped. "It might work."

"The same Spino that was taken down by the things?" Bergis said. "Assuming it's even still alive, I doubt it would be of much help."

"It helped us escape," Irrfan said.

Bergis pivoted to look him in the eye. "Not on purpose. Besides, the thing was too dumb to torch the hive before they could swarm it."

"Eh, we all make mistakes," Hoover said. "That, and I have a theory about that. I think the dinosaur needs gaps between uses of its fire breath. Like, maybe it needs to recharge, or something. I've noticed how sparingly it uses it. My guess is it probably needs a few minutes or so to replenish its breath."

The rest of the group nodded. All except Bergis.

"It doesn't matter, because the thing was on death's door last we saw it. Even if it's still alive, there's nothing we can do to heal it from the venom in its system."

Riley took another look in the direction of the Chem Lab. "There may be one thing…"

Hoover pointed enthusiastically. "The anti-venom! They said you were working on one. Were you able to synthesize something?"

"I developed a prototype," she said. "I haven't been able to run any tests."

"Are you confident it'll work?" Hoover asked.

Riley hesitated a few moments before replying, "It's a fifty-fifty chance." She looked back at Bergis. "It's our only chance."

The corporal's jaw tensed. All of a sudden, his own feelings of bitterness and vengeance began clouding his judgement. The creature had killed his friend and nearly killed him in the process, and here he was, being talked into *saving its life*.

Riley stepped in front of him and put a hand on his face.

"The Spino is not responsible for what happened today. It was Dietz and his schemes. Had he gone through the proper channels, had he performed a more competent dig instead of trying to sneak the specimens off to a competitor, they would not have destroyed its eggs. None of this would have happened. Furthermore, we would have been aware of the possibility of other predators, and could have prepared ourselves for the insects. Maybe even evacuated the island altogether. The point is, the Spino's not the enemy. Maybe we can convince it we're not its enemy as well."

"You think that thing's open to reason?" Bergis asked.

Riley shrugged. "It's got a large brain. There's potential for intelligence." She lowered her hand and took a step back. "Or, you can do nothing and condemn all of these people to death."

Bergis' ears took in the sounds of fright within the enlarging crowd. These men, as highly trained as they were, were not ready for such a horrific conflict. The war was supposed to be over.

Security for Globus was supposed to be nothing more than a job, with maybe a minor conflict here and there. For the most part, they just wanted to collect a paycheck and go home to their families. Not become chow for a hive of crazed bugs.

He thought of his team back in Algiers. All this time later, he could never shake the guilt of letting them die. He had lived to see another day, but at a cost someone else had to pay. And now, he was considering doing the same thing to all of these people here, many of them veterans of the same war he fought. They had paid their dues to the Alliance and had hoped to live good long lives in relative peace. At this rate, none of them would get their wish. An evacuation to the ship would be easily intercepted by the swarm. Holing up here and defending the compound would eventually fail, especially considering how fast the bugs replenished their numbers.

Their only hope lay with the Spinosaurus and the people who could maybe get it back to full health.

Colonel Tarsus was willing to sacrifice everyone under his command in favor of his grudge. Bergis refused to stoop to the same level.

He looked at his new friends. "Any of you know how to fly a Dragonfly?"

Blake shut his eyes and hung his head down. "Oh, great."

That was enough of an answer for Bergis. The guy didn't want to, but he wasn't going to say no.

"Let me get the sample," Riley said. She went to hurry into the Chem Lab, but returned to Bergis once more. "But first..." She grabbed his face and pulled him in for a kiss.

Irrfan smiled. "Aw. Look at that. True love at its finest!" He whipped out a handkerchief and dabbed his eyes.

"Oh, for crying out loud," Colin groaned. He glared at the lovebirds as the kiss persisted. "Um, I hate to kill the dramatic moment, but we were just talking about how those things out there would kill everyone in here if we didn't act fast."

Riley broke away. "Right. Let me grab the sample." She ran into the Chem Lab.

Bergis exhaled. He could feel himself blushing like a teenager.

"Do we get an invite to the wedding?" Irrfan asked.

Colin stared at his fellow smuggler. "For god sake! We could be eaten alive at any moment, and here you are gushing like a girl at a chick flick movie. They literally just had their first kiss. Let him at least get to second base before—"

Bergis found some discarded rifles from injured soldiers and handed them off to the group.

"You three know how to handle these?" he asked the smugglers.

All three of them checked the magazines and cocked the levers.

"Grab some ammo," Bergis said. "We're gonna need it. Hoover, until further notice, you're our mutated-prehistoric-animal-and-any-other-random-shit specialist. How do bugs communicate?"

"Bees use pheromones," Hoover said. "It's possible the ones outside do the same. Why?"

"Even if we're successful, I'm worried we won't get the Spinosaurus back here in time. But if we can locate that second hive and hit it with explosives, do you think the new queen might send a distress signal?"

"And recall the swarm..." Hoover completed his thought. "I think so. They wouldn't travel a distance where they would not be able to keep in contact with the hive."

"Good. We'll look for the nest first," Bergis said. "Now that we know what we're looking for, it probably won't be all that difficult to spot."

Riley returned with a large glass cannister with an orange fluid inside. She had a bag full of tubing and other medical supplies in a bag strapped over her shoulder. She secured the cannister in the bag and grabbed a rifle Bergis had gotten for her.

"We're gonna have to move fast," she said. "Those things are gonna be on us as soon as we're out the door."

Bergis reflected on the battle at the west beach.

"Not unless we smoke them out. I'm sure someone in here has some gas bombs."

He pushed through the crowd in search of supplies. After a few minutes, he returned with some grenades, stick flares, and a good old fashioned can of kerosene.

"This is the best we'll be able to do. Let's move."

CHAPTER 20

The process of getting from the compound to the helideck was as hectic as they expected. Though most of the swarm had congregated on the north side of the structure, plenty of them were quick to try and intercept the group as they went for the aircraft. Bergis' strategy of using the smoke bombs and kerosene proved effective enough in deterring them long enough for Blake to get the Dragonfly up and running.

The flight out was equally as chaotic. Bergis and Colin made good use of the door guns to take down their assailants, buying enough time for Blake to gain some distance from the swarm. At a quarter mile, they gave up in favor of resuming their attack on the compound.

From then on, they commenced a search for the second hive. All the while, they monitored radio transmissions from Command Central to be updated on all developments. As expected, things were going from bad to worse very quickly. The rhino bugs were ramming the damaged section of the building where the Dragonfly had collided, widening the main breach. At the same time, the warriors were attempting to make their way in through any vent or window they could find on the upper floors.

Not once did they hear a transmission from Colonel Tarsus. His name was only brought up by security operatives, who were confused as to his whereabouts, and trying to determine a new chain of command. At some point, Major Hood's body was discovered, and his cause of death was quickly surmised to be a bullet from a .357 magnum.

Further alarming the compound were reports of the last Dragonfly having gone missing.

"Is it destroyed?"

"No! Not destroyed. They're all just... gone!"

Irrfan scratched his nose. "They're not talking about us, right?"

"There was one other Dragonfly on the deck," Colin said. "And Bergis was nice enough to inform the dispatcher we were taking this one. They may not have been pleased, but still."

"Stay focused, people," Bergis said. "We need to find that second nest ASAP."

"My eyes are glued to the window," Irrfan assured him.

Colin knelt by the door gun and watched the wilderness below with bitter eyes. "It was supposed to be a quick job. Drop some bombs in a hole, leave, and get paid. But noooo. I've got to save the world from mutated bugs. With the help of a giant dinosaur, of all things." He began looking across the fuselage. "Is there beer in this thing by any chance?"

"There's one thing we did not quite consider," Bergis said. "Assuming the anti-venom is successful, how do we know the Spino won't try and squish us? It may be intelligent, but are we certain it will put two-and-two together?"

Riley was seated with the briefcase. One benefit of Colonel Tarsus getting a look at the computer was he was able to get someone to override the security features and access the files. She scrolled through some more images which had not been printed out.

"There might be a way."

Bergis hated dramatic moments of silence before the explanation finally came out. "And?"

She spun the laptop for him to view the screen. On it was a high-resolution image of one of the Spinosaurus' eggs.

Bergis took a closer look. The shell was broken, the newborn inside plainly visible. It was curled up like a sleeping cat, complete with a claw covering its face.

He shrugged. "Okay?"

Riley swiped the screen to display the next image. The date and time revealed it was taken only a minute later.

The newborn's posture was mostly the same, but the claw was lower and its foot had lifted a few centimeters.

It was a detail that could have easily been missed. Even Bergis had to compare it to the previous image for a couple of minutes before he noticed. But the change was there.

"It moved?"

Riley nodded. "I think it might still be alive. These images are only a day old."

"It could've died since then," Colin said. "A lot could've happened in a day."

"The other offspring were clearly damaged beyond saving," Riley explained. "This one seems to have suffered some injuries from the dig, but they appear fairly minor from what I can see. The Spino probably thought it was dead as with the others. But if we can bring the young one to it, maybe it can serve as a sort of peace offering."

"Aren't we anthropomorphizing the thing a bit?" Bergis said. "Seems a little far-fetched."

"Based on what?" Hoover said. "The fact this group lived in a family contradicts what we thought we knew of the species. It clearly understands sentimentality. If you ask me, it's our best shot at getting the thing to help us."

Bergis turned his eyes back to the outdoors. "This has been one strange day."

"It's about to get stranger!" Blake called from the cockpit. He slowed the Dragonfly and turned it to port, giving them a view of a rock ledge a quarter-mile from the dig site where the Spino originally emerged.

The hive was a similar shape to the other one, albeit a little smaller. Like the first, it was incomplete, with its top section entirely open. Several bugs crawled over it, acting as the colony's construction workers. A few warriors patrolled overhead, while most of the swarm worked to assist their grandmother.

Bergis peered through a set of long-range binocs. The new queen was inside, attached to a large brown sac where the eggs birthed from.

"That's... gross."

"Anyone having second thoughts?" Blake asked.

"Been having those since we first arrived," Colin remarked.

"Blake, fire four rockets. Land one on the hive itself, the others close by. We don't want to kill the queen just yet. We need her to withdraw her swarm." Bergis looked to Hoover. "How fast do those pheromones travel?"

"Something this size? The others should realize something's wrong in a matter of seconds."

"Works for me," Bergis said. "Blake, do it!"

The pilot made an exasperated sigh.

"Here goes nothing."

He unleashed the four rockets. As instructed, one of them hit the nest on the lower right side, rupturing a section of wall. The other three landed close by, sending fire and shrapnel into the interior of the nest.

A screeching hiss echoed from the upset mother inside.

Blake reversed the Dragonfly to distance them from any retaliatory force. Behind him, Bergis turned up the volume on his radio to catch any significant transmissions.

For nearly a minute, everything was steadily getting worse. The rhino bugs had nearly collapsed the eastern portion of the main compound. Multiple transmissions relayed the fact that several warriors had gotten through the top floors and were infiltrating the hallways.

Bergis began tapping his foot. A natural instinct to blame somebody started welling up inside of him. He had hung on Hoover's theory of how quickly the swarm would respond. It was going on two minutes now, and there appeared to be no change.

Even if they got the Spinosaurus up and moving, there was no way they could get there in time. From the sounds of it, the remaining defenses were about to falter. All two hundred people in that compound were about to be massacred.

He needed to take his rage out on something. May as well be the hive.

"Blake, arm the rest of the rockets and all hellfire missiles. Blow that thing to hell."

"Wait!" Riley called out. "Listen."

The fuselage went silent, save for the barrage of radio chatter.

"They're pulling back. The two big ones are expanding their wings. Jeez, they're huge."

"How are things upstairs?"

"They're withdrawing. Every single one is taking to the sky."

"The big ones are lifting off. They're heading north… and the one with the big tail is digging a tunnel. They're leaving."

Riley smiled and shared a high-five with the group.

"Holy crap!" Hoover exclaimed. "It actually worked."

Bergis lifted the radio. "Command Central, the swarm is regrouping at their nest. This is your one opportunity. Evacuate to the freighter right now. Do not wait. We don't know when they'll attack again."

"This is Lieutenant Riker. Who is this?"

"Corporal Lon Bergis. We're at the nest right now, Lieutenant. I suggest you take my word for it."

"Well done, Corporal. We're commencing evacuation now."

Colin nervously watched the horizon. "You know, since we did our good deed and saved everybody, we can probably go ahead and make a run for it."

"No," Riley said. "We need to destroy these things today, or else they'll proliferate out of control. Bomber squadrons won't get here in time. Our only hope is the Spinosaurus." She brushed some hair out of her face. "Admittedly, that's not a sentence I ever thought I'd say."

Colin hung his head low. "Ugh. If you insist."

"We need to get that egg fast," Irrfan said. "The mine is not far from here. We'll be in the path of those things."

Blake turned the aircraft around. "You'll hear no argument from me!"

***

Bergis secured himself in the full-body suit. Stored in the management building for the dig, they were relatively undamaged from the Spino's attack. They were snug outfits, more resembling a dive suit than anything else. His movements were slow and strained, the mask foggy.

"This better freaking work."

Riley strung a second harness over his torso to allow an easy grip on the egg. "Just have a little faith."

"And move fast," Colin added.

Bergis looked down at the gaping pit below him. The Dragonfly hovered in the middle, its nose level with the surface ground. The deepest point was over two hundred feet down. There, a few gaping pits marked the entry points of the caves where the mineral was extracted, and the Spino was discovered. Its emergence had displaced much of the soil, destroying the ceiling on one of the caves. The bedrock had slid back into place, sealing the area of rest.

"Gosh, I'm not sure I'll be able to find it in all of that. The whole thing has collapsed in on itself."

"You've got to try," Riley said. "Please."

"You have to!" Irrfan said. "Our survival depends on it. If you are not successful, how would we get to attend the wedding?"

Bergis closed his eyes. *Not this crap again.*

"You guys better have a buffet at the reception," Colin said.

"Yeah!" Hoover called. "I've been to some receptions where you are stuck between two crappy choices. Oh, and if you don't have an open bar, you're a dick."

Colin nodded in agreement and put an arm around Hoover. "I think you and I just became best friends."

Bergis glared at them, then looked at Riley. "Gosh, they move so fast, I'm shocked it's not the 1920s."

She smiled. "We'll discuss it at dinner. First, let's save the world."

Bergis took one more look at the pit.

"This has been a strange day indeed. And it's not even over yet."

With that said, he fast-roped into the mine. The first hundred-and-seventy feet was pretty much a complete freefall, with the remaining distance slowed by the winch.

Bergis set foot at the bottom of the mine. He stood amongst some battered digging equipment—the first casualties of the dinosaur's revenge. Unclipping his harness, he moved to the mouth of the cave. As he noted in the Dragonfly, the roof was gone, transforming the cave into a gorge.

He could see the tunnel where it went farther underground. Activating a spotlight on his helmet, he passed through the gorge and entered the tunnel.

Bergis entered a world of violet walls, glistening with millennia of energy carried from beyond the stars. These crystalline objects had been on this earth for over a hundred-million years, and had probably been drifting in space for a billion years before that.

The surrealness never hit Bergis until now. He never saw his time on the island as anything more than a job. More specifically, it was an opportunity to keep the last part of his Scorpion team with him. The significance of the find was not something he cared about.

Here he was, a part of a whole new team consisting of a medical doctor, a young science enthusiast with no formal education, three smugglers with hearts of gold. And, if things went well, a mutated, fire-breathing Spinosaurus.

He had lost everything, but had gained so much more. Not only had new friends entered his life, but also a new sense of purpose. Since the end of the war, he slogged through each day, with no other goal than to make it to the next morning. For the first time since that horrible day in Algiers, he found himself thinking about the future. While he would never excuse his cowardice in the face of danger, he now believed he was being given a second chance.

That newfound optimism gave him the confidence of finding that egg.

It paid off three hundred feet into the deep pit. He was inside the fragment of asteroid, surrounded by its crystalline magnificence, when he discovered the skeleton of the Spino's mate. She was only half the size of what her life partner would grow into. The bones had the same damage shown in the photographs. She had burrowed her way into this pit with intent to give birth and hopefully heal. The latter wish did not come into fruition, and it was man's interference that ultimately sabotaged her goal.

The ceiling here was surprisingly intact. Bergis could see the claw marks on the ground where the big one had crawled out and emerged through the pit.

Near the wall were the offspring, surrounded by an assortment of manually operated excavation tools and a pair of rovers, both of which were crushed. It was difficult to look at the first three eggs. Dietz and his crew did not exercise caution when digging them out of the rock.

The fourth one, as Riley suggested, was a different story. There was no blood or yolk. The little thing was near the point of hatching when the shell was ruptured.

As surreal as the sight of its father was, it was somehow even more astonishing to see the little one. It was the size of a full-grown Labrador Retriever. Coiled within its egg, the baby Spino was still. Its eyes were closed.

For the first time, Bergis felt a wave of compassion for the species. The poor thing was just a helpless soul waiting to live out its life, only to find itself displaced in time, and nearly killed by the dominant species of the New Age.

Bergis reached inside the egg and put his hand on its head. His touch answered the question of whether it was alive.

The baby weakly lifted its head. It looked at the human kneeling above it and let out a cry. There was no effort to bite him. Either it was too weak or too scared, or both.

"How's it coming?" Colin said through his earpiece.

"I found it. It's alive. We're heading out right now."

"Make it fast. Blake's got radar contact. The swarm's coming, and we're in the path."

"Copy." Bergis looked at the large hole in the egg. There was no point in trying to bring out the whole thing. He widened the opening and wrapped both arms around the baby Spino. "Sorry kid, but we're in a bit of a rush."

It strained in his grasp, but failed to outmuscle the man it perceived to be a captor.

Bergis turned around and ran as fast as he could out of the cave into the sunlight. Up above, the Dragonfly was in place, the fast rope swaying where he had set down.

He placed the second harness around the baby's middle, then attached it and himself to the clip.

"Go! Go!"

The Dragonfly took off to the west, getting out of the swarm's path as the crew reeled him and their new passenger into the fuselage. Colin and Hoover were right there at the opening, both astonished to see a miniature version of the sail-back reptilian.

Riley, true to her loving personality, could not help but smile.

"Oh, my gosh! Look at it!"

"You two already have your first pet!" Irrfan said.

"Not a chance," Bergis said. He yanked his helmet off and stood by while Riley tended to the newborn.

"It's malnourished," she said. "We need to get some food and water in its belly. I can get an IV going. Are there any rations in this ship? Preferably something meat-based."

Irrfan opened a cabinet. "We've got some Spam." He tossed it to Bergis.

The corporal chuckled at the tinned portion of salted pork. As sophisticated as Globus was, they went cheap when it came to field provisions. It made him think of tales from soldiers from World War Two and Vietnam. Many of them liked to use the cans as target practice.

He peeled it open and used a knife to pry the cube of meat out. He cut it into slivers and extended one to the baby's mouth.

"Might not be the most nutritious thing you've ever eaten, but it beats an empty stomach."

The poor thing recoiled, lacking trust in the strange creatures surrounding it.

Riley took one of the slivers and held it to its mouth, only to get the same result. The frightened dinosaur squeaked and tried to crawl away. Having an IV needle in its leg did not help matters.

"Oh, come on, fella. This'll help you."

The words did nothing to calm the animal. Now, it was trying to bite. The jaws came shut inches from Riley's hand.

She retracted. "Whoa!"

"Maybe this won't work," Colin said.

"Relax, relax," Bergis said. "Everyone relax. Let's not quit because of a little misunderstanding."

He held his slice of the Spam in front of the dinosaur's eyes. He waited until its gaze was on it, then took a small bite.

"Mm-mmm." It was a lie—cold Spam was not necessarily his idea of a yummy snack. But for a starving lizard, it may as well have been Thanksgiving dinner. All it needed to understand was it was food. For millions of years, its definition of food was raw meat from recently slain animals. Not something from a cupboard.

The baby calmed. It sniffed the salted meat. The fear began to subside and curiosity took hold. Curiosity led to the return of hunger.

Bergis gently moved the slice to its mouth. The baby parted its jaws and slowly took the meat. It jittered its head, surprised by the taste. Nonetheless, it was happy to eat the stuff. Swallowing the biteful, it looked at the one in Riley's hand.

Chuckling, she placed it between its jaws. This time, the baby took it with much more enthusiasm.

Before long, the rest of the can was consumed.

"Any more of that stuff?" Bergis asked.

Irrfan tossed him another can. "If you've been asleep for a hundred-million years, you'd wake up hungry too."

"Well, he's young. After a while, he'll discover some better food," Bergis replied. He began feeding the little Spino the contents of the second can. It had completely warmed up to him now and had completely forgotten about the IV in its leg. "But first, we need to see your dad."

CHAPTER 21

The adult Spinosaurus was on its side, its jaws clenched, arms tucked close to its torso. A shift of its head at the arrival of the Dragonfly confirmed it was still alive.

Blake set the Dragonfly on the ground and lowered the aft boarding ramp.

Lon Bergis and Riley McKeon stepped outside with caution. A smell of charred bug and resin permeated the air. Smoke rose from the decimated hive as though it was the crater of a volcano. Dead insects, burnt or bashed, littered the entire clearing.

Bergis held a T-4 Python automatic rifle, muzzle pointed downward, ready to be utilized in the blink of an eye. He and Riley reached the bottom of the ramp and gauged the aggression and energy level of the Spinosaurus.

An angry growl filled their ears. Claws grazed the ground and the tail rippled with strained motion. Its head lifted and pointed those angry eyes at them.

Naturally, Bergis put a hand up to demonstrate peace. Immediately, he felt like an idiot.

Yeah, right. Like this thing is gonna understand any gesture I make.

Riley put a hand in front of him. "It's alright."

"Alright? Are we looking at the same dinosaur?" Bergis responded. They watched as the creature's head bobbed. The venom in its veins was wreaking havoc on its respiratory and circulatory systems. Its immune system, as incredible as it was, appeared to slowly be losing the battle.

Despite its weakness, it was ready to take on the humans who, from its perspective, were here to take advantage of its condition.

They took a few steps closer.

The creature shook and bellowed. Its tail smacked the ground.

"I'm starting to have second thoughts," Colin called from inside the Dragonfly.

"Where's the baby?" Bergis asked, refusing to break eye contact with the adult.

"It's still eating," Hoover replied.

"Yeah! It really likes our rations," Irrfan added with his usual glee.

"Very cute," Bergis replied. "Except, if I remember correctly, I asked you to bring it out with us. Not continue to feed it."

"It went maybe its whole first twenty-four hours of life without any sustenance," Irrfan said. "You'd be hungry too."

"I'm gonna be the main course if you don't get that thing out here!"

Irrfan took a couple of steps down the ramp. "Technically, given the size of the dinosaur, you'd be an appetizer."

Now Bergis broke eye contact with the beast to shoot him a glare. Colin soon emerged behind his fellow smuggler.

"Hang on. It's almost done. I think…"

Bergis turned his gaze back to the dinosaur, then leaned toward Riley. "Maybe we should get back in the ship. This idea you had of making a show of peace doesn't appear to be working."

"Hold your ground," Riley said. "With or without the newborn, it needs to understand we mean no harm. If it's as intelligent as I think it is, it will recognize the fact that we could easily have attacked it, but did not."

"You're giving an awful lot of credit to a lizard."

"A 'lizard' that's managed to outsmart the entire security force on this island," she replied.

Bergis sighed. They truly were in a relationship; he was already losing arguments.

"What do I do?"

"Talk to it."

He scoffed. "Talk to it? About what? The Super Bowl? Price of gas? Favorite movies?"

"Just do it," she said.

Bergis sighed again. He kept one hand raised and slowly approached the creature. A gust of wind spewed from its nostrils. Another growl shook his soul. Crippling terror was seizing his entire body, inducing shakes he had not felt since the start of the war.

Somehow, he could sense the Spinosaurus was hesitating. Even though it was in critical condition, it could easily muster up the energy to squash him in the blink of an eye. Maybe it was curious as to what this display from the humans meant.

Bergis, following Riley's advice, tried to think of a meaningful statement. With the adrenaline free flowing through his veins, he decided to go by the seat of his pants.

"Uh, hi."

He hoped the creature was unfamiliar with the sense of awkwardness. How could one not be clumsy when trying to talk to a hundred-plus-foot fire-breathing dinosaur?

"Listen, it's been a rough day to say the least. Right? Listen, I get it, you don't like us. I'm not exactly your biggest fan either. I had a buddy on this island. You killed him this morning. Even as I say it now, I question whether I'm doing the right thing by trying to help you. Part of me still thinks I should let that bug venom finish you off."

He stopped in his tracks after receiving a growl in response. Maybe the creature did not understand the words, but it seemed to know the tone.

"But, I think about what Galloway would do if he were here and I was dead," Bergis continued. "He was a tough guy, but he was good at keeping a rational mind. If he were here instead of me and knew what I now know about you, he would insist we do what Riley here insists. Okay, that was kinda wordy, but my point is this: You lost your family and you think us humans are at fault. Us shooting at you probably did not help matters. But you thought we were your enemy. Only a small handful of us were. Still, you killed a lot of people who did not deserve it."

He took a breath.

"But maybe, in the eyes of some, you can balance it out by helping us. Those wasp things are still out there, and they're gonna kill you, me, and everything else on this island if we fail to do something about it."

The creature huffed again. Oddly enough, it appeared to be listening. Again, Bergis did not believe it literally understood the words he spoke, but its aggression appeared to be decreasing.

Maybe it was optimism bias, but he started to think the gist of his message was getting through.

"I guess you probably feel like you don't have a stake in the fight. After all, everything you've done up until now was revenge for what happened to your kids. Except, you might have a second chance at fatherhood."

Just as he hoped, he heard fast footsteps coming down the ramp.

"Whoa!" Colin exclaimed. "He ate all his food and now he's looking for you, Corporal. I think you made a buddy."

Bergis turned around and made eye contact with the little one as it reached the edge of the ramp. The youngster, rejuvenated by the sustenance it had ingested on the Dragonfly, sprinted in his direction without any hesitation.

"Slow it down, kid," Bergis said.

It brushed against his leg like a cat. A bright red tongue stuck out of its mouth and touched his hand.

Bergis pursed his lips and looked at the drool on his fingers. "Lovely."

"His version of a kiss," Riley said with a laugh.

The adult raised up with newfound energy at the sight of the little one. It inhaled deeply, taking in the familiar scent. There was no doubt in its mind it was the same offspring it had slumbered with for millions of years.

Bergis knew the look. The thing appeared flustered as though it had seen a ghost. The intimidation display was gone. Seeing its young, the last of its species, interacting with the humans shed the Spinosaurus of its blind hatred.

The youngster stood beside Bergis and looked at its father for the first time. A long moment of silence fell between them. At the end, the baby trotted up to its father and snuggled near its neck.

Colin, Irrfan, and Blake stepped off the ramp and watched in fascination as the seemingly terrifying beast displayed its parental instincts.

"Well, would you look at that," Blake said.

"He's happy now," Colin said. "Give it time. The kid'll start pestering him for food, waking him up in the middle of the night… Dad'll be stocking up on beer real soon."

"You think it'll let you apply the medicine, Doctor?" Irrfan asked.

Riley raised the cannister and the syringe for the Spinosaurus to see. This was the really tough part. The needle could easily be mistaken for a deadly stinger or some other harmful weapon. Worse, the only flesh soft enough for it to penetrate was inside the mouth.

Bergis walked with her.

"Listen, man," he said to the gargantuan beast. "You see this? This'll make you feel better. Just let us get it in your mouth." He pointed at the large syringe, then at the roof of his own mouth.

"You really think it's going to understand that?" Colin called out.

Bergis looked back at him. "Excuse me, it's my first time acting as a veterinary assistant to a freaking dinosaur."

"And it'll be your last time too."

Bergis knew that voice well. Way too well.

He swiveled on his feet as Colonel Tarsus emerged from the tree line. A rifle was pointed directly at Riley's chest. Even if he was not aware of their newly blossoming relationship, Tarsus knew Bergis well enough to know he would not roll the dice on her safety.

"Drop the rifle, Corporal. Then remove your sidearm and place it on the ground. *Slowly.*" A slight, but noticeable twitch in the colonel's rifle conveyed the deadly consequences of defiance.

Emerging next to him was Godfrey. He had a rifle pointed at the trio of smugglers.

"Best not to make a move," he warned them. Godfrey turned his eyes to Bergis and Riley, noting the cannister of anti-venom in her hands. "Just as we thought. She took it, Colonel."

"Like it would have done you much good," Riley said. "I would have needed at least another two days to make it suitable for your purposes. Not that it matters anyway; Command Central was overrun. Only thanks to *us* do the people there have any chance at surviving."

"Somehow, I don't think the colonel cares about that," Bergis said.

"Step towards me," Tarsus snapped.

Bergis and Riley gave each other a supportive look, then complied. The doctor kept the cannister close to her chest and her arms wrapped tightly around it.

A heavy downdraft pummeled the area. Moving over the tree line into the clearing were the two remaining dragonflies. They moved slowly, each one sporting a towing cable from their underbellies.

Bergis recognized the shape and the chipped green paint of the M3 Scorpion *Old Buster.* The war machine-turned-tunneller had been given the repairs Bergis had been conducting before the start of today's events. Tarsus' intent was clear; he intended on using the powerful laser cannon technology to kill the Spinosaurus and complete his vengeance.

The two aircraft, piloted by Munro and Sagara, gently moved the huge machine west of the group and set it down. The attachment hooks parted and the cables retracted into the dragonflies.

"All set," Munro said through the radio.

"Good. Watch the perimeter," Godfrey replied, keeping his weapon trained on Hoover and the three smugglers.

"The two of you walk over here on foot?" Bergis asked.

"Nah, that would only happen if you were driving the dragonflies," Hoover remarked, pointing at his own sore feet.

After failing to understand the context of that statement, Colonel Tarsus replied to Bergis with, "We suspected you had returned here after we discovered the prototype anti-venom sample was missing. We had to approach as though you were a hostile group, so Godfrey and I roped down a quarter-mile back." After giving a look to the dying Spinosaurus, his face tensed. "I see it has come to this, Bergis. First, you are insubordinate. Now, you are a full-on traitor."

"A traitor?" Bergis shot back. "Says the guy who got tens, if not over a hundred people killed to fulfill his own vendetta."

"At least I'm not trying to save the life of the monster who killed them," Tarsus said.

"No," Bergis said. "I'm trying to save our only chance of stopping the hive before it gets out of control. This operation here on Delta-5 Caprona is over. That meteorite is something else entirely, Colonel. God only knows what else we might unearth."

"Thank you for supporting my argument," the colonel replied. "You are correct; we cannot risk awakening any new creatures, *and* we must destroy the ones that have already emerged. Like this one here." He shifted his head at the Spinosaurus. In doing so, he did a double-take. "And its offspring. I don't suppose you all have anything to do with the sudden appearance of this second Spinosaurus."

"Uh, let's not get off track," Colin interrupted. "Frankly, Colonel, your argument is bullshit. You seriously expect us to ignore the fact that you shot two people in cold blood back at the compound?"

"Not to mention he was gonna pin it on Bergis and I," Hoover added. "He'd probably blow your guys' brains out in retaliation for contracting for Dietz."

"This has nothing to do with ethics," Irrfan said. "You are pathetically trying to justify your revenge. You could not care less about the swarm. To you, they are just a speedbump, an inconvenience, in the path of your personal crusade to destroy the Spino."

Godfrey silenced the two of them with a kick to Colin's abdomen and a strike of the rifle barrel to Irrfan's jaw.

Tarsus shifted his rifle muzzle to Bergis' head. The corporal gnawed on his lip, literally biting the urge to tackle the colonel whom he once respected and give him a much-deserved beating.

"I see the way you're looking at that M3," Tarsus said. "On that note, I suppose it's appropriate that you're here. You can make up for your betrayal and insubordination, Corporal. I was hoping of doing the honors myself, as I'm familiar with the controls of the Scorpions. That said, I'm content with watching while you do it instead." He nodded at the huge machine. "An energy cartridge has been loaded into the tail cannon. Board the cockpit and burn a laser right through that thing's head. Try any funny business, like pointing the cannon at my associates or myself, and your friends will each get a third eye-hole before you can follow through. Do as I say, and I'll let you walk out of here."

The answer to what the colonel would do if Bergis refused was clear. It would be a simple matter for Tarsus and his mercenaries to execute all six 'traitors' and chalk their deaths as casualties of the mutant creatures.

"Yeah? And again, I have to ask what you plan to do about the hive?"

"We've got the firepower, and thanks to the attack you conducted, the location," Tarsus said. "Once the dinosaur is dead, we'll destroy the insects. Plain and simple."

"Unless they destroy you first," Riley said. "They went through the defense forces at Command Central pretty easily. I think they'll make short work of a handful of dragonflies."

"Then we'll evacuate the island and return with long-range weapons," Tarsus said. "I understand your smuggler friends have a boat nearby. We'll use that to evacuate and get in touch with the East Pacific Navy. I know some of the admirals. They'll direct their carrier strike groups to this island and launch missile attacks."

"By then, another queen might escape the hive and set up another nest. Maybe even off the island," Bergis said. "We don't have time for this. Our best shot at ending the threat is to get the dinosaur back on its feet and let it do the job for us."

"Nonsense." Tarsus thrust the gun muzzle into his face, knocking Bergis down. "Enough talk. I'm not gonna keep debating the issue with you people. The decision is made. All I'm offering you is a chance, Corporal. Kill the Spino, or I'll shoot you right here. Who knows? Maybe your demise will inspire your friends to see the value in being a team player."

Bergis stood up and looked to Riley. She turned her eyes toward his. He received the message they conveyed. She did not trust the colonel to stay true to his word. Even if she did, she had no desire to betray her conscience and give in to the mad colonel's demands.

It was a sentiment shared by Bergis. The decision was still his, however. Refusal meant guaranteed death.

Bergis reflected on his life, particularly the mindset during his failure in Algiers. At the time, he thought he had gone through too much hell to deserve to die at the last minute.

He looked Tarsus in the eye.

"Well?" the colonel barked.

"Here's what I think," Bergis said. "You can march into that thing's throat and become kiryu chow."

Tarsus gave a half-sneer. On the one hand, he was eager to make good on his threat. On the other hand, he had no clue what the hell Bergis was referring to.

Even Riley in this moment of crisis was stunned with confusion.

"Um…" Howard waved one of his raised hands. "Do you mean 'kaiju'?"

"Kaiju?" Colin perked up. "Is that what those Japanese monster things are called?"

"That's right," Hoover said.

"Hmm." Blake nodded, hands still clasped behind his head. "I guess Bergis just made up a word and hoped for the best."

"Well, technically the word '*Kiryu*' has a place in the genre, as it was the name for the 2002 iteration of—"

"Oh! My! God!" Bergis exclaimed. Even with death staring him in the eye, he could not escape all of Hoover's nerdy bullshit. Even worse, he brought this one on himself in an effort to get one more insult at Tarsus before biting the farm. "You know what, Colonel? Just shoot me now. It's a mercy at this point."

Tarsus gave a rare laugh. "Maybe I should keep you alive a little longer and have your friend recite more trivia if you consider it the worst degree of torture."

"I can do that, Colonel," Hoover called out.

Bergis squeezed his eyes shut. "Great. Thanks."

"Nah, you'll like this one," Hoover said. "In the *Jurassic Park* franchise, there was talk of people imprinting on dinosaurs when they're born. Helps to earn trust. It's one of many factors that's debated in the films and in actual science. But, recent evidence suggests that such a bond actually exists."

Tarsus, his weapon fixed on Bergis, glared at Hoover. There was a look of regret in his eyes, as he didn't expect the operative to actually follow through on the 'threat' of burning their brains with useless trivia.

"And what evidence is that?" Colin asked him.

Hoover smiled. "You'll find out in just about… three… two… one…"

Tarsus growled. "The hell are you going on about—JEEZ!"

Bergis picked up the sounds of rapid footsteps behind him, and the violent snarl of the baby Spinosaurus as it jumped through the space between him and Riley. Like a loyal canine, it threw itself at Bergis' attacker. Tarsus was put on his back, twisting and kicking wildly as he tried to wrestle those jaws from his left forearm.

Godfrey turned to aim his weapon at the small reptilian. Hoover and Colin seized the opportunity and charged the mercenary, knocking the rifle from his grasp as they tackled him to the ground. Hoover managed to grab ahold of the merc's sidearm and unholster it. Godfrey was quick to retaliate with a kick to the young operative's wrist, flinging the weapon out of his grip. A second kick struck Hoover in the groin and knocked him backwards. The other two smugglers joined in the brawl. Godfrey was able to get back on his feet and exchange blows, accomplishing a few knockdowns before his four opponents overpowered him.

Tarsus received a similar treatment from Bergis and Riley, in addition to their dinosaurian friend. It kept its jaws clamped on his arm, even as he rolled to his feet.

The attack and pain kept his attention long enough for Bergis to get behind him and get ahold of his sidearm. He fired two warning shots skyward then placed the muzzle to Tarsus' head.

Yelping with fright, the baby Spino let go of the colonel and jumped back next to Riley.

Near the boarding ramp, Hoover and the smugglers pulled a bruised and agitated Godfrey to his feet. The paper-ranked lieutenant had a look of bitterness on his face. He didn't care about the job at this moment; he just wanted to continue the fight. But, like his two accomplices piloting the dragonflies above, he did not want to derail his gravy trail.

"Riley? You wanna give me a hand here?" Bergis pointed at the colonel's radio with his chin. Obliging his request, she unclipped the radio and held it to Bergis' face while he gave his warning to the pilots. "Here's how this is going to play out: you two are going to land your aircraft. Then, you're going to step outside and lay any weapons on the ground. Then you will stand with my crew with your hands on your heads while the doctor administers…"

Machine gun fire rang out.

Tarsus cringed, thinking the pilots were sacrificing him to get at Bergis. Their shots were horizontal, going over their heads at a target to the east. An all-too-familiar droning sound filled their ears.

Munro and Sagara made distance from each other, maintaining steady gunfire directed eastward. Through the rotating of barrels and bursting of gunpowder was that rapidly increasing droning sound.

Their source arrived.

Shadows passed over the clearing as dozens of angry insects arrived. They had come with murderous intent, drawn by the sound of aircraft engines and other chaos that occurred in the last few minutes.

Like hail falling from a terrible thunderstorm, several flying warriors nosedived at the startled humans. Simultaneously, several others went after the large flying machines, sparking a dogfight a hundred feet high while those on the ground dispersed.

Tarsus took advantage of the confusion and delivered an elbow to Bergis' ribs, freeing himself from his grip.

Behind them, Godfrey delivered a flurry of punches at the four men around him. Irrfan and Blake hit the ground, their lips bright red with fresh blood. Colin took a kick to the shin and an elbow to the jaw, flooring him alongside his partners. Hoover, distracted by the horde, was too busy trying to secure one of the mercenary's fallen weapons when Godfrey sucker-punched him in the face.

Grabbing his weapon off the ground, the merc pointed the weapon at the four men, finger on the trigger.

Bergis extended the colonel's pistol and fired. His shot ran wide, skidding over Godfrey's left shoulder. All the same, he was successful in preventing him from executing his friends. Godfrey jolted, his shots going wide. Bergis fired a second time, his bullet right on course to striking the target's center mass, had the rifle frame not been in the way.

There was a *CHING!* sound of the weapon getting hit and falling from Godfrey's hands.

Bergis cursed. He thought only in movies could such a ridiculous thing actually happen. Then again, it was fitting, since this whole freaking day felt like something straight out of the cinema.

"Lon!"

Bergis looked north. Riley was making a run for the adult Spinosaurus, simultaneously trying to get the anti-venom into its mouth while also trying to protect the baby from the bugs.

Four of them hovered just a few feet over her head, positioning their tails for a fatal sting.

Bergis shifted his aim from Godfrey to the insects and fired twelve of the pistol's remaining thirteen bullets. His shots were on point, punching holes in the thoraxes of all four assailants and rupturing the internal organs inside. The four bugs hit the ground, wings fluttering and legs twitching as the life parted from them.

A fifth insect lowered itself in Riley's path. She stopped, one hand wrapped over the cannister, the other on the baby, following a motherly instinct to guide it behind her back.

Bergis fired his last round. The bug shifted right as he pulled the trigger. The bullet, aimed for its head, passed through one of its wings instead. Though failing to kill the insect, it was enough to cripple its ability to fly.

It fell to the ground a few feet ahead of Riley, immediately throwing itself into a frenzy as it tried to get its wings to function adequately again.

In that moment, more bugs gathered near her.

Bergis looked at the locked slide on his pistol. His mag was empty and he had no others.

He felt the urge to scream. It seemed too cruel for it to play out this way, for them to come this far and fail at the most crucial moment.

A tremor steadied his turbulent mind. Several yards beyond Riley, the adult Spinosaurus shifted its weak body, balancing its weight on its right knee and two forearms. It pivoted counterclockwise and swung its tail over the doctor's head, smacking the group of insect warriors out of existence.

Its strength spent, the Spino rolled onto its side and let out a deathly exhale.

Riley attempted to move forward, but was stopped when the fifth bug Bergis had shot righted itself. It stood on its legs and bent its flexible tail over its back. Both claws cocked back near its head, ready to strike.

Riley gasped, anticipating the agonizing attack, then gasped again when her sail-back friend darted past her. Following the same instincts that enabled its father to be an alpha predator, the little one lunged at the insect. Its stinger slashed for the baby's head, going high as the baby went low for a tackle. Fingers and toes raked the insect's underbelly, breaking apart its exoskeleton like thin ice chippings. The jaws dug into the soft flesh beneath the opening, tearing a mouthful of yellow flesh free.

Bergis sprinted up to Riley and watched in astonishment as the baby Spino stood over its dead opponent, enjoying the thrill of its first victory.

"Takes after his old man," he quipped.

She smiled back at him.

At once, they turned their eyes skyward as a massive shadow passed overhead.

That smile vanished.

The giant rhino beetles had arrived. Their incredibly long wings created sonic waves that brought all people on the ground to their knees. Moving at rapid speeds, they moved directly at the two dragonflies. Their horned faces connected with their metal opponents, sending both aircrafts into a literal downward spiral.

Bergis threw himself over Riley and tucked her head down.

Munro and Sagara met an explosive end as their dragonflies crash-landed on the west side of the clearing. Two massive balls of fire lifted into the sky, the thick black smoke forcing much of the swarm eastward. The rhinos joined their smaller companions and landed on the far side, now interested in the last remaining aircraft resting near the trees.

At the top of the boarding ramp was Hoover, Colin, Irrfan, and Blake, all seeking shelter in the aircraft. Colin could see the giant beetle-shaped insects through the window. They were between a rock and a hard place; either they stay there and get trampled by the enormous bugs with rhinoceros horns, or run outside and get swarmed by the drones.

Bergis helped Riley to her feet and took the cannister from her.

"Get back to the ship!"

"What about you?" she said.

"Is it not obvious?" Bergis said, holding up the cannister. "I just need to dive this hypodermic needle through its gums, right?"

"Yeah."

"Then that's what I'll do. Now, go!"

There was no time to waste. Riley leaned towards the baby and clapped her hands.

"Come on, hon!" She began moving to the Dragonfly. Fortunately, the little dinosaur responded to the gestures and started following her.

Bergis faced the adult Spinosaurus.

"You better not make me regret this."

"Way ahead of you!"

Bergis turned to the sound of Godfrey's voice, just in time to see the fist coming at his face.

BAM!

The corporal was knocked to the ground, the cannister rolling from his hand. He scampered backwards, avoiding the stomp from the mercenary's boot.

Behind Godfrey was Colonel Tarsus, carrying a large knife dripping with yellow blood after physically taking on some of the drones. Another one swept down to sting him, forcing Tarsus to delay joining in on the brawl in favor of self-defense.

"Get that cannister!" he shouted to Godfrey.

The merc landed a kick on Bergis' chest, driving the wind from his lungs. Huffing and puffing, Bergis retaliated with a few jabs and an uppercut, all of which were parried by the stronger merc.

The flurry of attacks concluded with a frustrated right hook. Godfrey raised an arm, blocking the swing and grabbing ahold of Bergis' sleeve and collar. He rammed a knee into the corporal's stomach, drove an elbow down onto the back of his neck, and landed a haymaker of his own.

Bergis went down hard. His vision was hazy and his own mouth tasted of blood. Godfrey stood over him, the heat of the flames keeping the swarm at bay for the moment. He hit Bergis with a kick to the ribs, rolling him on his back.

"You should've gone with the colonel's offer." He planted his boot on Bergis' throat. Both hands clutched the toe and heel, but lacked the strength to push him off. Godfrey grinned with joy. "Now, you and your friends can join the big lizard in hell."

A new tremor swept under Bergis' back.

Godfrey's eyes went to the Spino. His smile twisted into a mishmash of shock, confusion, disbelief, and pure terror.

The Spino, drooling from its mouth, pushed itself onto its hands and knees. It pointed its enormous snout at the merc and parted its jaws.

Godfrey lifted his foot from Bergis' neck and started backing away. He was not fast enough.

The Spinosaurus lurched, sliding on its chest and stomach to close the distance.

SNAP!

Only Godfrey's legs could be seen twitching from those intertwined teeth. From within those jaws, the merc was screaming. Only his legs were damaged. The rest of him was laying atop the dinosaur's long wet tongue.

With a swing of its head, the Spino tossed Godfrey into the burning Dragonfly wreckages. There, the screams intensified. The rest of his life was spent in sweltering fire—appropriately transitioning him to his eternal afterlife experience.

The Spinosaurus remained on its belly. Its breathing was labored and its eyes were beginning to shut.

Bergis scampered to where the cannister had fallen and scooped it up. Now back on his feet, he hurried to the Spino's jaws. He smacked the thing on its nostrils.

"Hey! Open up! Hello?! I need you to say 'Ah!'" *My God, I'm talking to a dinosaur like it's a five-year-old.* He kicked its chin. "Come on! Open up!"

The creature shook its head in annoyance, then exhaled through its mouth. Bergis saw the red gums between its teeth.

He cringed in fear. "Don't hate me please."

The needle went into the soft flesh, rapidly delivering the antivenom. Bergis jumped back as the beast shuddered from the sting. The needle remained lodged between its teeth, allowing for all of its contents to enter its bloodstream.

When it was all over, the Spinosaurus rested its head once again.

Bergis watched the swarm and the two rhinos. They were making their approach to the Dragonfly. Blake was in the cockpit, getting the engines ready for a quick getaway.

Several warriors crawled over the hull in search of an entry point. The fuselage doors and boarding ramp were closed. Inside, the five occupants were torn between making a desperate escape, in which the entire swarm would be on top of them, or praying for the medicine to work.

"Come on," Bergis said to the Spino. "I was under the impression this stuff was supposed to act fast. Come on, we need you on your feet."

There was a sound of motion coming from his right. Bergis turned and raised his hand in time to grab ahold of Colonel Tarsus' wrist, stopping his knife from making its plunge. The colonel, high on his own rage, stared Bergis in the eyes, his jaw bared and bloodied, brow furrowed, eyes bloodshot.

Even now, with his men dead, giant carnivorous insects buzzing about, and his plan ruined, he was still hellbent on his ultimate goal. Only now, his satisfaction also required Bergis' death.

He landed a headbutt against the corporal's nose and began pulling him into a circle, ultimately wrestling Bergis to the ground. Bergis kept both hands on the wrist, keeping the tip of the blade at bay.

"Now I know where your loyalties lie. You failed your unit in Algiers, you failed them here—Yeah, I know about that. How you allowed the enemy to kill your Scorpion team, and you managed to walk away with a medal. You let the enemy win then, and you're letting it win now. Every person that beast kills from now on will be on your head. I guess, in a way, I'm giving you mercy by ending your life here."

He put all of his weight on the knife, bringing its blade gradually closer to Bergis' throat.

Bergis maintained direct eye contact with the colonel.

"I did fail back then. I failed to help my team and by not getting into the Scorpion, I allowed the enemy to inflict many casualties." His eyes went to the Dragonfly. Through the windows, he could see the faces of Blake, Colin, Irrfan, Hoover, and Riley watching in repulsion. They were not scared because of the bugs. They were scared for *him;* they wanted nothing more than for their friend to survive.

"I'll forever carry that with me," Bergis continued. "I miss those guys. I'll miss Galloway—my one friend from those days. But today, I've gained a new team. New friends. Some of whom I've only known for a few hours, but I've got their backs, and they have mine."

Tarsus sniggered. "So much for your team. They're all trapped in that Dragonfly, soon to be crushed by the beetles. None of them can help you."

Bergis tilted his head up. "You forgot to count one."

Thump!

Tarsus looked over his shoulder. Standing on its hind legs was the massive Spinosaurus. Its breathing had normalized and its strength had returned. The colonel suddenly felt as though he was an inch tall. Compared to the creature, he was not much more than that.

His anxiety did not erase his anger. Tarsus applied as much pressure on the knife as possible, hoping to at least get the satisfaction of killing the man who revived his enemy.

A slash of the creature's claw put an end to the colonel's ambitions. In the blink of an eye, he was no longer on top of Bergis, his mangled body joining Godfrey's in the burning wreckage.

Bergis rested on his elbows and watched the Spino. It stood over him, watching the human whom it had fought tooth and nail at the beach. Any grudge held between them dissipated in this very moment. The Spinosaurus, now recognizing not all of the humans were responsible for the death of its other young, turned around to face the real threat.

The sonic wave rained hell on Bergis' eardrums as the two rhino beetles expanded their wings. They took to the sky to gain an aerial advantage over their new opponent.

Surrounding them was the horde of warriors, each of them ready to sacrifice their lives in service to the colony.

What they did not know was how futile that sacrifice would be.

Bergis saw the change in coloration in the massive sail. Recognizing what was about to happen, he got on his feet and began to make some distance.

The Spinosaurus reared its head back, then thrust its jaws forward. A stream of flame entered the swarm, incinerating most of the smaller warriors on contact. A tornado of fire began to swirl.

Rapidly, the soundwaves generated by the beetles dissipated. Like giant phoenixes, they fell out of the fire tornado, their wings ablaze.

Bergis caught a glance of one of the huge beetles tumbling out of the sky… in his direction. It barreled in mid-air, legs kicking, wings smoking and falling apart.

"Shit!" He broke into a sprint. "SHIIIITTTT!"

The creature landed behind him.

Bergis felt himself lifted off the ground by the shockwave. He felt the weightlessness of being airborne, and the *SMACK* of landing on the ground. Next thing he knew, everything went black.

CHAPTER 22

"Lon! Lon! Wake up!"

Bergis felt the tapping of a hand against his cheek and a tightening sensation around his arm.

The darkness parted and in its place came blinding sunlight. Bergis winced as the thunderous sounds of literal tons of violence rocked his world. His senses returned, bringing to view the clouds of smoke passing between him and the blue sky. Kneeling over him was Riley, her hand on his face, her eyes on the brink of tears.

She smiled with relief. "Thank God!"

The others were gathered around him. On his left was Hoover, who was busy applying a bandage on his left arm. Behind him were the three smugglers, all of whom were leaning forward to lift him up.

"Not a good place to take a nap, Corporal," Colin said.

Booming stomps ahead of the group solidified his point. Bergis' vision cleared and he beheld the sight of the gigantic Spinosaurus in mortal combat with the two rhino beetle creatures.

It had its jaws on the horn of the beetle with the red scar. Pivoting its feet, the dino dragged the bulky adversary in a tight circle. The second beetle was righting itself, having been knocked on its back during the few moments Colin had blacked out. It was on its feet for no more than two seconds before the Spino's tail whipped across its face, sending it tumbling backwards again.

The one with the red scar kicked up dirt with its six legs, unable to outmuscle the angry reptilian pulling it by its horn. After two complete passes, it came to a stop. It tilted to the right to allow its left foot to rise and come down hard on the scarred beetle's side. The huge insect attempted to resist the powerful blow, but lacked the strength and the leverage. The foot struck and the beetle rolled onto its left.

Meanwhile, those jaws remained clamped. The Spinosaurus, growling with anger, twisted its head back and forth.

Bergis heard a mild *crack*. Moments later, there was another one. The Spinosaurus paused for a moment to inhale through its nostrils and summon energy for one more jerking movement.

CCCRRRAAAAACCCCKKK!!!

The Spino's head raised high, the severed horn of the red-scarred beetle in its jaws. Below its chin, yellow blood spurted from the insect's face. Its many legs flailed clumsily with no purpose other than reacting to the intense surge of pain shooting through its nervous system.

The Spino spat the horn into the distance and slammed another kick into the beetle, fully rolling it on its back. Claws and teeth came down hard on its underside. Armor coating, relatively thin and weak compared to the rest of the beetle's carapace, gave in easily to the pointed instruments. Huge black shards separated from the writhing insect, making way for an eruption of blood and guts.

Six legs thrashed uselessly, striking nothing but air while the beetle endured an agonizing whirlwind of carnage inside its body. The Spino had buried its snout deep within its abdomen, its teeth ravaging everything inside.

After several moments of butchery, the dinosaur pulled its head free, entrails dangling from its teeth. Below those strands of guts was a massive hole in the middle of the beetle's stomach. Its whirling legs slowed to a permanent stop as life parted from the giant insect.

As it had done with the horn, the Spinosaurus spat the guts out, simultaneously ridding itself of the vile taste and conveying its disdain for the bested opponent.

Behind the large reptilian, the second beetle righted itself. Immediately, it attempted to charge the Spinosaurus in hopes of catching it off guard.

The Spino turned on its heel and engaged the insect directly. To the dismay of the bug, it charged with superior force. Tucking its head to the right, it avoided impalement from the large horn in its direct collision with the beetle.

Bergis stepped back with the rest of his group, watching in astonishment as lizard and bug tussled. The beetle attempted to angle its horn to penetrate the dinosaur's trunk. Its efforts were countered by the Spino's leverage of two long arms. Claws slashed the bug's face, lacerating its eyes and driving it backward. The Spino stomped after it, not allowing the beetle to gain distance.

It moved in with a massive bite, securing part of the crest behind the bug's head. As it had done with the beetle with the red scar, the Spinosaurus dragged the beetle into a spin. It only completed one complete turn before using the momentum to literally throw its opponent.

The beetle rolled over its side, its shell parting to release its wings. Charred stubs, burnt from the Spinosaurus' fire breath, protruded from the openings, flapping ineffectively in a failed effort to airlift the insect. Kicking its legs and hissing frenetically, it opened its elytra flaps a second time, using the rigid shell casings to get itself back on its feet.

Scraping the earth with its feet, the beetle turned to face its dinosaurian opponent, ready to attempt another attack.

The Spino had backed another sixty feet away and was cocking its head back. Its human observers recognized the posture as well as the shifting in colors on its marvelous sail, and held their breaths in anticipation of what came next.

Stomping the ground like an elephant in the African savanna, the beetle charged the Spino head-on.

Huffing smoke from the corners of its mouth, the Spino lurched forward. Its jaws parted one-hundred-and-twenty degrees. From the back of its throat came a jet of fire, hot as molten magma from the earth's core.

The beetle had halfway closed the distance when it was engulfed. Its exoskeleton ignited easily, the heat bringing its insides to a literal boil.

Eyes red, the Spinosaurus kept the stream going. It stepped forward, keeping pace with the beetle as it backtracked.

A cry of agony pierced the air. Entrapped in the horizontal vortex of fire, the beetle reeled backwards. Fluid bubbled through the chitin in its joints. A rumbling sound reverberated from its center mass. From where Bergis and his friends stood, it resembled the sound of a hungry person's stomach growling.

Riley was able to quickly connect the dots.

"Oh, God." She turned around. "Take cover."

Before anyone could ask "why?" they were showered with the answer. The beetle's shell came apart like fragments of a broken vase, its insides bursting from within.

Bergis put his hands over his head, anticipating the wetness of blood raining down on him. He heard droplets splattering all around him, their vile smell invading his nasal cavities. Miraculously, he remained untouched.

He lowered his hands and looked at the battlefield. The Spinosaurus had ceased its fire breath and began filling its lungs with much-needed oxygen. In front of it, the beetle rested in pieces, having decorated the clearing with its insides.

Riley. She looked back at him, also untouched by the yellow insides. A smile stretched over their faces and they broke into a laugh.

"At least one thing went our way today, huh?" she said.

"Can't argue that," he replied.

She ran at him, threw her arms around his neck, and planted a kiss on his lips.

"Glad someone's happy."

Bergis and Riley parted their faces and looked at the miserable Colin Sermon, his dust jacket... and face... smothered with huge globs of bug guts.

Irrfan waved a hand over his nose. "Whew! You need a shower."

Colin shot him a look. "Oh really? What gave it away?" He took off his jacket and tossed it. Blake handed him a handkerchief to wipe his face. Colin did so and looked at his five companions, all dry as a whistle. "Wait a sec; how is it *I'm* the only one who got drenched?"

Bergis smacked him on the arm. "Luck of the draw."

Together, they looked to the Spinosaurus. The colors of its sail were going through their usual shift. It turned its head to the group and watched as its youngster trotted from the safety of the Dragonfly to join them.

It rubbed up against Bergis' leg and shoved its head against Riley's hand, anticipating to be petted.

"Gosh, you two have been together for like five minutes and already you have a pet," Hoover remarked.

"Two pets, if you count the big one," Irrfan added, pointing at the adult.

Bergis pursed his lips at that statement.

Riley, on the other hand, was delighted at the idea. "It's remarkable, actually. We can partake in a research project. The Spinos can get a home somewhere isolated, and we can observe how they interact with the environment."

"On top of that, we can develop a way to help it avoid contact with civilization," Hoover added. "Maybe we can host a fundraiser of some sort, or get someone to give us a grant."

"If we do, we can get a PhD to help us study the creatures," Irrfan exclaimed with joy.

Colin shot him another look. "We? What 'we'?" He looked to Blake to assist in dogpiling their colleague, but got a shrug and a 'meh' sound instead.

"I mean, if they can figure out a way to get the funding going, it might beat what we do now. Let's face it: this year alone, we've almost been killed six times. Yeah, it pays well, but we're not necessarily in the friendliest business."

"We almost got killed six times *today*!" Colin replied.

"Yeah," Blake said. "But mostly from the bugs." He gestured at the field of smoldering bodies. "As you can see, I don't think they'll be much of a problem anymore."

Hands tucked in his pockets, Colin tightened his lips and exhaled through his nose. "So much catharsis right now. You know, coming to this island was supposed to be an easy payday, not a course of events to make us reshape our entire futures." He hung his head down in defeat. "I suppose I'm outvoted."

"So, you're game?" Hoover asked.

Colin shrugged. "Join a bunch of people we've known for three hours in a life-long venture to study mutated dinosaurs and whatever else gets unearthed? What could go wrong?" After a sigh, he followed his statement up with, "But at least it won't be boring." He looked at Riley. "That pizza better be damn good."

"Hmm?" Riley looked at Bergis. "Pizza? Did I miss something?"

Bergis, remembering the 'bargain' made earlier at the discovery of the hive, chuckled. He opened his mouth to explain, but was cut off by a sudden series of tremors passing deep below their feet. All eyes went to the ground and followed the moving epicenter to the northern part of the clearing.

"Oh, crap," Blake muttered. His remark about the bugs not being much of a problem anymore was said a little too soon.

A large fissure took form. The edges rose and split apart. From the center rose the Queen, angry and looking for a fight.

The Spinosaurus bellowed. Large feet stomped the ground beneath it. Its arms swiped the air, warming up for the upcoming clash.

Its foe pulled herself from the massive hole in the earth. Her mantis-like body rose tall at a forty-five-degree angle. Both claws stretched open and snapped at the air in response to the Spino's motions. Her tail unwound and stretched its entire two-hundred-foot length at the sky, arching into a crescent shape to point its deadly stinger at the reptilian.

Colin gulped. "There won't be any more of those things during our research adventures, will there?"

"Depends on how this turns out," Bergis replied.

In contrast to their crippling tension, Hoover clapped his hands and pumped a fist over his head.

"Smack her around, Spino!"

As though in direct reply, the Spinosaurus charged at the Queen bitch. Like a galloping horse, she met the reptilian head-on.

They collided with a resounding *smash!*

Pincer claws went for the Spino's face, their edges marking the tough flesh covering its snout. The stinger vaulted overhead for a deathly sting.

Anticipating this, the Spino leaned forward and raised its own tail upward, smacking the stinger to the side before it could make its plunge.

A swipe of its claw struck the Queen across the face, much to Hoover's delight. It followed up with a second slash in an uppercut motion. The Queen stumbled backwards, her chin lifted from the impact.

The Spinosaurus hit her in the face with a third slash, its talons parting one of the mandibles from her jaw. The still-twitching appendage reeled from her face onto the ground, its broken end oozing blood.

Yellow droplets dripped from the Queen's face. She retaliated by snapping one of her pincers shut on the Spino's left wrist. The jagged edges dug into the flesh, verging on cutting deep into the bone.

The Spino shrieked in pain, then promptly brought its jaws down on the Queen's forearm. Its incredible bite force punched its teeth through the armor, triggering a nervous response that opened the pincers and freed its wrist. The Spino refused to release the Queen even as she tried pulling away.

Blood trickled from her arm. She lashed out with her other pincer, only for the attack to be deflected by the Spino's claws.

It was her tail that managed to deal a blow. Her stinger vaulted overhead and drove its tip into the Spinosaurus' left shoulder.

The beast recoiled, releasing the Queen's arm and pulling loose from her toxic appendage.

"Shit!" Colin yelled. "She stung him!"

"It should be fine," Riley said. "He's got our antivenom in his bloodstream. It should counteract the dosage she injected him with."

Hoover blew a sigh of relief. "But if she stings him repeatedly?"

The question seemed to make Riley shrink a few inches.

"If she gets too much into him, it might overwhelm his immune system, even with the antivenom."

Hoover went back to feeling tense, especially as the giants resumed their brawl.

The Queen waved her tail like a cowboy's lasso. After a few whirls, it lashed at the Spino's face, whipping it right above the left eye. The mutated dinosaur staggered backwards, roaring in frustration. A second lash struck its face, drawing blood along the snout.

Hissing, she went for a third slash.

The Spinosaurus parted its jaws, ready to snatch the tail out of the air and chomp down on it. It was in this moment the Queen proved she relied on more than just killer instinct. She was intelligent and understood how to adapt.

Her third lash went low. Her tail, like the tentacle of a giant squid, looped around the Spinosaurus' ankle.

She yanked back, literally pulling its foot out from under it. The Spinosaurus flipped onto its side, hitting the ground with an ear-splitting crash. It kicked its foot, freeing itself of the segmented tail.

The Queen went for another sting. A swipe of the Spino's tail deflected the attack, redirecting her stinger leftward where it wedged itself into the ground.

It provided enough of an opportunity for the reptilian to right itself. Now on its feet, it faced the Queen. She yanked her tail free and readied herself to perform another attack.

The Spino was not having it.

It charged like a quarterback, even tucking its head down and putting its shoulder out.

BAM!

It connected with the Queen. A raspy scream parted from her jaws as she was knocked backward. A cloud of dust kicked up as she landed near the fissure where she rose from her tunnel. Legs and forearms frolicked, the tail rising as though it was its own entity.

She rolled herself rightward, feet digging into the dirt to resecure balance.

The Spinosaurus pivoted on its heel with the grace of a Taekwondo black belt, whipping its tail in a complete hundred-eighty-degree pass. It cracked the Queen across the chin, knocking her back onto the ground.

"There we go!" Hoover shouted.

Even Colin was getting into it. "Yeah! Serves her right."

Bergis felt himself sporting a grin as he watched the colors of the sail begin to shift. Whatever combustion system the Spinosaurus had within its body had recharged and was ready to spew another round of its signature weapon.

The fight was almost over.

So he thought.

"Wait…" Irrfan pointed to the northeast. "What's that?"

Bergis heard the droning sound and saw the shape appear from over the trees.

"You've got to be kidding me!" he snarled. "It's the queen from the second hive."

Her mantis-scorpion shape was near identical to her mother. She was smaller, maybe two-thirds the size of her mom, but maintaining the gift of flight. Wings, like those of a dragonfly, carried her huge body at a frightening speed. Having lost almost all of her guard in service of her mother, she was unable to rest in her own damaged hive until the threat was neutralized.

She swooped down like an eagle, coming within a few feet of the ground before angling upward, right at the Spinosaurus' chin.

The dinosaur absorbed the full brunt of the five-ton insect moving at seventy miles per hour. It reeled backward, its fire breath redirected at the sky.

An orange-red tornado extended from its mouth and traveled hundreds of feet skyward. The Spinosaurus rolled to its hands and knees to get back up. The daughter swooped down again, smacking its sail and knocking the dinosaur back on its side.

The Queen was back on her feet. There was no acknowledgement of her daughter's assistance. As far as she was concerned, such things were owed to her, for she had given her flying offspring the gift of life and power.

"That's cheating!" Colin exclaimed.

"If they were both on the ground, the Spino could probably manage it," Riley said. "But with the second one having the advantage of flight, he's overwhelmed."

"Not sure what we can do," Blake said. "The Dragonfly is damaged, so we can't give him aerial support."

Bergis looked to his left. Beyond the grey veil of smoke was *Old Buster*, standing on all eight legs, waiting for its operator.

Over a hundred yards ahead of it, the Spinosaurus was crawling on its belly, desperately trying to fend off two attackers who had a tactical advantage, both in numbers and position.

A ping of fear went through him. He had survived so many encounters on this island already. Going into that machine would undoubtedly draw the attention of the two queens. So many times today, he had barely avoided death. An all-too-familiar feeling crept up his spine, warning him this would be the time his luck would run out.

All he would have to do was turn around with his friends and go the other way. He had done enough.

The only thing he hated more than the feeling itself was how tempting it was. That, and the feeling of guilt it resulted in.

He shook his head in defiance of his inner demons.

Not again.

"No, not air support," he said. "But we can provide ground support."

Having said that, he started running toward *Old Buster.* He reached the stern side and opened a panel in one of the legs. He tapped the access code, opening the boarding ramp.

As its end touched the ground, he noticed the rest of the group assembling.

"What are you guys doing?"

Colin made a face. "What? You think we're gonna let you do this alone?"

"You guys know how to operate one of these things?" Bergis said. "Have you ever loaded a plasma cannister?"

"No, but I imagine it's something you can talk us through," Hoover said.

Bergis looked at him. The young security operative, whom Bergis had looked negatively upon for most of this assignment, had more heart than most soldiers he had known in the West Atlantic Army. It was a shame he did not serve, for he would have made an excellent soldier.

Even the baby Spinosaurus had joined them at the ramp. It was whimpering out of concern for its father, but being so young, it had no clue what to do other than stay with its human friends.

"Alright. Get aboard," he said.

They hustled up the ramp and assembled in the main body of *Old Buster.* It was not a luxury vehicle with comfortable seats, but rather a confined space with all sorts of slots and mechanical components for support crew. Everywhere they looked, there were instrument panels and lights.

For Bergis, the stale smell was very familiar. For the people behind him, it was a bit of a shock to think people worked in this thing for months on end.

The ramp slammed shut and the interior lights came to life.

Bergis typed a code into one of the computers and opened a large unit on the aft side of the chamber. It was shaped like a tube in a waterpark, except made of steel and layered with materials the group did not recognize.

He typed another code.

A slot in the port side opened up, revealing the first of many objects which resembled three-foot-long capsules.

Bergis snapped his fingers to get the attention of his friends. "Pay attention, because I only have time to explain this once. Take this capsule… it's an energy capsule; that's where the laser comes from… load it into the slot, and pull this lever to seal the firing chamber." He pointed at a manual lever on the tube thing on the aft end. "When all LED bars go red after firing, pull the dual levers down here…" He referred to a pair of metal levers near the loading tubes. "This'll eject the empty plasma capsule and open the loading chamber. Pull the lever on the wall to access the next one, and repeat. Understood?"

"A lot of lever pulling," Colin remarked. "I think we're good."

They went to work loading the first cannister while Bergis made his way to the cockpit.

He took a seat and started the ignition process. While the scorpion-shaped battle mech came to life, he watched the progression of the battle taking place up ahead.

The Spinosaurus was on its side, kicking its right leg at the flying insect as she hovered above it. She attempted to jab it with her stinger, but failed to find an opening through the flailing of limbs.

It attempted a bite, missing the stinger by inches. The young Queen ascended, while her mother advanced toward the fallen dinosaur. The Spinosaurus pushed up with its claws, getting itself upright for a grand total of half a second before it was struck from behind by the matriarch Queen.

Roaring angrily, the Spino fell on its stomach.

"Hang on, you overgrown gecko." Bergis went through the startup process, *Old Buster* coming to life with some loud whirring sounds.

A hand touched his shoulder.

He looked up and saw Riley standing in the cockpit with him. The message conveyed by her eyes was clear: *Wherever you go, I go.*

It was a sentiment shared by the newborn Spinosaurus, apparently. It stood behind her, watching concernedly as its father was double-teamed by the two insects.

The Spinosaurus scampered on all fours to gain some distance from the two empresses. Behind it, the prime Queen's tail came down and drove its barb through its hip. A cry of agony filled the air. The Spino swung its tail, dislodging the stinger.

Immediately after, the flying Queen descended. She slashed with her tail, striking the base of the Spino's sail. It fell to its side, overwhelmed and lacking the advantage of reach and leverage.

"Capsule's loaded!" Hoover shouted.

Bergis grasped the controls.

Old Buster moved forward, quickly gaining the attention of the prime Queen.

Bergis primed the main gun for firing and moved the center joystick to take aim. The targeting computer came on and automatically detected the movements of the younger queen. With the tap of a few keys, the gun locked on to her.

A humming sound filled the interior of the M3 Scorpion.

Bergis confirmed the target to the computer, then put his finger on the trigger.

"How's *this* for a sting?"

He unleashed the laser.

A concentrated stream of red energy, capable of slicing through the hull of an aircraft carrier, streamed from the tip of *Old Buster's* tail. A puff of yellow burst from the flying Queen's abdomen as the laser punched through her.

Screeching in agony, she spiraled out of the air and struck the ground.

Bergis panned the laser to the right to slice the prime Queen. Recognizing the danger, she turned around and retreated eastward. She reached the entrance of her tunnel and dove underground, the laser nicking a segment of her tail as it passed over her.

"Damn it!" Bergis exclaimed. It was a marvel how something so large could move so fast. He leaned back to call into the fuselage. "Reload!"

"You did good," Riley said. She nodded at the Spino. "Look."

She was correct. The Spinosaurus was back on its feet and madder than ever. Its feet stomped deliberately as it made its way to the younger insect. She had rolled to her front, smoke billowing from her torn abdomen. Her tail was limp and stretched across the landscape, the nerves and muscles controlling it seared by the laser.

Sensing danger, it reared up to defend itself against the dinosaur. It was a futile effort, resulting in a mighty stomp landing on its back and pinning it to the ground.

The jaws slammed shut over her head. Wings flapped and legs spasmed as a major compressive force compromised the integrity of her skull.

The Spino jerked its mouth back and forth, then pulled upward with every ounce of its energy.

A *SPLAT* sound accompanied the separation of the young queen's head from her thorax. The body went limp, save for a few automatic twitches.

Her head was fully intact between the jaws of the Spinosaurus for a grand total of seven seconds before a second *SPLAT* erased any semblance of its original form.

Spitting brain tissue from its teeth, the dinosaur turned around in search of its final threat.

"One down," Bergis said.

"Nice," Riley replied. She looked around. "Where's the other one? You think she retreated?"

Seismic monitors alerted the Scorpion pilot to tremors directly below *Old Buster.*

"Don't think so…"

His attempts to move *Old Buster* came too late. The Queen burst from directly underneath the machine, striking its belly and lifting it off the ground.

"Brace!" he shouted. He grabbed Riley's arm and held tight.

Old Buster hit the ground. Everyone unsecured to a seat fell to the ceiling. Riley's fall was softened thanks to Bergis' grip, allowing her to 'backflip' into a decent landing.

Everyone else had a hard landing.

"Oooh! Son of a—" Colin complained.

The baby Spinosaurus took the fall fairly well. It was back on its feet and immediately started nudging Riley. It was astonished to see Bergis seemingly 'floating' above it.

Looking at the upside-down world outside the windscreen, the corporal was unsure whether or not it was a good idea to have strapped himself in the seat. One way or another, he was doomed to fall on his head. There was no getting the *Old Buster* back on its feet without the help of a crane.

The Queen pulled herself out of the ground and towered over the cockpit. Big black pincers slammed shut outside the glass, threatening the insignificant lifeforms inside.

Stomp! Stomp! Stomp!

She pulled away and swiveled on her feet, separating her attention from the mech to the charging Spinosaurus. She raised her claws to engage the beast. Once again, her right arm was caught between those powerful jaws. Blood splattered the windscreen as the Spinosaurus pulled the Queen away from the *Old Buster.*

The Queen's attempts to resist were futile compared to the superior strength and anger of the theropod. Her tail came down for a sting, but missed after her entire body was swung counterclockwise.

She was taken for a complete pass and forced on her left side. The Spino grasped her forearm with both claws while its jaws sawed at the wrist.

The Queen screeched in agony at the removal of her pincer. It was tossed aside, freeing the jaws to come down on one of the front legs. It met a similar fate in a fraction of the time, much to the dismay of its owner.

She pushed back on all seven of her remaining legs and slashed with her tail. The Spinosaurus tucked its head down, avoiding the pointed tip.

Inside the *Old Buster,* the rest of the crew joined Bergis and Riley in the cockpit. They helped Bergis out of his harness and lowered him to the ceiling without the misfortune of landing on his head.

"So much technology that went into building this big machine and yet they couldn't be bothered to add seatbelts for the crew," Colin muttered while nursing a fresh bruise on his forehead.

"Nothing compared to what that bitch is gonna get," Hoover replied.

Together, they watched the conclusion to the quarrel between reptile and insect.

After gaining some distance from her adversary, the Queen whirled her tail in preparation for another slash.

The Spinosaurus watched carefully, anticipating the trajectory. It peeled its lips and bared its teeth, challenging the bitch to do her worst.

She gave it her best try.

The stinger came at the Spino, the tip dripping with venom.

With a shift of motion, the therapod caught the tail in its mouth. The Queen stood dumbfounded, her tail taut as a wire. Her attempts to free her primary weapon from that of her opponent proved futile. That is, until the Spinosaurus applied additional pressure and crushed the stinger in its mouth. Rivers of blood and venom poured out from each side, carrying fragments of the shattered barb.

She retracted her tail, leaving a long yellow trail in its path.

All hope was lost. One pincer was gone, as was her ultimate instrument of war. She was intelligent enough to know her odds at victory had significantly dropped. Her only viable option now was retreat.

Even that was unlikely. Her wings were gone, making flight impossible. Additionally, the loss of one of her pincers meant her ability to dig was severely impaired.

She reared up and screeched at the Spinosaurus. It was at once a cry of defiance and a scream of horror. The battle was lost.

The sail completed its color changes.

A river of burning energy flowed from its mouth and encompassed the insect.

She rose on her rear legs in a fit of madness, her scream traveling into the high heavens.

Over the course of the next few minutes, the humans inside the mech witnessed her exoskeleton deteriorate and her bodily fluids erupt through every orifice, including new ones formed in its joints as the internal pressure mounted.

She fell on her back, writhing in anguish.

The Spinosaurus moved closer, keeping up the punishment until the heat within her met its peak.

In a burst of black fragments and yellow guts, the Queen exploded.

Ceasing its fire breath, the Spinosaurus looked upon its work. Its enemy was defeated and its son was safe.

Basking in the warmth of the dead queen, the Spinosaurus roared in triumph.

CHAPTER 23

It took a little bit of creativity for the group to exit the upside-down *Old Buster*. With the boarding ramp now overhead and the topside hatch jammed shut, they had to climb out through the cockpit to get outside.

Once on the ground, the baby Spinosaurus ran to its father and stood on its huge foot, where it was gently nuzzled. After their embrace, the two dinosaurs turned their eyes to the group of humans. They were more than spectators. They were even more than allies now. They were considered family.

"Well, can't say today was boring," Hoover said.

"Certainly not," Bergis replied.

"There's still the larvae inside the remains of that other hive," Hoover said. "If we can get our new friend over there, it'll make short work of the rest of the swarm."

Bergis looked at the soldier standing beside him. It may not have been official, but in the eyes of the corporal, being a soldier was more than a patch on the arm and a few checkmarks on a sheet of paper.

"At least you can tell your girlfriend's dad you fought in a war. Better yet, you can tell him you helped save the world. If that doesn't win him over, I don't know what will."

"Ha! One can only hope," Hoover said. "The guy's a rich bastard. He's on the board at Globus. He could keep me here to the end of my days if he wanted."

The statement sparked a shared thought.

"Hmm. Rich... part of Globus..." Colin said. "I doubt they'll want to continue the mining operation here. Especially not after learning the truth of what lies within the rock."

"As long as we can gain some public support, we can probably pressure the company to keep a small outpost on Delta-5 Caprona," Riley said. "That way, we can monitor the Spino's activity. It's unlikely it would leave the island for long periods of time. Not with a youngster. The little one will have to remain here. Dad might go fishing and bring back some seafood. Other than that, I doubt they'll interfere with the outside world." She looked at Bergis. "What do you think?"

"Beats working as a digger," Hoover said.

Blake nodded. "And, when you're not being attacked by dinosaurs and carnivorous bugs, it's easy to appreciate the tropical paradise. There's worse places to work."

"Can't deny that," Colin said. "Plus, at least I won't be making shipments to… let's just say, less than desirable clients who will shoot you if the payload is five kilos off."

"You think it's a viable solution?" Blake asked. "I mean, even with the full context of what happened, the big lizard caused a lot of damage. You don't think Globus might consider it a threat?"

"It's a dinosaur in the 21st Century," Bergis said. "As long as it isn't rampaging through Tokyo, it's too scientifically valuable to exterminate."

Riley leaned against him. "So, you up for long-term commitment?"

He returned her gaze, smiling at the double-meaning behind her question. Riley grinned ear-to-ear. She had her answer.

"You think the dinos will be good with us sharing the island with them?" he asked her.

Right then, the baby Spino sprinted over to him. It put itself between Bergis and Riley, making sure to nuzzle its head against each of them.

Its father watched without a worry in the world.

"I think we have our answer," Riley said with a laugh.

The group took turns petting the youngster. It started sniffing their hands and their pockets.

"Geez." Bergis recognized the behavior. "It's looking for Spam."

"Hungry again, huh?" Hoover said. "Can't blame it, really. Now that I know I'm gonna live to see the end of the day, I'm starting to feel a little hungry myself."

"That reminds me…" Irrfan looked at Riley. "You think it'll like pizza?"

The other three smugglers murmured with enthusiasm and watched the doctor eagerly.

She chuckled and turned to Bergis. "What's this story about pizza?"

The End

Check out other great

Dinosaur Thrillers!

Rick Poldark

PRIMORDIAL ISLAND

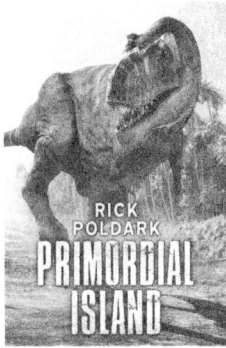

During a violent storm Flight 207 crash-lands in the South China Sea. Poseidon Tech tracks the wreckage to an uncharted island and dispatches a curious salvage team—two paleontologists, a biologist specializing in animal behavior, a botanist, and a nefarious big game hunter. Escorted by a heavily-armed security team, they cut through the jungle and quickly find themselves in a terrifying fight for survival, running a deadly gauntlet of prehistoric predators. In their quest for the flight recorder, they uncover the mystery of the island's existence and discover an arcane force that will tip the balance of power on the primordial island. Things are not as they seem as they race against time to survive the island's man-eating dinosaurs and make it back home in one piece.

P.K. Hawkins

SUBTERRANEA

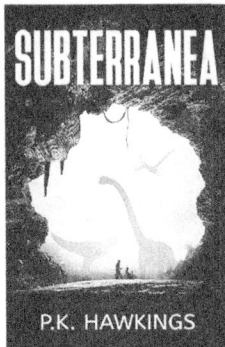

Fall, 1985. The small town of Kettle Hollow barely shows up on any maps, and four young friends are used to taking their BMX's outside of town in an effort to find anything interesting to do. But tonight their tendency to go off by themselves may have saved them, and also forced them into the adventure of a lifetime. While they were away, Kettle Hollow has been locked down by the government, and a portal to another world has opened on Main Street. It's a world deep below the ground, a world where dinosaurs roam free, where giant plants and mutant insects hunt for prey. It's also a world where all their family and friends have been kidnapped for sinister purposes. Now, with time running out before the portal closes, the four friends must brave the unknown to save their loved ones. Time is running out, and in the darkened tunnels of Subterranea, something is hunting them.

Check out other great

Dinosaur Thrillers!

Julian Michael Carver

TRIASSIC

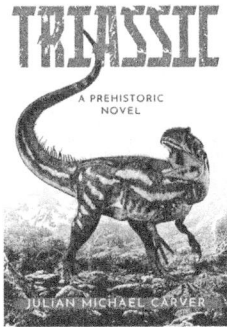

After spending many years in artificial hypersleep, a handful of survivors of the exploration vessel Supernova awaken to find their ship torn to shreds. They are unsure of what happened in space or how they crashed into an uncharted planet. Upon exploration of the new world, they soon realize their destination: The Triassic, the first chapter of the Mesozoic Era. A plan is formulated to escape this terrifying landscape plagued with dinosaurs and prehistoric beasts. The survivors soon discover that there may be an even larger threat looming under the trees than just the dinosaurs, threatening to cut their mission short and trap them all forever in the primitive depths of the Triassic.

Hugo Navikov

THE FOUND WORLD

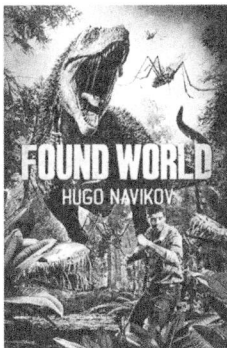

A powerful global cabal wants adventurer Brett Russell to retrieve a superweapon stolen by the scientist who built it. To entice him to travel underneath one of the most dangerous volcanoes on Earth to find the scientist, this shadowy organization will pay him the only thing he cares about: information that will allow him to avenge his family's murder. But before he can get paid, he and his team must enter an underground hellscape of killer plants, giant insects, terrifying dinosaurs, and an army of other predators never previously seen by man. At the end of this journey awaits a revelation that could alter the fate of mankind ... if they can make it back from this horrifying found world.

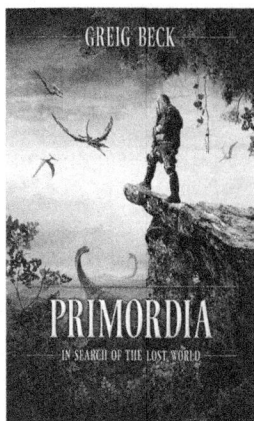

CHECK OUT OTHER GREAT DINOSAUR BOOKS

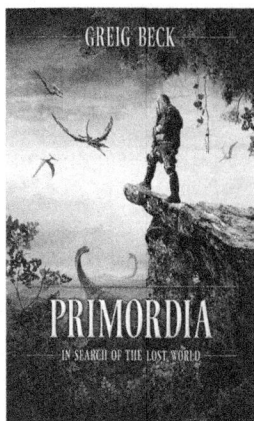

PRIMORDIA
by **Greig Beck**

Ben Cartwright, former soldier, home to mourn the loss of his father stumbles upon cryptic letters from the past between the author, Arthur Conan Doyle and his great, great grandfather who vanished while exploring the Amazon jungle in 1908.

Amazingly, these letters lead Ben to believe that his ancestor's expedition was the basis for Doyle's fantastical tale of a lost world inhabited by long extinct creatures. As Ben digs some more he finds clues to the whereabouts of a lost notebook that might contain a map to a place that is home to creatures that would rewrite everything known about history, biology and evolution.

But other parties now know about the notebook, and will do anything to obtain it. For Ben and his friends, it becomes a race against time and against ruthless rivals.

In the remotest corners of Venezuela, along winding river trails known only to lost tribes, and through near impenetrable jungle, Ben and his novice team find a forbidden place more terrifying and dangerous than anything they could ever have imagined.

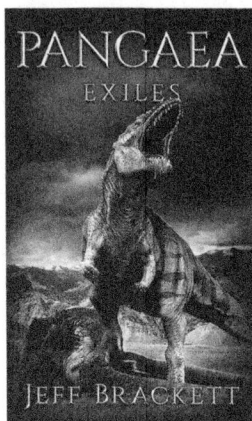

PANGAEA EXILES
by **Jeff Brackett**

Tried and convicted for his crimes, Sean Barrow is sent into temporal exile—banished to a time so far before recorded history that there is no chance that he, or any other criminal sent back, has any chance of altering history.

Now Sean must find a way to survive more than 200 million years in the past, in a world populated by monstrous creatures that would rend him limb from limb if they got the chance. And that's just his fellow prisoners.

The dinosaurs are almost as bad.

Printed in Dunstable, United Kingdom

66120357R00121